THE JOURNEYS OF MCGILL FEIGHAN combine the epic sweep of *The Lord of the Rings* and the tight suspense of the *Dune* trilogy with the wry humor and techno-fantastic imagination of *Stranger in a Strange Land* . . .

Book Two: REEFS

Welcome to a world of unlimited possibilities, in a universe of no escape!

Second in the new series by
KEVIN O'DONNELL, Jr.
Author of MAYFLIES

Berkley books by Kevin O'Donnell, Jr.

THE JOURNEYS OF MCGILL FEIGHAN
BOOK I: CAVERNS
BOOK II: REEFS

MAYFLIES

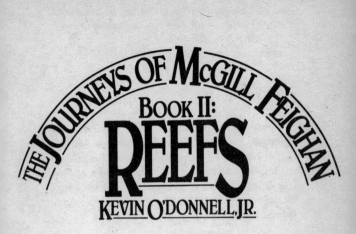

THE JOURNEYS OF McGILL FEIGHAN

BOOK II:
REEFS

KEVIN O'DONNELL, JR.

BERKLEY BOOKS, NEW YORK

To Kevin and Ellen O'Donnell,
who gave me the courage to risk this fine madness
by the gambles on life they have taken themselves,
I dedicate this book with love,
appreciation, and enduring gratitude.

I would like to thank some of the people who are coming to know McGill Feighan almost as well as I know him, and whose insights have helped me to tell his story better: Mary Kittredge, Mark J. Mc-Garry, Joel Rosenberg, Victoria Schochet, Cherry Weiner, and last but really first, my wife, Kim Tchang.

REEFS

A Berkley Book / published by arrangement with
the author

PRINTING HISTORY
Berkley edition / October 1981

ISBN: 0-425-05059-9

A BERKLEY BOOK® TM 757,375

PRINTED IN THE UNITED STATES OF AMERICA

▪ Chapter I ▪

As McGill Feighan materialized on the marble-topped Flop Table, he said, "Dammit, Greystein, love hurts!"

"Puppy love always does," said his roommate, then bent back over the keyscreen at the far end of the living room.

"No, it's—"

Every light in the penthouse flashed; a siren keened wild and shrill. The apartment computer boomed: "Intruder. Intru—"

The blast of sound almost knocked Feighan off the table. Covering his ears, he said, "Hey!"

Marion Jefferson Greystein purpled. "Oscar, cue: shut up; do it now!" The siren cut off. Greystein's energy tunic still flared angrily. "Sorry, McGill; there's a bug in my program. Hold on just a minute." He spoke into the microphone: "Oscar, query: do you recognize the second person here; answer it now."

Wondering if he had just been declared *persona non grata*—by a machine, yet—Feighan glanced at the ceiling grille that hid Oscar's speaker.

"The second person here is McGill Feighan."

Feighan said, "Then why—"

Greystein held up a finger. "Oscar, update: McGill Feighan is authorized always; file it now." The lights blinked off. Greystein sighed, pushed himself away from the keyscreen, and spun his chair around. "I am truly sorry about the cacaphony, McGill; I've been putting a watchdog program into Oscar and hadn't gotten around to listing the people who shouldn't trigger it." Standing, he stretched. "Now, what were you saying?"

"Why a watchdog?" Feighan crossed the room in two huge strides, and sprawled on the onyx force couch. It wheezed as

1

it accepted his ninety-five kilograms, then lenghtened to accommodate his meter-point-nine frame. "Aren't there enough guards around for your peace of mind?"

"Not any more." Though nearly Feighan's height, he was sapling slender; he had curly brown hair and a two-bump nose. Against a skin paled by too many hours in electronics labs, his dark eyes stook out like smudges on rice paper. "The NYPD called today; they've removed the guards and the surveillance cameras because, they say, you're out of danger."

"They're probably right. Word must have gotten around by now that nobody wants me dead any more."

"How do you know?"

"Aw, Greystein, the only thing I'm in danger of is a broken heart." He crossed his hands under his head, and lifted his feet to the far arm of the sofa. "Or marriage, I'm not sure which, yet." Closing his eyes, he took a deep breath and sighed it back out. "Jesus, love's hell."

"McGill, McGill, my young daffodil, what in the world can a nineteen-year-old possibly know about love?"

"Hear the ancient impart his wisdom." Feighan snickered. "Tell me, oh venerable twenty-two-year-old, all your arcane lore." He laughed, but was too depressed to make it sound real.

"I'm not kidding." Blinking in the dazzle of April sun through the window-wall, he said, "Hey! Look at this."

Feighan craned his neck to see outside without getting up.

Beyond the window hovered a balloon five meters in diameter. It was green and purple, and a propeller held it steady against the gusts of New York City.

"Yeah?" said Feighan. "So what?"

"So have you ever seen a Ua'litscha tourist before?"

"What?" He looked again. "It's a balloon, probably broke loose from Central Park."

"McGill, those colors aren't the plastic's, they're the gases."

"Huh?"

"The Ua'litscha are sentient gases . . . or gaseous life forms, or whatever. And this one," he said, his tone sharpening, "is taking pictures of us. Oscar, cue: polarize windows; do it now."

The windows opaqued; two floor lamps snapped into brilliance.

"Greystein! If you wanted to live underground, you could have said so—Manhattan's got lots of basements—I wouldn't have rented a 124th story penthouse if I'd known you had this thing about sunlight."

"What else did you have to spend your money on? When you've got ten million in a trust fund, don't begrudge us a little luxury. Besides, I hate having my picture taken by strangers; they never get my best profile. You want a drink?"

"Sure, a beer."

"Oscar, cue: pour two beers; do it now."

Behind the bar, glass clinked; pressurized liquid hissed.

"I got some new mugs today," said Greystein, sauntering over. "From Inta Leina—Canopus XIV?—incredible world, McGill, you'd enjoy it. I special ordered these last week, and picked them up at lunch today. Remind me to teach you the route sometime."

"You're not supposed to make interstellar Flings for personal reasons."

"So who'd tell on me?" He winked.

"They're going to catch you one of these days, Greystein, and when they do, they'll figure out that you gimmicked the indoctrination machines—and then where will you be?" A sudden thought alarmed him. "Jesus, where will *I* be?"

"With me," said the other teleport, "somewhere else." He tapped the latch on the bar. "I don't care what the FNC wants, I won't be brainwashed like the rest." The wood-grain panel slid up to display two cut glass steins of beer, each with exactly three centimeters of head. He brought one to Feighan, and held the other before his eye. "Look at it real closely."

Feighan did. His own face, brown-eyed, square-jawed, and Roman-nosed, stared back at him. He shrugged. "So?"

"Turn it around, look at the other side."

He did. This time, no face: just tousled black hair that tumbled over ears and down a neck that widened into broad shoulders— "Hey!"

"Neat, huh?"

"Yeah, but how?"

"I'll be damned if I know—the Inta Leinans sell glassware, not trade secrets." He wiped his lips. "Now. Tell Uncle Greystein: who are you in love with?"

Feighan blushed. Given his earlier comments, he felt like a fool when he had to say, "Well . . . there's two of them."

"A polygamist yet!"

"No, I mean—" Uncomfortable, he fingered the facets of

the stein. He was reluctant to explain how he felt, even to himself. Wasn't it enough that he did feel? Did he have to analyze it like a math problem, setting limits and deriving exact quantities for each variable? He wasn't that kind of person. He would never repress his emotions—he expressed them whenever appropriate—but he'd grown up believing that to stress the emotional at the expense of the intellectual was undignified. Uncivilized, even. "Never mind."

"I'm not letting you off that easy. Come on. How can you be in real love with two women at once—and who *are* they?"

"Ah . . ." He brushed his hair back up his high forehead. He liked Greystein, and wanted to impress him, but first he had to overcome instincts which said that discussing an emotion would etch it too clearly in his consciousness. That, he didn't like. It gave his feelings too much importance, too much authority over him. And he'd be damned if he'd let his heart rule his head. "You know."

"No," said his roommate, "I don't know. That's why I'm asking."

He surrendered. "It's different for each of them. See, one's Gina Maccari—"

"The telepath? She's nice, for a Minder."

"To put it mildly. So easy to talk to—and smart? Like you wouldn't believe. She's comfortable, makes you feel she really cares about what you're saying, what you're thinking . . . the thing is, the other's Nadia Liang."

Greystein's dark eyes widened. "You've got to be kidding."

"No! I mean, she's just so—" He knew the feel of the adjective, but not its sound.

"Sexy?"

"Yeah . . ." What he could more truthfully have said was that Nadia Liang was so pretty that looking at her hurt—that when she smiled he wanted to genuflect—that aching happiness paralyzed his voice any time he came within five meters of her—but those are not the things you say to your roommate, not when you wish to appear worldly and sophisticated. So he looked into his beer, all bubbly amber, and said again, "Yeah."

"The Snow Queen of the North American Consortium herself . . ." Greystein made a face, then snorted. "I asked her out last year; she said—not outright, but between the lines—she said if she didn't have time for the Senator from Texas and the

Governor of New York, why should she make time for me? Think *you* can get into her pants?"

He jerked upright. "Hey, she's not—"

"That kind, I know, I know." Greystein grinned, apparently pleased at disturbing his roommate. "This isn't history's most liberated age, but she is that kind. Under the right conditions, everybody is. You're playing the old idealization game—put her on a pedestal, pretend she's better than human . . . Tell you what would make you a lot more at ease with her, McGill my acolyte, is if you could bring yourself to visualize her taking a shit."

"Hey!" He balled his left fist and started to get up.

"I'm sorry, McGill. I also take pins to parties for the balloons. I didn't mean to hurt your feelings, and I'm not saying she's a teletagger, but—"

From the ceiling grille came: *Ding*

Greystein held up a hand. "Lemme check this. Oscar, report: reason for signal; say it now."

"The incubator calipers have expanded past notification point."

"Fantastic!" He bounced to his feet. "McGill, it's your egg! C'mon!"

"Huh?" He set down his beer and swung off the couch. "What do you mean?"

Greystein disappeared into the bedroom on the left; his voice came through the door: "That egg from the Flinger on Throngorn II, what's her name?"

"Sahaang," he said, sibilating it properly. "What about it?" He entered his bedroom and found his roommate staring at the display case which, months earlier, he had mounted on a dial-studded stand. Inside rested a cream-colored egg almost as big as a football: its soft, leathery skin was stretching and sagging. "Is it hatching?"

"I don't know. You said she said that it would be ready when it got to be about the size of your head—so I instructed the incubator to measure it every eight hours—and you heard Oscar, it's now just a tad bigger than your skull. If what's her name—"

"Sahaang."

"—is right, then it should be sometime soon." He flicked a knob; from a speaker in the incubator's base pounded a muffled thumping. "Fetal heartbeat," he said. "Sounds okay, though I haven't the faintest idea of how it should sound, so don't put any faith in my diagnosis. And this—" He spun another dial. "—detects unusual motion, so we'll have some warning when it starts tearing at its shell, and you'll be able to get back here in time." Straightening up, he turned back to Feighan. "Oscar's been programmed to page you—wherever you are—when the system picks up hatching sounds. Keep it informed of where you're going to be for the next few days. All right?"

"Sure, thanks." He beamed. "This is fantastic, Greystein. How come you haven't been transferred to the Computer Section at Flinger Network Control?"

"I would have been," the other said, "but I flunked their test—accidentally on purpose, if you know what I mean. I don't want to spend the rest of my life at the Hub. A year or two, yes; I'd like that, because if I could access their files, I think I could find the Far Being Retzglaran for you—"

"You know I'm not interested in the Far Being any more," said Feighan calmly.

"Oh, *sure*."

He met his roommate's gaze levelly. "It's over, Greystein. Done with."

The other shrugged. "As you like it—and in that case, I wouldn't want to spend more than a week at a time at the Hub."

"I know what you mean—who needs New York squared?" He dropped onto the bed, laid his right ankle on his left knee, and jiggled his foot. "Ah . . . about this program. How do I tell Oscar where I'm going to be?"

"Simplicity itself. Just say, 'Oscar, update: McGill Feighan will be at X location from Y o'clock to Z o'clock; file it now.' Simple?"

"Yeah, sure. Thanks." The phone rang; he flopped across the bed to pick it up. "F&G Incorporated, Feighan speaking."

"Mr. Feighan?" The electronic secretary sounded courteous yet impersonal, like an engraved invitation.

"Yes."

"Please hold for Ms. Nadia Liang; thank you!" The line clicked into a silence that lengthened even as Feighan's nerves tightened. *Nadia! What could she— maybe— no, probably not, but—* Confusion, elation, and fright so filled him that when a low, husky voice asked, "McGill?" he could say only, "Uh-huh." And even on that his vocal cords threatened to knot.

"Are you all right?"

Humiliated by his awkwardness, he winced, and gave thanks for the unpopularity of vision phones. His cheeks burned. "Oh, sure, I'm— I'm fine."

"Could you come down to my office right away, please?"

"Sure!" He winced again. *Dammit,* think *before you speak— don't sound so easy.* "Ah . . . how come?"

"I've been going through the files—" She spoke so softly and expressively that it *felt* like she'd said, *I've been falling in love with you.* "—and there are a few items I believe we should discuss."

"I'm on my way," he said. "Ah . . . your office *is* the one with the purple force chairs in the reception room?"

"That's the one."

He was breathing hard. "Be there in a minute." He cradled the receiver so carefully, so lovingly, that it could have been an antique. Then he leaped off the bed. His Talent pulsed with eagerness to perform. "Gotta go, see you—"

"Wait!" Greystein held up his hands. "First, cue Oscar."

"Oh." He scratched his temple. "Oscar, update: McGill Feighan will be in Nadia Liang's office from now until . . ." He shrugged helplessly at the computer's programmer.

"Till further notice; file it now," said Greystein crisply. "Nadia Liang, huh?"

"Uh-huh. I'll see you—"

"Just a minute."

"What?" Impatience hyped him with adrenaline, which clenched and unclenched his hands. He couldn't bear to wait a second longer.

"Why's she want you?"

"I don't know, something about my personnel file."

"Hmm." He made it sound very skeptical. "Look, Mc-Gill . . . you haven't had much experience with women, have you?"

"No, but—" At Greystein's glance, he reined in his haste. "You know I haven't ever had time. I always avoided tele-taggers—who needs a woman who's only after your tunic?— and as for ah, normal women . . . well, what with the Academy and then Throngorn and all, I just, ah . . . I never got any practice. But now—"

"Things are going to change, right?"

"Yeah, that's right. Things are going to change. Why?" He sounded defensive even to himself, but didn't care. The pressure of his desire to Fling filled him like wind in sails, and he wanted to cast off. "Shouldn't they?"

"I'm not saying that, not at all. What I'm saying is simply that you should be very, very careful with Ms. Nadia Liang, that's all."

"Why? She's a—"

"A shark, McGill. A beautiful, sexy, seductive shark. Be very careful what you say to her, that's all. All right?"

"Yeah, all right. Now can I go?"

"Of course." He waved a negligent hand and stepped out of the bedroom. "See you later."

Closing his eyes, Feighan visualized his destination: the orange rug, the purple force chairs, the framed print of a horse and rider on the wall above the secretary's desk. At the same time he formed and held an image of himself: tall and broad in his sparkling tunic, white pants, and black boots. As the two pictures became juxtaposed, he *knew*, on a level beneath the conscious, how to transport the latter to the former.

It was a simple matter, really, just a little *pop* through the fabric of space and time, no momentum to adjust because the object and its destination were so close, then

*PI—

—it started, the Fling, the teleporting, in darkness grew Feighan till his elbows rubbed infinity while simultaneously he collapsed upon himself like the remnants of a nova falling into a black hole–

and for an instant that time didn't rule he was both the universe and the smallest portion thereof—

and stress began to shred his body, pulling half of it one way and half the other, and the pain had no ending because in teleportation there was no time, no space—

then before it had even begun, his largeness shrank and his smallness grew until they overlapped and the stress faded to let his body knit itself back together and—

—NG*

The Fling had ended. He stood on an orange rug, before a secretary's desk behind which hung a framed print of a horse and rider. "Hi," he said to the computer-generated simulacrum, "I'm McGill Feighan; Ms. Liang asked me to stop by."

The simulacrum, a creature of light and magnets enlivened

by the same technology that had spun the Flingers' tunics, had neither face nor definite form. Like a technicolor shadow, it glittered and flowed. "Please go in," it said in its sweet but artificial tones. A relay snicked; beside the print, a door swung on hitherto-invisible hinges.

"Thank you." He went in—blinked—and shielded his eyes.

Nadia Liang's office stretched six meters wide by ten deep. A window-wall filled the long side, and through it splashed a river of sunlight. The ceiling glowed like burning ice; its run-off dropped in a blinding lumen-fall.

The brilliance laved the plants she loved: trees in tubs and lilies in water and cacti in pots. A three-meter tall *dracaena fragrans* screened the doorway from the desk. To the right prickled a giant saguaro; to the left drooped a willow. Palms fronded and lemons ripened and on her desk at the window, a hundred-year-old jade bronzed its silver-dollar leaves in the sun. The air smelled humid, fertile. Flora and fixtures must have cost thousands, but the North American Consortium's administrators took good care of themselves.

Squinting, he edged past a rubber plant, and awakened a host of butterflies. Beyond it sat two people in lawn chairs. Nadia Liang rose to greet him. The fragile olive haze of a *dizygotheca elegantissima* blurred the other's face.

"Hello, McGill," said Liang in her throaty voice. Some ten years older than he, she had deer-soft eyes and a compact body. Her reddish-brown hair fell to a centimeter above her bare shoulders, then curled briefly. When she extended her hand, she moved like snowflakes on a gentle wind.

"H-h-hi." He released her cool, dry fingers quickly—not because he wanted to, but because he was embarrassed by how sweaty his own were. "What, ah . . . what is it you wanted?" *Jesus, Feighan,* he thought, *you're a social oaf. Shape up.* He hoped his turmoil didn't show on his face.

"I believe you know Gina Maccari?" With that same litheness, she indicated the woman in the other chair.

"G-gina?" His poise crumpled like a rain-soaked cardboard box. "Oh, yeah, sure. Hi, Gina." He wanted to die. He had no idea why the two women had invited him to their get-together, but it couldn't be good. *Maybe they've been comparing notes, now they're gonna tell me to get lost or something . . .* And even as he thought it, he knew it couldn't be, since he hadn't let either know how he felt about her—or about the other. "Ah . . . nice office you've got here, Ms. Liang."

"McGill!" Her laughter rang like joyous bells. "Don't be so formal; call me Nadia. I'm only an Administrative Assistant to the Director, not a Senior Flinger. Please, have a seat."

She pointed to a chair next to Gina's; when he dropped into it, it slithered back and thunked against the *dizygotheca*'s pot. "Oh, God, I'm sorry, I—" Flustered, he half-turned to see if he'd broken anything.

"It's all right," said Liang, easing into her own chair. "The plant's fine."

"Well, I ah . . ."

Maccari laid a hand on his. "McGill, relax." A short, stocky woman, she smiled reassuringly. Strands of black hair framed her good-natured face. Concern softened her voice, and her hand squeezed Feighan's. "I know you Flingers get nervous around Minders, but don't worry—I'm not nosy, and telepathy isn't a toy. Really."

Relieved that she hadn't mentioned the true cause of his consternation—but then, no one had ever suspected the Staff Telepath of misusing her Talent—he began, "No, Gina, that's not it, I—" and choked himself off. He couldn't tell her—or Nadia!—why he was nervous, so he sank back into his chair and hoped his cheeks would stay cool. They flushed anyway.

Liang cleared her throat; even that mundane sound delighted him. "McGill, the reason I've asked you here is to review what seems to be a dominant theme in your life: your involvement with the Far Being Retzglaran."

"Oh, that, I—"

"Please." She raised a finger. "The NAC needs to know that it can rely on your loyalty, that you're not in any way indebted to or allied with an alien which does not have formal relations with the Flinger Network. Gina is here to probe—"

"Wrong word," snapped the telepath.

The hostility that crackled between the two made Feighan even more uncomfortable.

Yet the administrator took the rebuke gracefully. "My apologies. Would you explain, then?"

Maccari turned to Feighan. "Here's the story, McGill. I'm going to monitor your responses—*not* probe you—just listen to your answers while I Mind your totality. As long as your words jibe with your feelings, I won't do a thing more. Promise. If there's a conflict, though, I'll point it out. If it continues, then—and only then," she said, with a quick sharp eye for Liang, "will I probe. And before I do that, I'll warn you. Do you understand? 'Cause I want this perfectly clear at the beginning."

"No, I, ah—" He squirmed on the webbing of the chair. "—I think I see what you mean."

"Do I have your permission?"

That surprised him. "Can I stop you?"

"Yes." She brushed back her hair. "Oh, you couldn't block me if I wanted to get in. But, if you won't give me permission to monitor you, I'll leave."

A butterfly fluttered between them. He watched it disappear into a weeping-fig before he said, "I do understand. Please, stay. Monitor all you like."

"Thank you." She inclined her head to Nadia. "Go ahead."

"To commence," said the Administrative Assistant, "please summarize your involvement with the Far Being Retzglaran."

"Summarize?" He raised his eyebrows.

"Yes."

He shrugged. "Okay. There's been none."

Liang's face jerked up. For a moment her eyes flashed hard as flint, then they switched their focus from Feighan to Maccari. "Gina?"

"Absolute truth," said the Minder.

"But your dossier says—"

"The gastropod?" The word tasted bad.

"Yes."

"*That.*" Weary, he sagged back; his sigh defined rue. "Briefly: when I was born, an alien tourist—a giant gastropod traveling on a forged passchip—broke into the hospital and seized me. At first people thought it was a terrorist, then that it had gone crazy or something, especially when it wouldn't communicate. Three days later, it gave me back and escaped. Before it left, it claimed to be acting on orders from the Far Being Retzglaran—but last year, it came back to Earth to die. Right before it collapsed, it confessed that the whole thing had been its idea of a practical joke." With his right fist, he thumped the chair arm. "Dammit, anyway."

"What causes you to say that?" Her voice was gentle.

"*What?*" He was too upset to keep his voice down, even though Liang recoiled from his vehemence. "Because it screwed up my whole life, that's why! When I was a kid, all

I did was worry about why the Far Being had ordered it to do that. Instead of playing floatball or collecting planetcards or—or dating, I was trying to find out why. And nobody knew. I—" From the north of his soul whistled a winter wind. Hunching forward, he cupped his hands and blew into them. "I shaped my whole identity around this thing, like an orphan who thinks his real father's a millionaire or something, you know? I used to fantasize that the Far Being had picked me for a reason, and it—it warped me! I'm just starting to . . . I don't know, live a normal life, be a normal person . . ." She opened her mouth; quickly he said, "There's more. See, I wasn't the only one who believed what the gastropod had said. The Organization did, too—and tried to capture me, make me work for them. I, ah . . ." Sorrow swelled up in him, tightening his throat and blocking his tongue. He clenched his teeth, blinked hard, then coughed. "They tried to kidnap me a buncha times—caught me twice, but the first time they had to swap me back for one of their own people, and the second time I was rescued. So they murdered my parents. They destroyed my favorite teacher. On Throngorn II, they killed my best friend." He spread his hands wide, and looked into Liang's concerned brown eyes. Inside, where he now recalled all the things he'd tried so hard to forget, everything hurt. "And it was all because of a joke. A malicious, stupid joke." He dropped his hands, and then his head.

Liang glanced at Maccari, who nodded. The administrator spoke in a voice as soothing as balm: "I'm sorry. There were . . . discrepancies in the records, and I thought to clear them up. I didn't intend to force you to relive your pain."

Still staring at the backs of his hands, Feighan ordered the words to come out smoothly. "That's okay. I, ah . . . I mean, it's history. It happened. I have to accept the fact that it happened, get used to it, till it . . ." He cleared his throat. "Anyway, is there, ah—"

"More?" She smiled, and the smile held such warmth, such sympathy, that it replaced his pain with something equally filling, something almost paralyzing in its sweet intensity. "No, that covers all my questions. Thank you very much." She rose from her chair like smoke off a fire. "And I am sorry."

He stood, too, as did Maccari. "No, it's okay." And it was okay, because even though he hadn't told it for that reason, his story had touched her. It had shown her that McGill Feighan was more than a callow nineteen-year-old with a Talent; it had revealed his depths, complexities . . . tragedies. And, with a flash of triumph that he hoped didn't show, he suspected that it might have made him attractive to her. "I'd better be going."

The Minder patted his arm. "Do you have time for a cup of coffee?"

"Ah—" He hesitated—he didn't want Liang to think he was committed in any way to Maccari—but the telepath was fun to be with. "Sure. Where?"

"The cafeteria downstairs?"

"Want to Fling?"

She shook her head. Something like fear flickered through her eyes. "Let's walk."

"Sure." He turned back to Liang. "Nadia, I'll, ah, see you around?"

"You can depend on it." And her smile said even more.

* * *

On the outskirts of Rome, in a quietly luxurious apartment that he shared with seventeen cats, there lived a man who had once stalked McGill Feighan. He sat before a computer screen and read:

PREREQUISITES TO OPERATION RECOVERY

☑ 1. Discontinuation of police protection and surveillance
☐ 2. Relaxation of subject's wariness
☐ 3. Installation near subject of decoys, lures, strike
team and other operatives.

Next to the second and the third he placed a check. He smiled. And rose.

· Chapter II ·

In the basement cafeteria of the Flinger Building, Feighan and Maccari, relaxed and joking, drifted toward a secluded corner. The Minder had the gift of putting him at ease, and he loved her for it. He could have hugged her, she made him feel so . . . appreciated? Maybe that was her secret—she convinced him that she enjoyed him as he was, that he didn't have to distort his reality to please her. It stood her in sharp contrast to Liang, whose air pressured him to excel, and insinuated that one whiff of mediocrity, one brief rough edge, would mark him flawed, unfit for her presence.

He winked across the small, square table while it filled their cups. She drank her coffee black; he took his with cream and three sugars.

"You'll get fat that way," she said.

He chuckled, finished stirring, and tapped his spoon on the cup rim. "Uh-uh. I put the sugar in to keep from getting thin."

"I'm jealous. Why?" Snapping a paper napkin out of the slot, she began to fold it origami-style.

"Nice," he said, as it formed into a leering vulture. "I don't know why. My system just, ah . . . I've got a fast metabolism or something, I guess. When I went to work here, I dropped like thirty pounds in the first couple months—Flinging's more strenuous than it looks."

"So's Minding." She penned eyes onto the vulture's face, then set it to roost on the charge box. "But it doesn't seem to slim me any."

"Doesn't do it to the other Flingers, either—just me. The doctor told me, milkshakes and double helpings and lots of sugar in my coffee. So I do. Makes it taste like syrup, though." He scowled into his cup.

She said, "McGill—" and stopped.

He quirked his brows. "Huh?"

"There was..." Her capable hands folded, twisted, and pinched another napkin into a free-standing question mark. "There was something odd about that 'review' in Nadia's office—I was Minding her, too, sort of off the side of my brain, and...she didn't feel right."

"Wait a minute," he said sharply, suspecting he might have strayed into a private feud. "If you've got something against Nadia—"

"McGill, I'm not saying anything *against* Nadia." She paused for a breath, and scanned his face. "I'm saying that the whole scene felt like an excuse for something totally different...I couldn't probe her—I mean, I could have, but I wouldn't. I won't, you know that; it's *wrong* to probe without permission, except in emergencies...but— are you in trouble or anything?"

That took him aback. "Me?"

"Yes, you."

"No, not that I, ah...not that I know of." Gently, he twirled the paper question mark. "Why?"

"I mean like, are you having trouble on the job or anything?"

"Monitor my answer." He touched her fingers with the tips of his own. "No. I am not in any kind of trouble. I'm not having any trouble on the job, or—" He didn't want to continue, but she would sense the reservation and doubt him if he didn't. "—or anywhere but in my social life."

"Your social life?" She smiled.

"I mean," he said hastily, "it's not an easy job—at the end of the day I'm exhausted, and grumpy, and always frustrated, you know? To be stuck here sending other people to places I'd like to visit myself...of course, the worst part is the boredom."

"You, too?" she asked softly.

"Oh, Lord. Visualize—concentrate—hold—know—Fling—adjust—" He drained his coffee, ordered another cup from the table, and pushed his thumb into the charge box. It prickled; the vulture wobbled. Then he remembered his manners. "Would you like some more?"

"No, thanks, I'm fine." She rested her chin on her clasped hands. "I wish I could travel...the job isn't what you expected?"

"Oh, no way." Stirring in sugar, he said, "I figured, hell,

it's a high paying job, classy uniform—" He brushed the glowing fields of his tunic with his knuckles. "—tremendous prestige, I figured, it had to be perfect. And I've got a need to Fling, too, you know? The Talent *wants* to be used; it *insists* on it. I take a day or two off, this incredible pressure builds inside, and only Flinging can bleed it away . . . but nobody ever told me how boring it would be. Even a bus driver can look out the window and see the scenery change—me, I'm stuck in a tiny white cubicle all day long, concentrating on pictures in my head." Glum, he licked the spoon. "You have the same problem?"

"You know it." Her shoulders drooped.

"But telepathy—"

"Can be a real kick, if you misuse it, but that's immoral. I refuse. And that's more than ethics, it's survival, too. Once a month, maybe, I probe—for a couple of seconds. The rest of the time, I just sit there waiting for speech not to match feelings . . . and let me tell you, McGill, you think Flinging is boring? At least it's *active*—my job is 99.9% passive." She took another napkin and creased it into an upright Y. "A tuning fork, that's all I am. It's making me wealthy, but God, it's boring."

"Your days last forever?"

"Oww . . . longer."

"Your free time?"

She snapped her fingers.

"Me, too." He sipped at the sugary coffee, and marveled again that he felt so much more comfortable with Maccari than with Liang. *It's their looks,* he thought. *Nadia's gorgeous, so she's got all those guys waiting, and you've got to compete. But with Gina, you don't have to try so hard . . .* the thought twisted away and he was too at his ease to pursue it. "What was that you said about survival?"

"Pardon?"

"You just said, ah, not ethics but survival. What'd you mean?"

"Oh." Her fourth napkin of the afternoon puffed into an acorn. "Every Talent has its anti-Talent. You Flingers have your Anchors; we have our Amps."

Since an Anchor immobilized a Flinger, he said, "They garble thoughts or something?"

"It's short for Amplifiers." In front of the charge box, beneath the vulture's laugh, she arrayed her three napkin sculptures: the tuning fork, the acorn, and the question mark. "See, some people, they think so loudly that probing them is like switching on a one hundred decibel noise source. If you monitor them for a while before you go in, you sense it, so you can put on 'mental earplugs'—but if you just sneak in quick, like a lot of Minders do . . ." She shrugged. "Some days you can get out in time; others . . . you overload. They say it's like having your brain burn down—but the fire, the pain, it never dies out. Just keeps on burning. People it happens to . . . most go crazy on the spot. The rest . . . kill themselves." She looked up. He sensed that she saw, not him, but lost friends. "One Minder in three overloads, sooner or later."

"Jesus," he breathed. "That's why you're careful, huh?"

"That's the physical reason why." She glanced at the time numerals on the far wall. "I should get home, start dinner."

It was a perfect opening for him to dart through: "How'd you like to go out for dinner?"

"With you?"

That startled him—and hurt. He couldn't keep it off his face.

"Dammit," she said. "That came out wrong. McGill, I'm sorry. I didn't mean it the way it sounded. What I meant was—" She opened her mouth then closed it, thought a moment, and tried again. "I was surprised that you asked me instead of Nadia."

"Was I that obvious?" He was tempted to Fling away.

"Let's say you could use more practice." She touched his hand. "Look, I'm a Minder—and when someone's as conscious of what he's thinking as you were in her office, it's like he's talking out loud. Your thoughts are shouting at me and I can't help but hear. Like right now—you're wishing you could melt into a puddle and let the sun dry you up."

"But I like you, too—" It sounded lame; he could have kicked himself. "I mean—"

"I know what you mean." She chuckled, and patted his wrist. "Really."

' "Well . . ." The atmosphere had changed—a new tension charged it—but still he wanted to be with her. "Will you go out with me?"

She nodded to the origami works beneath the vulture. "Read the rebus; there's my answer."

He frowned. "Tuning fork, acorn, question mark . . . this is definitely unfair, you know, giving me a riddle instead of a reply...tuning— Oh! 'Y nut?'" He grinned, and relaxed. "Thank you."

"You're welcome."

"What kind of food do you like?"

"Chinese?"

"Great. Stand up and hold your hat." Rising, he closed his eyes—

PING

They stood on a glossy parquet floor. "Hong Kong." He smiled. "I own a small condo here."

"Eerie." She shook her head to clear it. "But great! First time I've ever Flung...I thought after a hard day's work you were bored with Flinging."

"Not when I'm traveling myself." He led her into the corridor. "There's a superb restaurant just up the hill, you'll love it."

"But—" She stopped, and her face opened into an expression of awe. "God, the *space* this gives you!"

"Flinging's the freest prison going." Elevators and halls emptied them into a crowded, noisy street. It was six in the morning, Hong Kong time, and the towering buildings of Victoria blocked the dawn sun, but no one seemed to notice. Energy throbbed in the air; vitality and eagerness pulsed loud. He took her arm. They climbed the sloping sidewalk, and the crowds swirled open to let them pass through. Cars beeped, then hissed off on cushions of air; children chattered their ways to school. The sea scented the street. "Here it is," he said, gesturing to a dirty, cracked door with three ideograms on it.

"Are they open this early?"

"Twenty-four hours a day." He held the door for her, then followed her in.

A beaming maitre d' in a white coat approached, a sheaf of menus in his arm. "Mr. Feighan," he said, in a flawless Oxford accent. "How very good to see you again." He bowed slightly.

"Mr. Li," he said, returning the bow, "this is Ms. Maccari."

This bow dipped deeper. "Delighted to make your acquaintance, Ms. Maccari. Please." He gestured to the interior. "The usual?"

"Gina," asked Feighan, "how'd you like to picnic on the Great Wall of China?"

She seemed bewildered and enchanted both. "I'd love it!"

"Let's do that today, Mr. Li."

"Very good, sir. This way, please." He motioned them down a narrow, mahogany-paneled corridor, the fourth door of which opened inwards.

Maccari entered first. "McGill!" She spun round and around; her eyes got bigger and bigger.

He stepped onto the ancient stones and looked north, into Mongolia. The blue and cloudless sky hummed with clarity, like lightly tapped crystal. A gentle breeze blew across their faces, rippling the cloth on their picnic table. In the distance circled a hawk, but nowhere else did anything move. "You like?"

"It's fantastic!" She turned again slowly, looking at everything. "But how—?"

"Holograms, fans, some mild hypno-sonics . . ." He pointed to a white line on the stones. "Don't cross that, though, 'cause you'll run into a wall of the room, and that will spoil the whole effect."

She laughed, and sat at the table. "One question."

"Sure." He sat across from her. The tablecloth went transparent so they could read the menu that glowed below. He pressed the green button for tea. "What?"

"Doesn't the NAC frown on unauthorized Flinging?"

"Yeah, but they don't check up on us." *They don't have to,* he thought. *The rest're so brainwashed they'd never dream of a personal Fling* . . . Remembering he sat across from a telepath, he brought up their full teacups and tried to blank his mind. "Of course, if somebody reported me—"

"Hey!" Her dark eyebrows drew together. "What do you think I am?"

"Sorry . . . they have these rules and regulations, telling us how we can use our Talents and how we can't, but Jesus, it's mine, not theirs." For the second time that day, he felt obliged to define for another a truth which he'd been content to leave as a feeling. "Look, this . . . this power isn't a tool the NAC owns but pays me to use. And it's not a possession I can lay on a shelf when my shift is over, like a computer. It's mine like my arm is mine, you know? More so—the Talent is such an essential part of what I am that you couldn't take it away without destroying me." He thought he saw sympathy in her eyes, and felt better. "You do know what I mean, don't you."

She nodded. "I have a Talent, too, remember?"

"Yeah . . ." The scent of jasmine rose from his cup, but the tea was still too hot. "The way it is with me, I respect myself, and want to keep it that way. I don't plan to misuse my power— I mean, what I want is to use it as a 'force for good,' naive and idealistic as that sounds . . . but since this is me we're talking about, since the Talent is inherent in me and not in the NAC, *I* will be the judge of 'good' and 'bad' uses—not the NAC. Whew!" He slumped in his chair. "Sorry about the sermon; it sort of got away from me."

"That's okay, McGill." She touched the back of his knuckles. "Believe me, I know just how you feel . . . say—" She tapped her foot on the stones of the Wall. "Why an illusion instead of the real thing? You could have Flung us there, right?"

"Oh, yeah, no problem. Just that the real one's unbelievably crowded—and the restaurants are lousy." Anxiously, he looked from the holo-scenes to her face. "If you'd rather go *there*, though, I can—"

"No, McGill, this is fine." She turned her head slowly, and her eyes circled with the hawk. "I take it back. It's wonderful. And I'm *starving*."

*   *   *

They couldn't finish the shark's fin soup, not after four plates of dimsum and a heaping platter of beef lo mein. He offered her the last fried prawn, but she shook her head. "I'd explode," she said. "And isn't it getting sort of late?"

"Oh." He hated to see the evening end. "Would you like to leave?"

"Please."

He needed to see a place before he could Fling to it, so— since he'd never visited her apartment—he had to teleport them to an intersection he knew nearby. A wind chilled the New York night, and scuffed their feet with candy wrappers. "McGill," she said, as they walked to her building's door, "remind me never to go to dinner with you again."

"Why?" he asked, trying to conceal his hurt.

"Hey, I was teasing! I was going to say, I'll have to diet for a week, just to take off what tonight put on." She slipped her hand into his. "It was a lovely, scrumptious feast, and I enjoyed it thoroughly."

The switch from depression to elation left him dizzy. "I'm—

I'm glad. I had a good time, too."

"I know." She winced. The words had obviously slipped out.

"I'm thinking that loudly?"

She pushed back her hair. "That, and . . ." She exhaled noisily. "This is tricky to explain. I haven't been snooping, but— I don't know how it is with Flingers, but with Minders, tension triggers the Talent— You too, huh? Why'm *I* tense?" She laughed, with a catch and a quiver. "I'm attracted to you. I like you, but you're not sure about this aspect of me, and you're getting more unsure by the minute. So I'm nervous, and you're nervous about me so you think more loudly and my Talent reacts and . . . maybe the best way to put it is, the feedback cycles make me more attuned to you. You come through more clearly. Like right now. You're scared. So'm I, sorta. But you're standing here on this sidewalk trying not to wish you knew what to do, not to hope I'll ask you up, not to wonder how to get me to invite you without being crude about it—not even in your mind because you know I hear you—not to get a hard-on because you're afraid that'll show, too . . ." A taxi whistled past, leaking air through a torn skirt.

Numbed by his openness to her, he stood like a statue, unable to answer.

"Well, I'm standing here deciding I want you and wondering if you smell me and if you do, do I smell bad?" She opened the door. "Come up for a drink."

In the elevator he tried—quietly—to think of something to say, and—

Gina broke in: "You don't need to scrabble around for some way to impress me. I'm already impressed. Don't worry." The elevator stopped, and she strode out, calling him to follow with a toss of her head. "And stop worrying about should you try to kiss me—I do expect it; I'm in my twenties and it won't put me off, even if this is our first date . . . listen to me jabber." The lock on her apartment read her thumbprint and hummed a moment.

He stood behind her. A wisp of perfume floated up; he inhaled deeply.

"I'm glad you like it," she said, as the door opened itself. "And look, if it's any consolation, *your* nearness disturbs *me*, so we're even—I'm sorry to keep picking the thoughts out of your head like that, but I'm reading you so clearly I wouldn't feel right if I didn't tell you what I knew—and just to keep things balanced," she added, flicking on the light, "I'm being painfully honest and open about what I'm feeling, in case you hadn't noticed."

"Uh-huh." He stepped into the low-ceilinged living room with its bookshelf walls and deep soft couch. His arms felt stiff and awkward, like they had forgotten how to hang naturally.

"You're really scared," she said, peering straight into his eyes. "Relax, I won't bite . . . sure, it's the telepathy, my hitting you with it like this, you feel naked with nowhere to run. Look, if you'd rather call it a night, I wouldn't be hurt, really. I understand how you're feeling."

He shook his head, but couldn't get his throat to cooperate.

She came up very close to him, and slipped her arms around his waist. "It's okay," she whispered, "relax . . . don't *worry* that it's your first kiss, I won't hold it against you." She giggled. "I'll hold *me* against you . . . hey, you're shaking inside and out, you're more scared than before . . . relax, no matter what you think, I won't get mad or disgusted . . . and no, I *don't* think you're dumb or naive or any of that." She tilted her face up, and swiftly, gently, brushed her lips against his. "See, that wasn't so bad. I liked it, and you did too, even if your knees did wobble . . . I'm sorry I frighten you, and I *don't* care that those wild fantasies are flitting through your mind . . . oh, Jesus, I'm sorry, but don't be ashamed, I have my own . . . and besides, yours are going by too quick to comprehend . . ." Cupping her hand behind his head, she pulled his mouth down for a long and lingering kiss.

Blinking, he swallowed hard, but still could not talk. His knees felt ready to give way. He had to hug her tightly to keep his hands from quivering.

"I terrify you, don't I? I'm sorry. If you'd like to leave—of *course* I'm not asking you to, I *want* you, don't you know that? No, I *don't* finish up every date this way . . . again no, I'm not a virgin—don't be silly, why should I look down on you for that? Kiss me again, and re-la-a-ax," she breathed. As she raised her face to his, her right hand moved to the front of his pants and touched him, then began to rub. He tensed in her arms. She whispered, "Don't worry, don't—" but at the last instant shouted, "Don't you DARE—"

     *PI—

          "—FLING US—"

                    "Oh, Jesus!" he wailed.

                              —NG*

While he trod water—dark, cold water—he called, "Gina?"

"FEIGHAN!———WHAT THE HELL DID YOU DO TO ME?"

Hating himself, he swam towards her. "I'm coming."

"WHERE ARE WE?"

"Ah . . ." He sputtered on a mouthful of salty water. ". . . Long Island Sound, I think . . ."

* * *

Milford Hommroummy stroked the cat in his lap. A woman's voice came from the telephone amplifier: "The fish are running."

"Bait the hook and troll," he said. "But do not try to land it. Not yet. Let the line run free—let the hook sink deep."

The woman sounded hesitant when she said: "Perhaps another lure—?"

"Ah? Then you prefer to work off your, ahm, debt at the house in Marseilles, then."

"No!" After a silence she said, "I'll— I'll do it."

"I rather thought you would." He flicked a switch and dismissed her.

· Chapter III ·

"You've got to be kidding!" said Greystein the next morning, as the two walked the white corridors to their Flinger Rooms.

"Double fumbles I don't kid about." He wore glumness like a yoke; even his tunic was subdued. "Bad enough I klutzed up socially, but Jesus, to do it professionally, too . . . warn me if you see Gina coming; I can't face her."

"What did you do then?" He paused at his door.

Feighan scrunched his shoulders, embarrassed by the memory. "I Flung us back to her place, apologized maybe a million times, dripped all over her rugs, then got out of there before I could screw anything else up. What would you have done?"

Tapping his forefinger against his front teeth, Greystein gave that question his full attention. "Was she mad?" he asked at last.

"For a genius you ask real dumb questions."

"Flowers," said the other abruptly. "Tons of flowers, with a very small note saying, '*Mea culpa.*'"

"Huh?"

"*Mea culpa*—it's Latin—means, uh . . . 'it's all my fault.'"

Four musical notes chimed in the hallway. Through his depression, like wind through a screen, Feighan's Talent pushed to be used. "I better go," he said.

"Don't forget the flowers," called Greystein.

"She'd probably burn 'em." The door thunked shut behind him.

The cubicle was small and sterile white. The NAC said the color reduced the risk of distraction; the Flingers claimed the NAC Supply Officer had no imagination—and a brother in the paint business. Feighan himself thought a jealous environmental psychologist had helped design the building: only someone who hated teleports could have condemned them to such an Arctic ambience.

One step took him to the desk by the window overlooking the Fling Booth. He sat, and gazed down into a similar but larger chamber, where a red box rode a massive crate across the tiles. It floated to a halt in the mathematical center of the room. The magnetic pallet beneath them tilted one end to dump its load, then rose and glided out the freight door to the right. The left-hand door opened to admit two women, each slinging an oxygen mask and a mini-tank over her shoulder. Their heels rang on the floor as they walked to the crate. The thinner woman, a foreshortened blonde with thigh-boots, waved at Feighan. The microphone picked up her voice: "We're ready."

He activated his own mike. "Sit on the crate, please."

They obeyed.

The computer screen that formed his desktop flashed, "921."

"Ladies, you're three kilos overweight."

The taller raised her dark head. "We weighed in at 911 this morning."

He checked his screen. "You're sharing your Fling with ten kilos of tea," he said, "and you have—" He asked the machine for the countdown. "—one hundred twenty-three seconds to make adjustments."

"But we booked—"

"Ladies, McDougel Imports and Exports has a daily contract. They get priority, as I'm sure you were told when you made your reservations. Now, you gonna dump the excess baggage, or miss your chance to go to—" The upper left of the screen greenlettered their destination. "—Delurc?"

"But—"

"One hundred five seconds left, and counting," he said, snapping off his mike. Gusts of need-to-Fling thrummed the kite-string of his self-restraint. He watched the digits dance towards zero.

Below, the two women gesticulated to each other and at him, then sat on the crate, tore off their boots, and threw them into the corner. The screen flickered: "919."

He went back on the air. "One more kilo, ladies."

"Dammit," said the blonde. Adding, "You owe me for this, Allie," she slipped out of her coat. "How's that?"

"917.9. Well done. Thirty seconds, mark!" He closed his eyes, visualized the Flop Booth on Delurc, and imagined the uncountable tons of water that pressed down on that Booth's roof. Good, he had it, it felt right— keeping the image vibrant in his mind, he stared at the women and the boxes, checked the computer— *14 seconds* —stared and visualized and *felt* the way open up, *knew* how to send the one to the other, then— *3, 2, 1—*

PING

They vanished, but his duty endured. Still holding the images, he bled the momentum off the women and the cargo, dumping it all into the Energy Dimension, that glittery place that wasn't anywhere but paralleled everywhere, then drew from that dimension just enough impetus to match them with Delurc, so that when they materialized in that Booth ten dozen parsecs away, their velocity would be in all respects identical to that of the planet's surface. *No muss, no fuss, no bother,* he thought.

And opened his eyes. The countdown clock promised him 4:59 to rest until the next Fling; he punched a button and the screen gave him a crossword puzzle to take his mind off the remounting pressure.

On 8 Across the door opened. "Hello, McGill," said a throaty voice.

He spun— "Nadia!" —and leaped to his feet.

"I'm sorry to intrude on your this way—"

"It's no intrusion, really, please, have a seat." Waving to his chair, he clenched his jaws to keep himself from babbling on.

"I can't interrupt your work," she said with mock severity. "I'm just looking for Gina."

He colored, and wondered if she knew. "I haven't seen her, ah . . . today."

"Well, when you do—"

"I don't think I will."

"Oh?" She studied him with open curiosity. "This evening, then?"

"No, I, ah . . ." He shook his head and wished he weren't stumbling over his own tongue. "No."

"Poor Gina." She dazzled him with her smile, and made for the door. As it closed, she whispered, "And lucky me."

Couldn'ta been, he thought, resuming his seat and noting automatically that he had three minutes to the next Fling. *Musta been something else.* It was silly to think that Nadia Liang could have said . . . *uh-uh*. He fidgeted with his fingers: interlocking them, pulling on them, cracking his knuckles. *But what if she did say it?*

Though sure he had heard right, he couldn't convince himself that Liang had meant it the way it sounded. A woman wooed by holostars and politicians doesn't develop a sudden crush on a nineteen-year-old. It would worry him if she did, because he would suspect that she really wanted his Talent . . . or his tunic. *No, not that—Greystein said she's no teletagger, and he'd know . . . did she— why did she— could she have meant—* Calling back the crossword puzzle, he ordered himself not to dream.

And promptly disobeyed himself . . .

The breeze stroked the tree leaves, the light, bright leaves of spring. Sunlight washed the world with gold, and warmed them as they walked through a park that had no people, no borders. Her hand was firm and cool in his; it pulled him to a halt so she could raise her eyes and murmur, "I love you . . ."

He shook himself back to reality and sent a pair of blue-shelled diplomats to Delurc. He'd been assigned that run for the whole week; each load he dispatched made him think, *make a fortune there with my fantasies*. The Delu—large aquatic beings whose language no Terran had ever mastered—couldn't dream. Their brains could outcalculate anything going, could manipulate more variables than Greystein's favorite computer could even remember, but they had no souls. Or something. Probability theory they mastered before speech, but hunches came to them not at all. Emotions, yes; non sequiturs, no. Perhaps the most rigidly logical form of intelligence in the known Universe, they could not dream.

So they bought dreams, instead.

Yeah, thought Feighan, *I could really clean up with these . . .*

The first four-hour shift of the day continued in that slow, halting vein. He was eager to leave, to manufacture an excuse for running into Liang, but he had forty-eight Flings to make before his four-off, and the brass got upset over unFlung bookings. They had a point, of course—as they often did, since they in their own human ways were nearly as logical as the Delu. The Flinger Network held a mortgage on Earth. When the FNC had "discovered" the planet and incorporated it into the Network, it had charged five billion Flinger Network Credits for the privilege: it had to recoup its exploration costs somehow. It then loaned Earth another billion FNC's to cover the initial payments on the loan.

To repay it, the eight consortia of the world had FNC permission to charge up to 5O FNC's—roughly $750 US—a Fling, destination irrelevant. They operated on a very thin profit margin, which accounted for their irritation when a Flinger didn't do his full ninety-six Flings nine days out of ten.

So Feighan, though he ached to be elsewhere, had to stay on duty for the entire four hours, and teleport loads to Delurc every five minutes. It bored hell out of him, though as the shift wore on it did diminish the constant pressure of a Talent that, like a beaver's teeth, had to be worn down frequently to remain manageable. Having to return from his four-off without having seen Liang didn't improve his mood any, either.

I could take it easier if the damn NAC didn't spend so much money, he thought. *But no, they gotta have wall-to-wall carpeting, and deputies to the assistants to the undersecretaries . . . big ol' bureaucracy developing there, and we gotta earn the money to pay for it.*

At last he was done for the day. Rising with a yawn, he stretched, and considered strolling down to Liang's office. *Lessee, I could say I was, ah, looking for . . . no, what about, ah, checking to see if the files have my address right . . .* but he couldn't imagine a likely sounding excuse. Nor could he just walk in and say hi; that would be too . . . *admit it; it's too scary.*

He stepped into the corridor, leaned against the wall, and nodded to his relief when she arrived. A thin, fluttery woman who bore sixty-some years with an eternal air of preoccupation, she nodded back and slipped inside without a word.

Alone, though public, he smiled. *Funny. I spend nineteen years figuring out how to deal with the fear of people who were trying to hurt me, and I learn how, and I could go up against The Organization tomorrow and not be afraid, but when it comes to something I want—* An image of fawn-dark eyes flooded through him, racing his pulse and tightening his throat. *—then I'm so scared I can't talk straight . . . better go home.*

PING

"Greystein!" He hopped off the Flop Table. "Grey—"

"He's out for the evening," said a familiar husky voice.

He wobbled, then caught himself and turned, stiff with injured dignity. Someone was pulling his— No! There on the onyx force couch sat Nadia Liang, smooth legs crossed and a smile on her oval face. His *savoir faire* lost itself in fog, a victim of panic's amnesia. "N-Nadia," he croaked.

"Your roommate let me in before he left; he also cleared me with—Oscar, is it?" She extended an alabaster hand. "It's nice to see you, too."

His Talent tensed for a Fling farther, wilder, than the one the night before; he sensed it, and fought to reassert his mastery. *Never again,* he told it. *Once is an accident; twice is self-sabotage.* It resisted briefly before subsiding to quease-making billows.

Then he took the hand, unsure of whether to shake it or kiss it. She solved the problem by clasping his wrist and hauling herself to her feet. "I'm sorry," he said. "I—"

"That's all right." She smoothed her dress across her hips. Cut of irridescent flo-silk, a gossamer from Querithag VIII, it invited stares of admiration in a quiet, well-bred manner. Slit to mid-thigh and plunging at the neckline, it glittered like Feighan's tunic, and interfered with his breathing.

"Ah—" He looked down at her from his meter-point-nine, then pulled his gaze away from her cleavage. She stood too close. The scent of her reddish brown hair numbed him. He didn't know how to deal with her. "Ah . . . would you like a drink?"

Her eyes fastened on his. "Later." Her hands ran over his shoulders and behind his neck. Pressing against him, she lifted her face. "Kiss me," she whispered.

Talent firmly tethered, he exhaled his tension. Her lips warmed his; her tongue eased between them; her breath brushed his cheek. *I don't believe this!* It felt so good to hold her that he swore to himself he'd never let go. Yet it couldn't be happening—she'd turned down millionaires, Governors, Senators—her breasts pushed on his chest and the fog drifted back to his brain. He couldn't understand—it didn't make sense—he had to ask why she had settled on him. And he would. Just as soon as they finished . . .

When they broke for breath, he murmured, "Nadia, tell me—"

The doorbell rang.

"Oh, no!" She pulled away with a grace that doubled his desire for her. "Don't invite them in, McGill. Say you're contagious, leaving, anything. For me?"

He had to steady himself before he could find his voice.

"Sure." He stepped across the room, feet sinking into the plush carpet. "And if they won't go, I'll, ah, help them along."

"Good man," she purred.

He thumbed open the door and leaned against the jamb. On the other side stood a plump, black-haired woman with wrinkled eyes and a pursed mouth. "Yes?"

"McGill Feighan?"

"Yes."

She flashed a badge. "Iona T. Reed, US Department of Extraterrestrial Affairs." She lowered her head, ducked under his shoulder, and entered the apartment. "I have it on good authority that you're harboring an eetie here."

Flabbergasted, he said, "Me?" His concentration had focused in such a different direction that the copper-haired woman's question provoked only bafflement. He flapped his hand at Liang. "Just her, and she's, I mean, does she look—"

"An egg." Reed triggered her comp-clip and read the words on its smooth face: "A Rhanghan—" She pronounced it *Rangun*. "—egg, from Throngorn II." Shutting off the clipboard, she said, "Well?"

"Oh, *that*." The confusion cleared away and he relaxed. Embarrassed by his own incomprehension, yet amused, too, he gave a short, sharp laugh. "Yes, I do." He gestured to the bedroom. "In there. It's a present from—"

"You will have to surrender it." Tucking her clipboard under her arm, she dusted off her hands. "Bring it here."

"Surrender it?" He cocked his head while he stared at her impassive features. "Why?"

"It is the law. USDEA Regulation Num—"

"You've got no right." He squared his shoulders.

"She does, McGill," said Liang.

He whirled. "Why? Sahaang gave me the egg herself—it's her child, not the government's, and if she wants . . ."

Liang's upheld hand gradually silenced him. "I'm sure that on her planet it's perfectly legal. You're on Earth, though, remember? If the government's banned the importation of these animals for ecological reasons—"

"Animals?" He took a step toward her. "Nadia, the Rhanghan are intelligent beings—we have diplomatic relations with them!"

Her brows lifted. "Oh. I hadn't realized. That does make a difference—does it not, Reed?"

The AmerInd shook her head. "Not to me. The law says

no American shall possess an extraterrestrial life form. He does. Therefore, I confiscate it in the name of the USDEA."

"But I don't *own* it!" He raised his arms high in frustration. He wanted to grab the ceiling and pull it down on Reed's stupid head. "I'm like— like a guardian, a foster father, not an owner."

"Oh?" One obsidian eye unslitted fractionally. "Let me see the papers."

"What papers?"

"The adoption papers, duly certified by the appropriate Probate Court." At Feighan's dismay, she released a very small smile. "You don't have them?"

"No, I've never—"

"Then surrender the egg."

"But—"

Liang broke in: "Let me handle this." Patting Feighan on the shoulder, she nudged him towards a chair. "Sit down, relax." Then she confronted Reed. "My name is Nadia Liang, Administrative Assistant to the Director of the North American Consortium. I fully understand that you are doing your duty as you perceive it, and honestly, I don't blame you in the least. Here, however, we have a special situation. Mr. Feighan was granted custody of the egg by its parent—"

"Ms. Liang, I must impound it!" She slapped her clipboard angrily. "Now!"

Liang's ivory cheeks froze, and her eyes sparked. "Ms. Reed," she said, as smoothly as a dagger slices flesh, "depending on your behavior tonight, you will find on your desk tomorrow morning either a waiver of this regulation for Mr. Feighan—duly authorized by your superiors, all of them—or you will find your dismissal notice."

Reed's jaw hardened. "You could not—"

"I can guarantee that no USDEA representative will be Flung anywhere at all if you persist, and I think your superiors will believe me."

"But—"

"Postpone the seizure until morning. Play it safe, Ms. Reed."

The bureaucrat scratched the surface of her comp-clip while she thought. "He could move it tonight," she said.

"Seal the room—if it's broken when you return—" She shrugged.

Reed's grudging nod set her black hair to swinging back and forth. "Very well," she said, "but I want his word that he will not remove the egg from my jurisdiction."

Liang turned to the Flinger. "McGill?"

As if in a dream, he heard himself say, "Oh, sure. We'll leave it." He watched them cross to the door and affix a self-sticking computer chip to the jamb. He wanted very much to laugh—to point out that he and Greystein could enter the bedroom without disturbing the seal in the slightest—but he decided not to antagonize the government woman any more than he already had. He sat immobile until she'd left, then rose. "Thanks, Nadia." He stepped towards her, and opened his arms. "Now, where were—"

"Sorry, McGill." She side-stepped his hug. "Pulling strings without making enemies is a time-consuming art, and I must start now." She touched his cheek. "Don't worry that you'll lose the egg, though. Everything will work out for the best." She picked her coat off the sofa, and draped it over her shoulders. "Could you Fling me back to my office?"

He tried to master his disappointment. "Sure." Through waves of hurt that he knew to be immature, but couldn't suppress, he concentrated—visualized—felt—knew—

PING

And he was alone, scuffing the carpet. "Damn her!" He was not sure to which woman he referred. The quiet apartment swallowed his curse; its stillness intensified his loneliness. "And I never got a chance to ask..." He dropped into his chair, and kicked moodily at the coffee table until he finally fell asleep.

* * *

At nine o'clock the next morning, Reed arrived—tore the seal off the bedroom door—and stomped away, all without a word.

At ten, the egg began to hatch.

* * *

"Neat!" he marveled to Greystein.

Their heads almost touched as they stared through the glass wall of the incubator. Beyond their reflections rocked the egg.

No longer a perfect ovoid, it deformed and distorted in response to the struggles of the creature within. One minute it stood cylindrical; the next, it flattened into a thick pancake.

"It is," murmured his roommate, "truly one of the most fascinating sights it's ever been my fortune to observe. I've seen chickens hatch, and tadpoles, and snakes, and once even an alligator, but never have I witnessed the birth of an alien-American."

The computer's peripherals amplified a sound like rubber ripping. A minute hole appeared in the shell, and through it poked a tiny clawpoint. "It's coming!" said Feighan.

"What are you betting, boy or girl?"

Taken aback, he blinked. "I— you know, I never stopped to wonder." He realized then that what he'd been hoping for was Sahaang herself, with all her wisdom and humor. He shook his head at his own naivete. Then, slapping his knee, he chuckled. "You know something else? I'll have no way of telling which it is."

An entire foot tore through the shell, and dangled limply, wetly, in the open.

Greystein stood. "Take it to Sahaang; she'll know. I better go—it's supposed to imprint you, not me. You're positive it can eat worms?"

"Sahaang said it can, and I ate the food there without any trouble."

"Why is that?"

"Greystein, I don't know—it's bound to happen once in a while, I suppose—but right now I have other things to worry about."

"I better go."

"Going to watch on the monitor?"

"You think I'd miss something like this?"

He laughed again, a victim of irrepressible good spirits, but couldn't peel his gaze from the hatching egg. "I'll see you later, then."

"Uh-huh." The door hissed shut.

Everything began to happen quickly. Another foot crowded through the opening, widening it slightly, so a third could fit in, then a fourth. The speakers *br-r-ripped!* as two hands appeared. They strained, and separated, and a toothy, triangular snout emerged. It yawned and hissed, then with a shimmery slither the entire infant wriggled out of the limp shell, and rolled its half-meter length on the floor of the incubator. Except that it lay on its back, it reminded Feighan of a cat stretching. Its tail whisked from side to side, curling a bit at the tip. Its tiny scales glistened with newness and with perfection.

"Hi," whispered the Flinger, tugging a worm out of the box on the table. His breath fogged the incubator's glass.

The Rhanghan flipped right side up with a dexterity remarkable in one so newly born. Tail whipping, it turned to face Feighan.

Thirty-three of its fifty centimeters paralleled the ground, from the tip of its barbed tail to just forward of its stubby front legs. Then its body curved upwards, through a stomach plate that would harden into armor with age, past a scaly torso that would broaden as its muscles grew, to the flat slab of bone that crowned its head. Close-spaced teeth clicked and gleamed like bayonets on parade. Nictitating membranes traversed its green eyes. Six fingers flexed on each miniature hand. Fins flopped down its backbone, from its shoulders to its restless tail—in time they would stiffen into knife-blades. Its tongue flicked the air boldly: despite ten thousand generations of sapience, the Rhanghan had lost none of their predatory instincts. They emerged from their shells agile enough to fight, and hungry enough to kill.

Feighan undogged the front panel of the incubator. Saurian eyes followed his every move, and seemed, impossibly, to understand what they saw.

"Pleased to meet you," he said, reaching in to offer a wriggling worm.

It hissed.

"Now, now."

It snapped up the night crawler, and swallowed it whole.

"Feisty little thing, aren't you?" He slid his left hand under its belly and grasped its torso with his right. Then he lifted it— "You must weigh five kilos, kid" —and, ignoring its waving feet, brought it close to his face so it could imprint him, so it would know him as its "parent" for ever after.

"Hi," he breathed.

It nipped his nose.

Greystein's delighted laughter cut through the wall.

"Ow!" Holding the child at arm's length while he rubbed his nose on his biceps, he said, "Sahaang never said you'd do *that*, kid. What's the matter with you?"

Its feet stopped waving. Bending forward, it wrapped its arms about his wrist, and laid its snout along his forearm. Despite its awkward posture, it seemed blissfully content. Slowly, all its eyelids closed.

The door opened. Greystein came in, still chuckling. "How's your proboscis?"

"More prominent than ever, thanks." He rubbed it again. "Is it bleeding?"

"No." Staying carefully out of range, he peered at the baby Rhanghan. "Cute little thing—or ugly, depending on your frame of reference, I suppose, but to my eyes, it's beautiful."

"To mine too." He stroked the infant's neck with a fingertip.

"So you're off to Throngorn?"

"That I am."

Greystein stepped back—his Talent would feel a pull when Feighan Flung himself, a pull that lessened in proportion to the distance between them. "Remember, your shift starts in two hours. And don't forget the cigars!"

"With friends like you, how could I?" He winked, brought the sleeping infant close to his chest, and—

PING

—and stood in a stone-walled lobby whose flat ceilings hung four meters above the floor. He headed toward the far end, toward a heavy wooden door further laden with intricate intertwinings of bas-relief. Shouldering it open, he stepped into a long, wide corridor whose distant end cupped pale light. He took care to tromp his heels on the stone floor—both of Throngorn's intelligent species had martial habits, quick reactions, and a distaste for intruders.

The corridor let into the Flinger Building's dining room; before entering, Feighan checked his tunic. It sparkled as it reflected his joy. Cradling the baby in his left arm, he held up his right hand, palm open. Then, slowly, he stepped inside.

Eight heads snapped about to stare at him. Five were reptilian; three, big-eared mammalian. Every Flinger present wore an oversized automatic pistol.

"Greetings," Feighan called out.

One of the mammals unfolded himself from his chair. Just over three meters tall, he had hairy arms that dangled almost to his knees. Fur covered his broad chest. His chocolate eyes echoed the hugeness of his pink-lined ears; protruding from his back were furled "wings" which, outstretched, would each measure four or five square meters. The mammals—the Timili—used them as natural capes in winter. "Greetings, Guildsbrother," he said. "You honor this ramshackle hut with your presence. How may we serve?"

Feighan let out his breath. With a slight bow, he completed the ritual: "This great mansion honors me by offering me its hospitality. Nojono!"

The other broke into an ear-waggling grin. "Sun Spearer!" he bellowed. "Or shall we call you McGill Feighan?"

"Whichever comes more naturally to the tongue, my friend." On his last visit, he'd used the alias "Sun Spearer" to hide himself from The Organization, but Sahaang had learned his true name. Apparently she'd told it to her co-director. "It is good to see you again, Nojono."

"No better than it is for us to see you, Sun Spearer." He peered closely at Feighan's burden. "What? Do they infest your world as well as ours?"

"It is Sahaang's child," he responded, "and it is she whom I've come to see." He always succumbed to the formal cadences of Throngornian; it wasn't a language in which one could relax. "Does she stay in the Building?"

One Rhanghan slid away from the table on the other side of the room. Hissing, "I will fetch her, warmblood," it disappeared down another corridor.

Nojono studied the infant. "Never have I seen a baby lizard," he said. Hands on his knees, he stooped over, then grunted. "Just as gruesome as the old ones. Are you here to return it?"

"No." He was spared elaboration when the door swung in. "Ah! Sahaang."

"Sso, McGill," she rasped, approaching in the heavy-footed yet graceful manner of the Rhanghan female. "It has hatched."

He grinned in delight. "Yes! And that's why I've come. I, ah—" Suddenly embarrassed, he scratched his head with his free hand. "We were curious as to its sex."

Sahaang's magenta tongue whipped the air. "Let me examine it." Her six-fingered hands pried it off his forearm, then turned it belly-up and spread its hind legs. The child awoke. Its head swiveled to inspect the one who held it, but it lay still, as if it knew it was safe. "We are less exhibitionistic than you mammals," said Sahaang, in her deep gravelly voice. Her gentle fingers probed the infant's groin. "Aaah... a son."

"Really? How can you—" He choked the question off and

flushed. "That's wonderful!" he said, recovering his poise and exuberance.

"Not necessarily," she retorted, handing him back the boy. "Males make better guardians, but they are more reluctant to attack than we females." Her eyelids slowly nictitated. "Fortunately for you, young warmblood, they tend to be slightly smaller, as well." She herself measured some four and a half meters from head to tail; the difference would mean less to Feighan than to her. "Sso," she said, "have you fulfilled your quest on Delurc?"

"Oh." Abruptly sober, he pursed his lips. "You hadn't heard, then."

"What?"

"The gastropod was not the Far Being's." Swiftly, he related the tale of its revelation and subsequent death. "There is no quest."

"You mammals." She waggled her snout from side to side. "Always so sure of yourselves. Be less so."

"Why?"

She scrutinized him for a long time before replying, "Each life is a quest, McGill F-feighan. Each being seeks something— a prize, a peak, an answer. Your search is far from over."

"But—"

"I am on duty; I must go." She whirled with surprising agility, then over her shoulder added, "May fortune be with you, McGill. Visit when you can." Tail swishing, she headed for her Booth.

Feighan watched her go, wondering what she knew that he didn't—and aware that she'd never tell him if she thought he should learn it on his own. It frustrated him, but . . . he had learned to trust her.

"Will you stay for supper?" boomed a voice behind his back.

He turned. "Oh, Nojono—you startled me. No, I'm sorry— I would like to, very much, but I must report for work. However, I thank you." He bowed, and made ready to leave.

"You're certain," said the Timili, with a gesture to the baby, "that you don't want its neck wrung?"

"Positive." He smiled.

"Then here." Nojono thrust a fist-sized woven reed container at him. Inside something skittered and chirped like a cricket, or a katydid. "Genuine lizard food, lest it never know the tastes of Throngorn."

He took the box and concealed his astonishment. *A Timili doing a favor for a Rhanghan?* Then he remembered an autumn day in a chalk cliff cave when Sahaang had saved a Timili's life, and he bowed again. "Thank you."

"Cast safe," said Nojono, ambling back to his table.

PING

Expecting afternoon sun, he materialized in darkness. He tensed. The infant hissed. He scanned the room: his own bed-side clock read 1:00 PM. Puzzled, he glanced toward the win-dow—then relaxed at its polarized opacity. *Oscar must have glitched out again.* With an amused snort, he reached an elbow for the light switch. He missed.

A voice, low and throaty, said, "Leave them off, McGill. Join me."

"N-Nadia?"

"It's not Iona T. Reed."

"No, no, I just— where are you?"

"In bed. Waiting for you."

His blood boiled and froze in the same instant. Dizzy with surprise, he swayed and tried to speak. His throat constricted; his heart pounded; he opened and closed his mouth twice. Even his third try emerged inanely: "But I'm on duty in a few min-utes." It sounded so teen-awkward that he was afraid she'd laugh.

She didn't. "I re-arranged your schedule, darling. You've got six hours. Now come here." Sheets rustled in the dark. A soft hand patted a pillow.

He snatched up his nerve before it could desert. "Nadia— wh-why are you doing this? That's not a complaint," he said hastily, already terrified that he was fumbling away the person he most wanted to catch. "But for a year now we've only been nodding acquaintances, then all of a sudden we're— I mean— well, *this*." His arm fanned the darkness as he gestured to the bed. "I love it, but..." He trailed off thinking, *Jesus, I've screwed up again!*

Yet her voice caressed him. "Too fast and too strong?"

He managed a wry, "Too unexpected."

"But I've wanted you since we met!"

The bug-cage *thunked* on the carpet.

"What was that?"

"Ah . . . I dropped something." *Please don't let her change her mind!* "Since we met?"

"Yes, but . . . all those guards and surveillance cameras, I just couldn't—"

"I know *exactly* what you mean—"

"But now I don't feel so . . . you do understand, don't you?"

"Of course."

"Come here."

Anticipation weakened his knees—as did the fear he had yet to quell. *This is crazy, my pulse musta hit 200 by now and I'm shaking all over* . . . Carefully, he set the Rhanghan on his desk, then moved across the darkened room. Stumbling on a footstool, he threw out his hand to catch his balance. His fingers brushed the mattress—and warm skin. Bare warm skin. *God!* His tunic flashed wildly, and splashed the spectrum across her smile.

"You're still dressed." Rolling to her knees, she reached for his belt.

"Well . . ." He couldn't believe how good it felt to have her unzip his pants. When her knuckles grazed his stomach, he gasped, and half-giggled.

"What's the matter?"

"I'm t-t-ticklish." He wasn't. He was nervous. Yet he couldn't tell that to the night-draped woman whose breasts rounded out of shadows and who nibbled on her tongue while she eased his pants to his knees. He giggled again as her cool hand stroked the outside of his thigh.

"Do the rest yourself." She settled back and lay supine, one knee slightly bent. "Hurry!"

As he tore them off, his pants caught on his boot heels. "Damn." Blushing, he pulled off his boots and freed his legs and rolled toward her, wondering, *What do I do, kiss her, I touch her I'm gonna bust . . . foreplay, supposed to have foreplay, but I don't know how to do that* . . . so he wrapped her in his arms and kissed her. She kissed back with head and lips and tongue, with soft noises of pleasure and strong arms that held him close. His nervousness fell away, behind. Eagerness drove him now, eagerness and instinct and hunger.

She touched him. In sounds that weren't words she marveled at his manliness.

He touched her, and had never felt anything so good in all his life.

"OWWW!" She leaped to her feet and towered above him, a night-blurred pillar of ivory.

"God, I'm sorry!" He sat up. "What's the matter, what'd I do?" His face burned brighter than his tunic. He wanted to crawl into the closet, shut the door, and die there. *Feighan, you fool!* "Nadia, I'm sor—"

"Something bit me!" Then, in a gentler voice, she said, "It wasn't you, McGill—you didn't do a thing wrong—but something *bit* me."

A warm scaliness nuzzled his arm. "I think I know what it was." Sighing, he picked up the Rhanghan.

"What?" She rubbed her backside.

The motion thrust into his face something he tried not to look at. Which he knew was silly, since he'd been about to— but on the one hand he'd been raised not to look, and on the other he had probably ruined everything anyway, so he turned his head away and said, "The Rhanghan."

"The *eetie* bit me?" Her tone trembled with astonished outrage. "The eetie I saved from Reed?"

"Yeah . . . I didn't put him away. Sorry." Dejected, he rose, and fumbled through the darkness; his tunic now shone as dimly as the clock face. Once he found the incubator, he detached the saurian from his forearm and slid him inside, saying, "In you go— hush—" as it hissed "—can't go around biting people, so—" He closed the panel and dogged it shut. "There. Done. Ah . . . do you want first-aid spray or a bandage or anything?"

"No." And her voice, though briefly resentful, softened with forgiveness, lowered, invited: "Come. It's you I want."

His spirits soared; his tunic aurora'd. He bounded over and fell into her arms. Her lips burned away the last of his doubts, like the sun does morning fog. She moaned, and stroked him.

His blood surged. Exhilarated and hungry, he feasted on her warmth, her softness; she pulled his mouth back to hers and said, "Now."

Heartbeat thundering in his ears, he rolled atop her, careful of his weight. Her fingers, so cool and firm that they brought on shivers of delight, slid down his back, counting off his vertebrae. Then her hands cupped his cheeks and impelled him forward while she said, "Now, McGill, now!"

The excitement was more than he could bear. He felt one spasm of premonition— "Oh, no" —before, poised above her, he exploded. He could neither believe it nor control it. He spent his strength upon her belly and felt no pleasure, only shame. "Oh, Jesus, Nadia, I'm sorry, I—"

She made a sound, then said, "That's all right. If you could get me a towel—?"

"A towel? Sure, anything, just—" He sat up; beneath him, the mattress shook. "Are you laughing at me?"

"No!" She giggled. "Yes, I'm laughing, but not at you, never at you." Sheets around her, she sat up, too. She hugged him, and rested her head on his bare shoulder. Her hair tickled his neck. "It's just that the whole universe seems to be coming between us: first the government interferes, then a baby lizard interrupts, and now the male physiology gets impatient...I have to laugh, lover, because it keeps me from crying."

"Don't do that," he said anxiously. "I guess it is funny, sort of..."

Her fingertip doodled on his hip. "We could try again." She let the last word rise in a half-lilt, half-question.

He squirmed. He trapped her hand under his, and held it. Far from rekindling his ardor, it had extinguished it. And that, too, made him feel less a man. "Ah, I don't know if, I mean I can't...could we make it tomorrow night?"

"I don't know," she said slowly.

He listened to her voice for injured feelings, but heard none.

"I have about two weeks worth of paperwork to get done by Friday," she said. "Tell you what, you call me in the morning and we'll see what we can work out. Okay?" She kissed his ear, and rubbed her nose against his cheek. "We'll work something out. I promise."

He was relieved, but already scared: *what if I do it again?*

And as though she could read his mind, she said, "Listen, McGill—what happened tonight—don't let it bother you. It happens once in a while. That's all there is to it. I don't think any less of you, and I don't want you to think I do. Okay?"

"Thank you," he said. "I love you."

"And I love you, McGill Feighan—don't you forget it."

*　　*　　*

The chessboard on the disp-screen extended into three dimensions. Figures filled its squares, but Milford Hommroummy frowned. He touched his phone, and waited for his call to be answered.

"Yes?" said his agent.

"In regard to the fish—"

"I told you not to call me at work."

His caterpillar eyebrows lifted. He said nothing. A silent minute passed.

"I'm sorry," she said at last. "I— I spoke without thinking."

"Ah." He blinked. "A hooked fish must be landed carefully. Netting is preferable to gaffing, but netting requires peace, quiet, and privacy. Arrange a better location than New York. And do report soon." He touched his phone again, laced his fingers across his stomach, and moved a key piece on the board. "Yes," he murmured, "yes, that will do nicely."

▪ **Chapter IV** ▪

Seven mornings later, Oscar drew back the curtains. "Get up, Mr. Feighan," it said, depolarizing the windows. Morning sun flooded the room.

Lifting his head from the warmth of his pillow, he blinked. *It's my day off, why—*

The speaker clanged like a dented cowbell. "Get up, Mr. Fei—"

"Oscar, cue: shut up; do it now." Cocooned in sheets, he yawned, and scratched his nose. "Oscar, query: did I override today's SleepLate Program; answer it—"

Then his memory cleared and he sat up straight. Outside, a Rehmal rode the thermals of the city; the guidebook it studied fluttered pages in the breeze. "Oscar, never mind; drop it now." For he had canceled the program that, one day in ten, let him reward himself with drowsy dawdling. And for a reason so good that he didn't want to waste a second more.

He bounced out of bed and strode for the bathroom. With hurried care he washed, smoothed medicine over a pimple, brushed his black hair—then, tugging on his clothes, he said, "Oscar, cue: pour one coffee, cream three sugars; plate two raspberry doughnuts; do it now."

"Yes, sir."

He entered the kitchen to a fanfare of chiming china. Taking the cup and saucer from the server, he sat by the transparent force table and flicked on the holo.

The theme music of his favorite advenchacom percolated out of the hidden speakers. A long-jawed face with lively blue eyes filled the north corner of the room: Aimer Chantscamp, hero of "Hub Sales, Inc." The camera pulled back to show him at his desk, placating a thin-necked Ookinza. The alien held

45

in its feelerbeard the monogrammed keychip that opened Chantscamp's warehouse. Its voice bubbled like a waterpipe: "The keys in exchange for the coordinates."

"What coordinates?" said Feighan, wishing he hadn't lost track of the plot.

But he'd lost all track of everything, it seemed. Nadia Liang had occupied his entire week—because he couldn't see her even once. "I have ten megabytes of files to scan," she'd said over the phone, "so I'll talk to you later."

He'd thought she was putting him off, that he had offended her to the point where she wanted never to see him again. For most of the week he had brooded, agonized by longing and by self-loathing. Then she had called back, two nights earlier, and said, "I'm free for the weekend if—?"

"I've got the day off and—"

"Can you pick me up in my office at 8:30 that morning?"

"Can I ever!" And so for two days he had floated through joy and through dreams, dreams in which Nadia was more delighted than he that she had given him a second chance...

Greystein's sleep-frizzed head came around the corner. "Hiya, McGill." He yawned so widely that his jaws cracked aloud. "If you're not watching that dim-witted travelogue, how about turning it off?" Tying his bathrobe with a tasseled blue sash, he trudged to the table and drew up a chair. "Up sort of early on your day off, aren't you?"

"Yeah, I am, but ah—" He grinned. "—I'm picking Nadia up in ten minutes; we're going to the Moon. Hunting star pearls." He swallowed the last doughnut chunk and licked his fingers.

Morning still reddened Greystein's eyes. "I wish you wouldn't call them star pearls; they're just obsidian drops, no stars involved in at all."

"I know that, but star pearls sound a lot more romantic than volcanic glass droplets—come on, Greystein, where's your spirit of enchantment?"

"I can't stand pre-dawn cheeriness."

"The sun's been up for hours!"

"Not in my room, it hasn't." He squinted at Feighan's coffee cup as if it were something new. "God, I hate mornings...She's really got you, hasn't she?"

"Huh? What's the matter, you jealous? Oh. Can you babysit

the Rhanghan today? There's a jar of Japanese beetles next to the incubator."

"Sure. But don't you think you ought to name him? He's what, a week old now?"

"Geez, has it been that long?" Briefly, guilt clouded his mood—*I shouldn't be neglecting the kid like that*—but as he ticked the days off on his fingers, he thought of where he'd be in just a few minutes, and gave way to a sheepish smile. "Yeah, it has been . . . just I've been so busy—"

Greystein raised his eyebrows.

"All right, distracted, then . . . a name, how's 'Sam' strike you?"

"Sam?"

"Uh-huh."

"Kind of dull . . . but it's not dumb, or cutesy, either."

"Then we'll go with that." He stood, and drained his cup. "Gotta Fling, my friend. Nadia awaits."

PING

"Good morning, McGill." She sat behind her desk, riffling through hardcopy printouts. She had said the screen strained her eyes. "Sorry, but the budget is taking a bit longer than I'd expected. I should be done in a moment, though."

"No rush." That he felt no urgency surprised him, because just being near Liang made him nervous, and eager to mask his shyness by saying or doing something distracting. Wondering about this, he took the armchair beneath the schefflera, and rubbed a glossy leaf between thumb and forefinger. It struck him as odd that to sit quiet and passive could content him, if it let him watch the woman he loved. Then he thought, *But in a way, this is almost better—I get to be with her, but since she's busy I don't have to try to impress her, and there's no chance I'll—* Breaking that train of thought with a wince, he understood why he wasn't in a hurry to leave: the sooner they did, the sooner he'd have to prove himself. And if Nadia scared him, the thought of a repeat performance terrified him.

"Done," she said a minute later. She tucked a wisp of hair behind her ear; she looked tired, worried.

He stood. "Ready?"

"If you're sure you want to go."

"Of course I am!"

She moved up to him. "Then let's go."

PING

They stood on a platform carpeted in immaculate red-and-black wool; over their heads arched the dome of the Hotel Luna's lobby, polarized where sunlight fell on it. The nearest wall was fifty meters away, but wandering rows of date palms and yuccas broke the room into more intimate areas, each furnished with well-padded airchairs and coffee tables waxed to luminescence.

The uniformed Flop Attendant bowed, and with a sweep of her arm motioned them toward Reception, a twenty-meter-long counter carved from a waist-high outcropping of native crystal. Behind reception soared the convex arc of the tower itself, one hundred forty-three stories of metallo-glassine brilliance. It winked down on them like a giant's mirror.

"I should think this air's too dry for the plants' health," she said.

"Water's expensive up here—and aren't they desert plants anyway?"

She shrugged, and they walked on. An Occleftian skittered by on its many legs, leaving behind a whiff of must and library paste. A few ancient but impeccably-dressed Terran men broke off their conference with an Aronya sales rep to stare at them: her for her beauty and him, apparently, to discover how he had won her. The scrutiny delighted him, and he strutted to the desk as best he could in the low gravity.

"A suite, please," he told the attentive clerk. "We'll go up later. At the moment, we'd like two pressure suits." When the clerk slid the thumbplate toward him, he printed it without reading the charges. He meant the nonchalance to impress Liang—but genuinely did not care what the visit cost. Between the yield off his trust fund and his NAC salary, Feighan had never been able to spend more than he made.

The clerk held up a finger; a bellboy popped out of the floor. "Escort our guests to the tour lock." His computer chimed a mellow tone. "Mr. Feighan, your suite is 143-A; the thumblock is now keyed to your print. If the lady would like—" He offered her the plate.

"Thank you," said Liang, pressing down on it. "143-A, you said?"

"Yes, Ma'am." He inclined his head the degree her style demanded.

"Very good. Shall we go, McGill?" Again taking his arm,

she waved the bellboy ahead of them.

This is class, he thought, as a waiter bearing a tray of champagne glasses paused to let them pass. Even the one-sixth gravity enhanced the ethereality of their surroundings. Floating in every sense of the word, he relished the luxury and the chance to shower it on Nadia Liang.

At the tour lock, the bellboy surrendered them to a middle-aged woman with penetrating brown eyes and grease-stained hands. "Going outside, eh?"

Feighan nodded.

"Well, here are your units." She reached under the counter and pulled out two back packs. Each massed about ten kilograms, had shoulder and waist straps, and was about the size of an attaché case. "Got your air, heat, power, and field generator in here. Put 'em on, but don't turn 'em on, not yet. Got to put your headsets on, first." She handed a plastic bag to each of them. "That's the speaker, wear it like an earmuff. The mike goes on like a collar. These are tuned to each other and to my base station." She gestured to a console built into the rear wall of her office. "Don't get romantic, 'cause my computer's got a dirty mind and it might be listening in. Not that romance is possible in these suits anyway." She chuckled dryly. "Now, you wanna raise me in case of emergency or something, call 'Luna Base!' and my machine'll switch you through to me. I wanna talk to you, I'll just cut in on your frequency. Got that?"

Feighan nodded again, and loosened the throat strap.

"All right. Now, when you turn on that switch—not yet," she said, as he reached for it, "the generator throws out a force field that'll retain your air and your temperature. It'll mold itself roughly to your physical contours, leave a couple of centimeters between it and your skin, means your feet won't touch ground, but from the way you two are grabbing at each other, that's nothing new for you. Pressure sensor keeps you from turning it off outside, so don't worry about that. You got to blow your nose, do it now, 'cause you won't be able to out there. Or play touchy-touch, either, but if you've got a room here there's time enough for that later." She looked from one to the other. "Any questions?"

"Yeah," said Feighan, "how long's the power supply good for?"

She slapped her forehead with the heel of her hand. "That's

what I get for being cute, I forget to tell you something important. I'm sorry. You got an hour. The computer'll buzz you anyway."

"Safety factor?" he asked.

"There is one, but I'm not going to tell you how long it is, 'cause that might tempt you to run overtime. Get yourself back when the computer buzzes, and you'll be all right."

"Fine." He glanced at Liang. "Nadia, are you ready?"

She dazzled him with her smile. "Let's go!"

They flicked their switches simultaneously. Around each formed a sparkly shimmer akin to Feighan's tunic, but impermeable. It flexed freely at all joints; the life support package hummed to itself.

"Into the lock with you," crackled the earphone, while the brown-eyed woman pointed to a retracting panel in the side of the dome.

Feighan gestured for Liang to go first, and stepped in after her. The panel dropped down; the pressure meter counted towards zero as pumps inhaled the chamber's air. A bell tolled in their ear speakers, and the outer lock door cycled open.

Sunlight slashed in harsh and blinding. Their suits polarized a fraction of a second too late. "McGill, I can't see!" Panic tautened Liang's voice.

He touched her shoulder reassuringly—or tried to, but the force fields met and would not deform. He could come no closer than five centimeters. "Don't worry, your eyes'll adjust in a second. We can wait here."

"Oh, I thought I was . . ."

"No, just contracted pupils." He smiled to himself. The apprentice had taught the master, and that felt good.

When their visual darkness lifted, they stepped outside, shuffling so the low gravity wouldn't bounce them off the lock's ceiling. Behind them, the door swung shut. Vacuum stilled its motor's voice, but vibrations quivered the ground.

Ahead sprawled a rocky field that jabbed at them with knife-edged shadows. It was noon on the moon. The sun hung slightly to the south, a ball of fire in a black field scattered with crystals. Beneath Sol, gauze swathed a blue sphere: Terra.

"It's beautiful," she whispered.

"Yeah." No word was grand enough to match the view.

Though he'd seen it before, he was still stunned by its majesty—its silence—its . . . implacability. The sight dwarfed

Man in space and time. Here, more so than anywhere he'd been, the machinery of the universe displayed itself with distance-referents so vast that a mortal mind couldn't grasp their size. And clock-rocks kept time through the gradual pitting of the ancient boulders, while dust pools measured millenia in millimeters. Standing there, he felt very small, and very brief. He cleared his throat. "Let's look for some star pearls, okay?"

"Are they really here, or is that just a lure for tourists?"

"No, they're here. Most are pretty small, but there was a volcano around somewhere a billion years ago or so and . . ." He shrugged. The glowing force-suit exaggerated the movement of his shoulders. "Don't get your hopes too high."

"I won't." She laughed, softly. "They look like black marbles, right?"

"Only the round ones—but the teardrops are rarer."

"I'm going to hunt over here." She pointed west, and bounded into the air. "Wheeh!"

For an hour they used the hunt as an excuse to cavort on a rocky, sun-bathed plain. They played tag and leap-frog and follow-the-leader: children's games, really, but to that eternal landscape they were younger than children, and so it made them feel. It had a dignity so firm and overpowering that they couldn't approach it as equals; they had to come a-skipping and a-giggling because anything more pretentious would be beneath its notice.

As Liang did handstands on a flat-topped boulder, Feighan watched and wondered. Her sleek agility aroused his hungers; he wanted to press that firm body against his, to have those soft round limbs envelop his. And yet her face, her smile, her laugh—these were more girlish than her figure, more innocent . . . more fragile. He wanted to take that vulnerable part of her and cherish it, shield it. He was torn. With the lights out, she was Sex—at a distance, she was Love—but here, close yet unreachable, she became both, turning child-eyes on his lust, and blowing sultry kisses at his respect.

Cupping a pile of pebbles in his palm—the force-suit fingers wouldn't close well; they got in each other's way—he said, "The hour's almost up—let's go back."

"The computer'll buzz."

"Yeah, but—"

"You're thinking of something other than the time, aren't you?" She walked past him—very closely—swinging her hips and tilting her head. "Do you like what you see, big boy?"

Speechless, he could only make a sound at the base of his tongue, a growlish sort of noise that vented his feelings even if it failed to articulate them.

Pleased with her effect on him, she smiled, and almost purred. "Then let's go." She pitched her voice lower and throatier than usual. "I can't wait, either."

Minutes later, arms around each other, they tumbled into the living room of the suite. He hugged and kissed her—kicked the door shut with his foot—but when he reached for the throat of her blouse she said, "I have to shower."

Famished, he couldn't believe the chef thought dinner should simmer a little longer. "You don't need a shower." He tightened his grip.

"I'm all *sticky*." Her forearms pushed him away. "I'll be quick, though. Just wait here." She headed toward the bathroom, leaving in her wake the sound of snaps unsnapping. "Have a drink or something while I bathe."

He paced, instead, up and down the blue carpet of the sitting room. Something seemed wrong, but he didn't know what.

"Sit, sir!" said two velvet-covered force chairs.

"Get out of my way before I shut you off."

They scuttled back to the walls and huddled against them in silence.

The viewwall overlooked the plain; he went to it and peered down. Below, a pair of technicolor pressure suits held hands against the intimidation of immensity.

He put his own hand into his pocket, and rubbed the glassy stones he'd collected. He hoped that at least one was unflawed. Nadia needed a ring—his ring—and could it be set with a star pearl they'd found together, it would have more meaning.

For he had made up his mind: he wanted to marry this woman, this beauty, this remarkable creature with her magnificent brain and voice that goose-bumped his skin. He had to marry her, on whatever terms—if he couldn't bear being parted from her while she showered, how could he stand a life without her?

"McGill!" she called, as though she'd heard his thoughts.

He pushed open the bathroom door. Steam wisped out at him, coating his face with moist warmth, like a tongue-licking from a puppy. "Yes?"

"How'd you like to scrub my back?"

He laughed because it was the silliest damn question he had ever heard; his heart spiraled up into bliss. This time would be different. This time he would prove himself. "I am on my way!" He leaped through the door, and—

And night crushed his skull.

* * *

The Flinger's tunic glowed feebly against the bathroom tiles. Behind him stood Liang, her right sleeve damp from the shower. "I've kept my part of the bargain," she said.

Milford Hommroummy nodded, then stepped aside to let his assistants pick Feighan up and carry him out to the stretcher that whooshed patiently in the sitting room. "So you have," he said, "but I hope you realize that Sr. Abecasis died only after a most revealing conversation."

Paling, she touched her fingers to the wall. "The news called it a hit-and-run."

"But it was," said Hommroummy. "It was, indeed. He thought, you see, that we had set him free—rather than up." His shoulders lifted delicately, then receded. "You must understand, my dear, that we have done you *two* favors; you have returned but one."

She sagged. "What do you want, Hommroummy?"

"For the moment, nothing. Later—" He moved his head a fraction of an inch. "—we shall see."

Her jaw quivered, then firmed. "No. I won't—"

"We have the knife, you know. Your fingerprints, your father's blood—most convincing, as evidence."

The life went out of her. "I should have killed Abecasis myself."

"Oh, no, my dear—you simply should have brought us *all* your business." He snapped his fingers; an Ookinza snaked its head around the door frame. "Caltzyma—Fling Ms. Liang to New York City, please. And then you may go home—we shall proceed on foot."

The alien bobbed its feeler-bearded head. Liang disappeared. A second later, so did Caltzyma. And from the sitting room someone called, "He's waking up!"

· Chapter V ·

He had drooled on the pillow and his cheek was damp. Wincing, he tried to lift his head, but a horde of leprechauns beat it back down with cobbling hammers.

"Honest," someone said, "we thought he'd stay out for hours."

His eyelids parted painfully, like they had been glued together. He moaned. The world did a slow somersault, suspending him for thirty seconds from the ceiling of his hotel suite. Then cold hard hands seized his arm and peeled up his shirt sleeve.

He forced his eyes all the way open, and found his face mirrored in irises so cold and gleaming that they could have been star pearls. The man was almost bald, except for a fringe of bristles once black, now greying. Eyebrows thicker than most mustaches provided an air of good humor that the machine-hard planes of the lower face dispelled. He was nearly seventy, but his presence had the impact of a much younger man's. He held a hypodermic injector.

Though groggy and sore, Feighan reacted instinctively: he tried to Fling himself home. He visualized, felt, knew, Fl—and buried his face in the old man's vest. *What the hell happened?* he thought.

Bony fingers plucked at his wrist. Somebody shouted, "Don't shoot; seize him!" Feet pounded on the thick carpet.

He threw a punch blindly. The old man grunted, doubled over his shoulder, and jabbed for him with the hypo. Feighan jerked his head up; the top of his skull cracked the old man's chin. While phosphenes flashed in Feighan's eyes, the old man fell backward. Metal tumbled in a glittering arc: the hypo! It hit the carpet. He lunged.

Fingernails scraped his neck. Choking, he slipped the grip and jumped onto the injector. It crunched. And a squat, bearded man jammed a gun into his mouth.

He froze. Gagging, he lifted his arms slowly and held them above his head. His front tooth throbbed; it felt broken. An acrid, greasy taste swirled on his tongue. The bearded man asked, "Can I shoot him, Mr. Hommroummy?"

"Don't be an ass," said the old man, picking himself off the floor. "We want him alive."

The gunman retreated.

Hommroummy, Feighan thought, *Hommroummy, where*... he searched through the pain-filled recesses of his memory, drawing blank after blank until— his every muscle tensed. "The Organization! You're the one who—"

"Exactly." He smiled, but it gleamed as coldly as his gaze.

God, I gotta get out of here— He thought of his room, triggered his Talent, prepared again to Fling, and— *What's going on?* "Anchors?"

Hommroummy nodded. "Four of them." He pointed to the corners of the room, to the four wary men who aimed their guns at Feighan. Natural anti-teleports, they negated his Talent. By superimposing their locations on his destination-image, they made it impossible for him to Fling away. He was equidistant from all four. Any attempt to teleport would return him to exactly that place. "You're my prisoner, Feighan."

"But why?" He almost wailed it. Though he'd been The Organization's quarry for most of his childhood, their interest in him should have ended. Having them seize him again was like bumping into an enemy he'd buried himself. "Why?"

"Because of your association with the Far Being Retzglaran, of course."

"Oh, God." He let his head hang. "Didn't you hear about the gastropod?"

"Of course we heard." Hommroummy stepped away, a private joke toying with the corners of his mouth.

"Then you *know*—it had nothing to do with the Far Being— it was just a sick prankster."

Keeping a safe distance between himself and the Flinger, Hommroummy chuckled. "The gastropod that died was not the one that ingested you."

He stiffened, replayed that statement in his mind, and still couldn't make sense of it. "What?"

"It was one of our employees—old and ailing—we sent it down to make the statement and die. We estimated that the ploy would reduce the amount of, er, attention you were receiving—did the governments believe you had no connection with the Far Being, they would be interested in you only as a Flinger. We have waited these months for them to relax their surveillance—as they have. And for you to relax your guard— as you have."

"I can't *believe* this!" All his assumptions turned topsy-turvy, as they had such a short time ago, when he'd heard the gastropod had died. *I am special,* he thought. *I am! But that means . . .* "What do you *want* from me? You've had me before, you know I don't remember the gastropod, that I don't know a thing about the Far Being, that I haven't got—" Memory choked him off. He would have lunged at Hommroummy if the Anchors' guns hadn't been trained on him. "Nadia," he rasped. "What have you done to her?"

"Put her to sleep," snapped Hommroummy. "She will awaken in her New York office and not remember any of this. *If* you cooperate."

He stared at his captor. The promise seemed false. *Unless—* He frowned, thinking it through. Though relieved that she would be out of danger, he couldn't help wondering . . . "She set me up, didn't she?"

Hommroummy's eyes narrowed. "Of course not."

"She must have; nobody else could have! But why bother? Why did you—"

"We're going to examine you." Hommroummy examined his prisoner like a shark its dinner. Though his words were as flat and grey as rocks, menace hid under each. "Oh, not here— we haven't the equipment—or the time."

"This is crazy! What can you find—"

"We don't know," he said quietly, spacing his words with deliberate, chilling precision. "But if there is anything to discover, we shall."

"Look." He still hoped he could talk his way out of it. "You know I'm not going to work for you, not unless you mess up my brain, in which case my Talent goes, too. And I've been studied by experts—what could you possibly learn?"

"A clue to the Far Being Retzglaran, of course."

"We're back to that, huh?"

"Rather." Again he permitted himself that private smile. "What do you know of it?"

He shrugged. "Just what the books say: that it's immortal, close to omnipotent, nobody's ever encountered it, it does most of its work through subordinates—like the gastropod—and . . . I don't know. The rumors claim it's playing some sort of incredible game, and using the universe as its checkerboard."

"Very succinct," approved Hommroummy. "Of course, there's a one-word formulation that describes it equally well."

"What's that?"

"God."

"Oh." He pursed his lips, and thought about it. Seemed accurate enough, if not what the churches taught . . . "But why is The Organization interested in— in an almost-mythical, god-like creature?"

"It is not mythical," said Hommroummy. "It might even be a force for Good. Certainly it has thwarted us on a number of occasions. It constitutes a subject The Organization should investigate thoroughly—a parasite must learn the manners and habits of its host, yes? We have become the foremost anti-culture in the galaxy, but if the dominant culture has coalesced, consciously or not, around a living, breathing deity that can reach across parsecs to juggle an infant's fate . . ." The scalpels of his eyes probed Feighan's face. "We must be prepared."

The Flinger read his future in those words. The Organization would vivisect him to expose the knowledge it wanted. Sick at heart, he jammed his hands into his pockets, and fingered the stones that might have yielded a ring for Nadia Liang.

Nadia. He didn't want to believe that she'd come into his life only to betray him. Even now he wanted to think that she had cared, that . . . *Maybe that's why she wouldn't see me last week; why this morning she asked if I really wanted to go off with her . . . they must have had something on her, like a gun pointed at her head . . . but if they aimed a gun at her she should have . . . wish I had a gun, blow hell outta these bastards, just a simple little . . . gun?*

He froze. Carefully he scanned Hommroummy's angular face for gathering suspicion. Blank. Good.

For McGill Feighan had a gun, or at least two things that would function as one: His Talent. And his pebbles.

He'd never even heard of the method, much less tried it

before. Success would exhaust him because he couldn't rest between its four stages. Failure . . . the Anchors would kill him.

But he had no choice.

And he'd rather die there than on an Organization operating table.

His right index finger pressed a chunk of rock against the outside of his pants pocket. Mentally he drew a line between it and the Anchor in the far right corner. Perfect. Nothing in the way. He took a breath: a deep one.

"NO!" Snapping his head to the left, he gestured with his left arm to the man in that corner. The others reflexively followed his feint.

And while they squinted in puzzlement at the confused accusee, Feighan reached into the Energy Dimension. Chaos roared at him; he scooped from the cauldron enough force to hurl ten grams two kilometers per second. He poured it into the pebble in his pocket. It plucked at the fabric of his pants just long enough to burn through it. Whipping to its target, it pierced the Anchor's heart.

For a full two seconds the man stood silent and straight, bewilderment on his bearded face. Then, slowly, his jaw dropped and his tongue writhed—but no sound came out, not yet, even while his knees unhinged and he pitched forward. Low-g let him down like a leaf. Not until his face hit the floor did he grunt.

Feighan heard rather than saw that, for he had shifted, and brought a second rock to bear on the Anchor in the back right corner. Excluding all the world but hazy impressions—*Orgmen in two corners and a meter away, corpse-gawking; God I'm tired already!*—he reached, and injected, and began to turn again even as a hole charred the second man's sweater.

The third gasped. "Charlie!" He raised his left hand, his weaponless hand, and took half a step towards his collapsing comrade. When his weight came down on his foot, a tunnel burst through his brain—he drifted to the carpet in loose-jointed slow motion.

A battery sucked almost dry, Feighan couldn't keep the last thug in focus. Clumsily, he positioned another pebble, and swayed back and forth while he shook his Talent out of its stupor and plunged once more into the Energy Dimension.

"It's *him!*" The fourth raised his automatic. A perfectionist, that gunman was: he brought up his left hand to assume the police stance, and he braced himself with spread legs, and the barrel of his gun welled so large in Feighan's vision—

—that, giggly with exhaustion, he boomed a small stone right down that barrel at four kps, and the whole damn thing blew up in the Anchor's face.

"An' now f'you." He staggered about to confront Hommroummy.

The suite door shimmied in the breeze from the ventilators, and stillness claimed the corridor beyond.

"Damn," he said, and just had time to Fl—

PING

—ing

himself back to the bedroom of his New York apartment before a pile-driver of exhaustion hammered him into unconsciousness.

He awoke in darkness. The clock read 09:17. Remnants of a headache scuttled inside his skull. He groaned, rubbed his eyes, and pushed himself into a sitting position.

A hand brushed his thigh.

He was startled, first, and then suspicious, and then—"Oscar, cue: depolarize windows; do it now."—then, as the sun streamed in and he blinked, turning his head, he gave way to anger. To fury.

For Nadia Liang lay beside him, and her clothes littered the floor.

"You bitch!" Focusing on her pale cheeks and closed eyes, he thought, *What does she think I—? She sets me up and then comes back and crawls into my bed? I mean, how dumb does she think I am?*

He remembered one of the plants in her office. He touched the back of his head, still sore from Hommroummy's club, and studied the face she'd used to mask her secrets, and thought about her ivory body, undoubtedly nude— he checked the floor, *Yeah, her underwear's there, the whore—* and he let fly with his idea because he had to have revenge of some sort, and the only alternative to dropping her naked atop a giant saguaro cactus was to shake her awake and beat the living daylights out of her, and the notion of doing that disgusted him.

So he concentrated on her face, and he visualized, he felt, he knew, he—

PING

—Flung her to her office, but even as he automatically

adjusted the momentum he could feel it was wrong. The kinetic energies were far too small for a—

The bulge in the sheets had not flattened out.

Nothing lay on the pillow but a rusty smear.

He threw back the covers and— "Oh sweet Jesus." Nadia Liang's nude body sprawled beside him: headless. Involuntarily, he touched her. Her arm fell off. It—they—had been severed at the shoulders; her legs, at the hips. Above her breasts her executioner had incised the word: FAILURE.

He gulped. And blinked. And tried to edge away from the mutilated corpse, but his muscles would not work. Paralyzed, he could not even turn his head. His breath rasped harsh and ragged. He gulped again and his guts came up, bitter and acid as the tears that broke from his eyes. Vomit splashed the sheets, her belly, her— "Oh Jesus God!" He moaned and retched again and finally managed to scramble away.

Vision blurred, mouth foul, he turned his back on the horror in his bed. He had to hug himself to control his shivering. *What do I do? Oh my God, my God, what do I do now?* He reached for the phone, for the police, then yanked his hand back as if from a snake. *No, Jesus, they'll think I— a lover's quarrel, everybody knew we— oh my God.* He took a step towards the door. *Greystein, he'll know what to—* but stopped himself again. *This— no, I can't— he'd think— no, he wouldn't, but what—*

He saw a solution. A kind of calm came over him. Wiping his eyes, sniffing, he turned. The whole bed couldn't weigh more than a hundred kilos, headboard included. He'd just— he had to— he walked around to the far side and picked up her clothes, trying not to feel their silkiness, nor to smell their faint perfume. He held them a moment, unsure of what exactly to do with them, then finally just tossed them onto the corpse because they'd burn his hands if he touched them a second longer.

Then he concentrated—visualized—felt—knew—

And put the bed and its burden in the heart of the Sun.

He sagged against his desk, tired already, knowing he had a full day of Flinging ahead of him and wishing he could go AWOL. Wishing he could hide from the world. Wishing he didn't have to do that one last thing . . .

Again he dried his eyes. He wiped his mouth on a handkerchief. Drawing a breath that was closer to a sob, he—

PING

—Flung himself to Liang's office. As he pushed past the rubber plant, the butterflies burst out of it in a cloud of jerky color that spread and shredded and disappeared.

He came up to the giant saguaro, two and a half meters tall with branches that looked like human arms. It stood in a clay pot half a meter in diameter; coarse soil and colored sand filled the pot.

The head of Nadia Liang lay against the trunk of the cactus.

A long, unbloodied scratch marred the smoothness of her left cheek. Her jaw had dropped open. A bumblebee sat on her tongue.

He sent it all to the sun, pot and plant and bee and...

He shuddered, then, and wept some more, and bowed his head. *Lord, I— I don't know anything, anything at all, but I thought I loved her and she loved me and— and I hated her just a few minutes ago, before I knew she— oh Lord my God, why did they do this to her? Why?*

The door mechanism clicked. Someone was coming. He jerked his head up and *PING* Flung himself back to his bedroom.

And that door opened, too. A tail swished on the carpet as Sam scampered over to be scratched.

"Well, well, well, if it isn't my old roomie McGill," said a bright, familiar voice. "You look like you've been partied hard and put away wet, my friend; is Nadia Liang that luscious creature proving too much to handle? For if she is, just say the word, McGill my young daffodil, and I will move in to share the burden. What the hell happened to your bed?"

Feighan wanted to scream, but didn't dare. He had to act normally. He couldn't let anybody know. Anybody. Ever. "It's The Organization—they're after me again." He picked up Sam and shuffled to the bathroom. Only then did he notice the streak of blood on his index finger.

"So what happened?"

"I threw the damn bed out, all right?"

Greystein waved a hand. "I meant with The Organization."

"Look," he said wearily, "if it's all the same to you, I'd rather not talk about it, all right?"

Greystein paused for a full second. "No. It's not all right with me, my young roommate-cum-landlord. It might not have occurred to you, yet, but it is already obvious to me that if

The Organization is trying for you again, I might be exposed to situations with which I could most likely cope *if* I knew what had happened. Now. Tell Uncle Greystein. What happened?"

He peered into the mirror. Puffy, bloodshot eyes stared back. "You're right." Briefly, he described his capture and his escape—but did not mention his awakening. He did not even want to think about that.

Greystein listened intently until the tale ended. Then, rare uncertainty on his face, he shifted his weight from one foot to the other and cleared his throat. "Uh—no offense meant, understand—but has it occurred to you that Hommroummy might have had a little help in grabbing you?"

Feighan closed his eyes, but all he could see was the saguaro. "You mean Nadia?"

"Uh . . . yes."

For the love of God, fake it! He jabbed the faucet's temptrol button. "The thought has crossed my mind." The bitterness flowed naturally. "And I wanted to reject it 'cause—" His throat clogged; he had to cough it open. "But I can't keep lying to myself. She didn— doesn't love me; I was a job, an assignment. She set me up, no doubt about it . . . and our whole 'romance' was just a prelude to last night." He slapped the top of the sink; Sam scuttled back. "Dammit!"

Greystein put his hand on Feighan's shoulder. "Everybody gets suckered by a pretty face at least once in his life."

"Yeah, but—" *But everybody else gets a second chance— to make things better or to make things even—but me . . . pretty face? Uh-uh. No second chance for anything. Goddamn that bee . . .* "—you're right, I guess."

"You going to report her?"

Lilac perfumed the room as he soaped his hands thoroughly. "No. No, I don't think so."

"Why not?"

He glared at his roommate. "Bad enough I *was* a fool—do I have to tell the whole world?"

Greystein raised his eyebrows, then nodded. "How'd you come up with the pebble trick?"

"What do they say about necessity? I was looking at guns, I was thinking about guns . . . and I had a pocketful of star pearls."

"I'm glad for that."

"I wish I could say the same..." He saw her now doing handstands on that lunar rock, while he held up the biggest stone of all. He leaned on the sink; its plascelain cooled his palms. "But I feel sick—I mean, killing four people, it—"

"Self-defense, Feighan, self-defense. You had a right—and no court anywhere would judge you guilty."

"I know that." He struggled to express what he did mean. "What I'm saying, though, is ah... They had family, friends—innocent people who are going to gr— gr—" He caught his breath and held it till his turmoil calmed. "People who will grieve for them. Grief *hurts*, Greystein. It hurts like hell. And I—"

"But they were there to hurt *you!*" Greystein leaned forward, eyes blazing.

"Yes. No. I don't— Look." He dried his hands. "I'm not defending them, but they were hired to *hold* me. The one who wanted to hurt me is the only one who escaped." To forestall further comment, he said, "I haven't thought this through yet, so I can't talk straight about it... all I know is that, however righteously, I have hurt innocent people. And dammit, I have this feeling that I've done something wrong, that I've, ah... corrupted my Talent."

"But—"

"No more on that subject."

Greystein shrugged. "All right—how do you feel about The Organization being after you again?"

"I don't know about that, either," he said. "I mean, I'm not scared of them anymore, or at least not exaggeratedly so, like I used to be, but... damn." He shook his head, and winced: it felt like marbles rolling around inside his skull. "Remind me not to play soccer for a while... I was just learning how to lead as normal a life as any Flinger can manage, and now—geez, I'm back to Square One. It turns out I *am* connected with the Far Being, and The Organization's hot on my trail." He took the shampcomb from Sam and eased it through his matted hair. "Ouch!" The comb came away dirty, but left his mane clean and shiny. "Damn, I was really hoping I could be a *person*, you know? Not a somebody, not a celebrity, just a person." He stared at the reddened eyes of his mirror image. "It's going to take me a while to figure out how to deal with this. In the meantime..."

"Be careful for god's sakes, will you?"

He actually chuckled. "I'll work at it—but you do the same. You're close to me, man, and, ah . . ." He spread his hands. "The Organization hasn't been exactly kind to the people I love."

Greystein's jaw muscles jumped: not from nerves, but from determination—eagerness, even. "Don't worry your head about me, Feighan my fine-feathered friend." Softly, he said, "I'm a Flinger, too, remember? I *can't* wait to be attacked." And he winked.

"Thanks." He checked his watch. "Hey, I have to go—I'm on duty in an hour, and I want to visit the Luna Police, first. Watch Sam for me?"

"Sure." Greystein reached out and tickled the Rhanghan's belly. "I'll see you later."

PING

The Luna Police Station stank of anger and sweat and sickness. A zig-zag crack ran down the left wall from ceiling to floor; sealant glistened along its length. On the bench against the right wall, a burly, pallid miner with bloodshot eyes and bleeding knuckles sat tense and suspicious. Feighan stepped to the desk. Memory provided the name of an officer he'd dealt with before. "Is Commander Rostrovro in?"

"Top of the stairs, to your left," said the bored sergeant.

Staircases on the Moon rose more steeply than their Terran counterparts, and the risers stood taller, but he mounted them in a second to confront a denim-blue simulacrum.

"Just one moment," it buzzed, once he'd said who he was. "Let me see if the Commander is free."

"Thanks."

"You're very welcome, and the Commander is available. Please go in."

Beyond the sliding panel, in a rock-walled cubbyhole almost filled with a battered plastic desk, sat a bent-nosed woman in her late forties. She raised her head as he entered, and looked at him curiously. "Feighan, huh? Where do I know you from?"

"A few years back," he said, dropping into the only other chair in the room, "you had to rescue me from The Organization."

"Now I remember, you're a good guy. No wonder the crook-check didn't flash you." She slouched in her seat and regarded him with steady hazel eyes. "So what can I do for you today?"

"Well . . . I'm here about the deaths at the Hotel Luna."

She snapped erect. "What deaths?"

"The four—" He stopped, and cocked his head. "You didn't get a report of four dead men in Suite 143-A?"

"Tell me about it."

Tersely, he explained what had happened. Again he felt that twinge of shame; again he would not—could not—tell about Nadia. "So," he said, "I thought I'd come in, make a statement to get that case cleared up, then, ah . . . prefer charges against Hommroummy."

She consulted her computer. "According to this, there is no Milford Hommroummy on the Moon. Course he wouldn't use his real name, so let's pump a description through, see what it flushes out."

Verbally he sketched Hommroummy's appearance; she pointed to a monitor atop a filing cabinet. "Sing out if he shows up." Pictures flickered on the screen, disappearing each time he said no. Twenty minutes later she said, "That's the last of them."

"So now what?"

She yawned, and rubbed the bend in her nose. "We got no bodies, no suspect . . . maybe no crime."

"But—"

Her hand flashed up like a stop sign. "Feighan, we'll look for Hommroummy. I'll send a man over to your suite to eyeball it for evidence of a crime. But don't expect miracles. If they cleaned up good—and whatever else you say about them, you got to admit they're thorough—then we won't find a fingernail, even. And if we can't find proof that a crime's been committed, then there's not a damn thing we can do. You understand that, don't you?"

Rising, he said, "Yeah."

"I'll give you a call if we need you."

"Fine." He extended his hand. "Thanks anyway."

They shook, and—

PING

He stood in the corridor of the NYC Flinger Building, just outside his booth. He'd barely caught his breath before the four musical notes that signaled a shift-change chimed. Running his fingers through his hair, he went in. And wished he could stop imagining a cactus under a desert sun.

*　　*　　*

The villa was quiet. A six-toed cat slept in Milford Homm-roummy's lap while he sipped a scotch and stared at the computer screen. It was dark, except for one dot of light at its center; he focused on that.

Then he blinked, nodded, and touched his phone.

The man who answered said, "Sixty-first. Captain Paulson."

"A task for you: visit Feighan's penthouse, ostensibly to reinstate police protection—"

"But you told me to strip him!"

"Circumstances are now different. While in his penthouse, examine his bedroom most closely. Especially the floor. Should you find anything suggestive of violence—"

"Like what?" Paulson sounded exasperated and sarcastic. "A dead body?"

"Or parts thereof. Arrest Feighan on any reasonable pretext, and take him downtown. I shall handle it from there."

"Mr. Hommroummy, what are you trying to do here?"

His lips turned slightly up. "I am about to offer him a choice: drown in the deep sea, or turn to the devil for help." Another touch of the phone severed the connection.

"It will fail, of course," he told the cat. "But the point is simply to lessen his trust in his allies, and to harry him until he drops from exhaustion. When he falls, we shall be there, waiting."

The cat purred.

· Chapter VI ·

Shift over, Feighan pushed himself to his feet. He felt nauseous. His head throbbed. He was too tired even to yawn. But before he could rest, he had to get some advice.

He stepped into the corridor. Floor, ceiling, and walls were white; fluorescent lights recessed behind frosted panels kept cold vigil against the shadows. The hall extended so far in either direction that a figure at the end looked like a person seen through the wrong lens of a telescope. Yet he headed for Walking Mule's office on foot: he needed time to think.

He had three major problems, and wasn't sure how to deal with any of them. His resurrected relationship with the Far Being led the list, but Milford Hommroummy the Hunter demanded almost equal attention, as did that flaw in his own character exploited by Nadia Liang, false lover and secret agent.

He sighed and scratched his temple. The Far Being thing...he couldn't decide how he felt about it. Good, he supposed, insofar as anyone should feel good over having been singled out by the powerful. Little kids go hysterical with elation when a touring President shakes their hands; shouldn't he, McGill Feighan, be even more ecstatic that the most potent—if least-known—being in the universe had selected him?

But there the joy went bad: for he had no idea why he'd been tapped. Outside of his Talent—which cropped up once in every ten million Terrans—he was almost abnormally normal. A little taller than usual, perhaps a bit more handsome and a tad brighter, he could pass as the man in the street. And yet he had been chosen. Marked, somehow, as special to the Far Being.

All he knew, as he ambled through endless white sterility,

was that the gastropod's assault on him had made him attractive to The Organization. Maybe even for the reasons Homm-roummy had cited, not that it mattered. What mattered was that the galaxy's largest crime syndicate was pursuing him, and it had assigned one of its most brilliant administrators to his case.

His feet sluffed softly through the long beige carpet. He wasn't sure how to cope with The Organization—though through his uncertainty he did perceive a glimmer of maturity; a year earlier the mere thought of The Organization had been sufficient to panic him—but he could see, even as he began to outline his strategy, that his would have to be a defensive role. He would have to wait for Hommroummy to move, and then react, quickly and competently. He should be able to handle almost anything, as long as he kept his wits about him— and pebbles in his pocket . . . He chuckled sadly to himself, and drew a curious glance from a Deputy Director leading a tour of VIP's.

The chuckle subsided into uneasiness as he recalled the four sprawled bodies. *Self-defense, sure, but . . .* he couldn't escape the notion that he'd misused his Talent. Tarnished it. Blood-stained its bright and shining beauty. He shook his head unhappily. *Next time I've got to be cooler, more logical—find a cleaner way.*

But how, he demanded of himself, *how can I stay cool and logical when I run into somebody like Nadia? I should have seen it from the beginning, or at least from when Sam bit her . . . should have known that somebody like her wouldn't—* He couldn't even complete the thought, it hurt that much. She'd been his first experience with love and sex, and he'd adored her for her goodness. What a joke. *Damn hormones blinded me. Or immaturity, something . . . Greystein was right; I should have visualized her taking a shit—all over me.* He punched his right fist into his left palm. *Damn!* His stride lengthened.

Rounding the corner, he bumped into a stocky, dark-skinned man with a hawkish nose and gleaming black braids. "Walking Mule! I was just coming to see you."

"Social call or business?" asked the middle-aged AmerInd.

"Business, I'm afraid."

"Figured it would be." The Senior Flinger spoke with a dry, Southwestern drawl. "Don't see much of you these days." He retraced his steps and thumbed the lockplate of his office door. "Hear you got a good-looking girl friend."

"Had," he said, realizing again just how carefully he would have to phrase his explanations.

"Come on in." He gestured Feighan inside, and followed close behind. "Lover's spat?"

"Huh." A computer terminal and two thousand pillows adorned the office. The keyscreen resembled every other one in the building, but the pillows came in all shapes, sizes, and colors. Covering the floors, they mounted halfway up the walls on either side. Straight ahead, a huge window-wall overlooked Manhattan. Feighan took a running leap onto a man-high stack of softness, and landed on his back, arms outstretched. "I wish that's all it was," he said, staring at the ceiling.

"You forgot to take off your shoes," said Walking Mule, still in the doorway.

"Damn. I'm sorry." Sitting up, and keeping his balance with an effort, he yanked them off. "Can I toss 'em to you?"

"Sure." He caught them neatly, set them by the door, then removed his own. "So what was it?"

"She set me up for The Organization." For the third time that day, he recounted his story. "And now..." The truth loomed up before him, arms raised. He dodged it. "Now she's disappeared."

"She'll turn up again."

"I hope not," he said, because it felt like the sort of thing a betrayed lover should say.

"Guess you really hate her, huh?"

"I—" Catching a sob before it could break free, he took a deep breath. "Look, Nadia Liang is the last of my worries right now."

"I'd have to agree with you there," said the Senior Flinger slowly.

"Walking Mule, I came to you because you're the only person around here I trust—you and Greystein—and...and now that this whole thing's started up again..." He shook his head. "What do I *do?* I've got a full-time job. Not that I need the money, but—" The puzzlement on his mentor's face reminded Feighan that all other Flingers had been programmed to feel that they did need the jobs and its rewards. He floundered. "Ah, I mean, *Earth* needs my earnings, I can't just drop my responsibilities, I can't go scavenging around for my link to the Far Being."

Walking Mule bobbed his head. "Go on."

"But what the Far Being did to me, the plans it has for me, that could be important. And if The Organization gets me . . ." Folding his arms under his head, he wriggled deeper into the mound of cushions, and let his eyes half close. ". . . then I might have to kill again, and the thought makes me sick to my stomach."

The AmerInd grunted something sympathetic.

"Did you ever have to kill somebody?"

"Nope." His hooded eyes gazed towards the past, and dulled with pain. "But I did anyway . . . Sooner or later, we all get in a squeeze and wind up pitching somebody into the sun." He did not react to Feighan's wince. "It's just most of us don't have to do it all that often." He shook himself back to the present. "Guess in your case you'd have to steer real clear of The Organization."

"Sure—but chained to a booth in New York, I'm a sitting duck."

"True 'nuff. So what do you want to do?"

"I don't know, just . . . geez, I feel—" He tried to arrange his thoughts, but fatigue kept scattering them. "I'm back to where I was before. The assumption is that there's something about me, ah, intangible or latent or whatever, *some* result of the gastropod . . . it's probably just rationalization, but what happened to me got my parents and my best friend killed, and . . . I mean, it wasn't my fault, but *if* the Far Being made me special, then maybe their deaths had some value—like, if I'm part of a long-term plan, where I'll be needed to do something next week or next year or forty years down the road, then . . . then Rothono was sacrificed for the Cause, and not just for . . . for a whim." He took a deep, ragged breath. "God, it's frustrating! I endanger my friends, and I don't know the original why."

"'Cause The Organization wants you?"

"No, that's not what I meant." Surreptitiously, he wiped his eyes with his fingers. "What I mean is, I don't know why I was chosen. What if my assumption's wrong? What if, ah . . . say the whole thing was purely for the Far Being's benefit—it wanted to study an infant Terran or a baby Flinger or whatever. Then I was just a lab rat, you know? There not for my own edification, but for someone else's. Well, if I *knew* that—"

"You'd feel like shit."

"Yeah, maybe," he said glumly. "But if there were proof to convince The Organization, maybe it'd back off."

"So what you're saying is that you want to go hunting again."

"Exactly." He sighed.

"Got any leads?"

"Sure." He maneuvered himself into an unsteady sitting position. He tried to prop himself up with his hands, but they sank into the cushions. "The one I came back from Throngorn with—that the gastropod had last been on Delurc."

"Pretty slim." Brown eyes on Feighan, the Senior Flinger chewed a thumbnail. "But Delurc . . . maybe . . ." With a lithe motion, he uncrossed his legs, rose, and went to the computer. "Wake up," he said.

"Yes, sir."

"Isn't there an NAC Flinger on loan to Delurc?"

"Yes, sir." It hummed for half a second. "Mary O'Higgins, on 18-month TDY."

"How much time is left on her tour?"

"Three months."

Walking Mule turned back to Feighan. "There's your answer," he said, spreading his small, square hands.

"Mary O'Higgins?"

"Uh-huh." He dropped with grace into his tailor's squat, and didn't dislodge a pillow. "Not her, exactly, but her tour."

"I don't understand."

"The Delu are short on Flingers—nobody's sure why—but there's a lot of traffic to and from their planet. The Consortia worked out a deal with them a few years back. We station a Flinger there on permanent loan, and they fine-tune our money supply to eliminate inflation. The assignment rotates from one consortium to another; O'Higgins is from the NAC."

"So what you're saying—"

"Yup. We replace her with you. It'll let you shake The Organization temporarily—not permanently; we have leaks just like everybody else—and give you three months to figure out what the gastropod was doing there. What do you say?"

He thought for a while, stroking the embroidered silk cover of a blue lap pillow. "All right," he said at last. "Sounds like it'd be my best bet. Can you set up a briefing for me?"

"No," said the AmerInd. "The contract says we can't do that at all."

Feighan blinked. The FNC never sent people to alien planets without warning them about what they faced. "But—"

"The Delu want you to come in cold."

"That's idiotic!"

"Well, hell, McGill, you don't have to tell *me* that. That's the way the contract's written, though." He shrugged. "It's not all bleak—Harry Sherman's based on Delurc."

"*The* Harry Sherman?"

He nodded. "You subscribe to his service?"

"Doesn't everybody?"

Walking Mule laughed. "Only the hundred million interested in Network economics . . . anyway, he's on-planet. If you can get in to see him, do. He's a one-man outfit, but he's got more bits and pieces of data in his files than most news organizations. Rumor has it he's partial to Flingers, too."

"Why's that?" Feighan was suddenly wary that the newsman might turn out to be another celebrity teletagger. Or worse.

"Sherman depends on us to get his datachips home fresh. In that business, an hour's delay can kill your profits."

"Can I trust him?"

The Senior Flinger seemed instinctively to know what Feighan meant. "He's had a few dustups with The Organization himself. I don't expect he's on their payroll—but it wouldn't hurt to sleep with one eye open. Just in case."

"I'll look him up—carefully."

"You do that." Walking Mule rose. "Go on home, get your things packed. I'll talk to the Director and put the paperwork in motion."

"Thanks." He held out his hand.

Walking Mule took it, and squeezed it firmly. "Don't forget your shoes."

Grinning, he picked them up. "I'll wait for your call."

PING

His stockinged feet touched the Flop Table; a green hiss sped between them. Sam had been drowsing in the day's last sun, and Feighan's unannounced materialization had terrified him. He raced twice around Feighan's ankles, then leaped to the middle of the room, where he took up a defensive stance:

tail poised to club, arms cocked, jaws open. He hissed again, and his whole body shook with its force.

"I think you scared him," drawled a voice from the corner.

"Hiya, Greystein. I guess I did." Stepping down, he crossed to the young Rhanghan and dropped to his hands and knees. "Hey, Sam—" His tone approached a coo. "—it's all right, it's only me. See? Smell?"

Sam's magenta tongue tasted the air, but his tiny fists stayed clenched.

"Seems like he's forgotten who you are."

Feighan's conscience twinged. Defensively, he asked, "Are you saying I've been neglecting him?"

"Who, me? Accuse you of neglect? Tsk-tsk, McGill. *I'm* not the one who's hissing at you."

Slowly Feighan extended his hand, palm up, fingers spread. Saurian eyes glittered as they studied it, but the muscled jaws did not snap. He grazed Sam's stomach plate with a knuckle, then rubbed up and down until the Rhanghan relaxed. "Yeah," he whispered, "yeah, that's right, it's me. Sorry I haven't been around, kid, but I've been busy." Even to him it sounded lame. Then he blinked. "But we're going to spend a lot of time together from now on."

"I could swear he understands us." Greystein micro-goggled his eyes and went back to work on the circuit he'd been tampering with.

"Not yet," said Feighan, rising and stretching. "He hears the voices, and they intrigue him, but I don't think he's comprehending much of anything."

"What was that line about 'a lot of time together'? Your vacation isn't for another six months."

"Oh, that—" The phone rang. "I'll get it. Hello?"

"McGill," said Walking Mule, "the Director approved the idea—even if he is displeased with you for losing his Administrative Assistant. You can leave any time you're ready. Before you do, drop by his office, pick up a formal transfer notice for O'Higgins. The bureaucracy bends, but it will not break."

"Fantastic! Ah...I'll be over in about an hour, once I get packed. And...Walking Mule, thanks, huh?"

"For a protégé," said the AmerInd, "I'll go to very great lengths. See you then." He cut the connection.

Greystein shoved the goggles back to his forehead. "Packed?"

"Yeah, see— c'mon, I'll explain it in my room." As he passed Sam, the infant grabbed hold of his pants leg and scurried up his body to sit on his shoulder, like a maharaja on his elephant.

Feighan opened a lightweight suitcase on his bed and started wrenching out drawers. "Shirts," he muttered, seizing a stack and tossing them into the case. "And pants, and..." While he ransacked his bureau, he explained the situation. "Don't worry about the rent, though—the trust fund credits the landlord's account automatically, until I order it to stop. Just don't fill the place with machines, that's all I ask."

"They make very good roommates," Greystein said. "Neat, quiet, efficient—and they're not always running off to the far ends of the galaxy on some weird quest."

"Dammit! It's *not* weird. It's...it's essential, huh? And besides, it's moving the line of fire away from you, so you ought to be happy about it."

"Hey, McGill—" He put a hand on his roommate's shoulder. "—I was teasing; I'm sorry. I didn't mean to set you off."

"Yeah, I know." He sighed. "Things've just been happening too quickly. I'm edgy." He laid a travel alarm on the pile. "And I'm packed, so—" He took Greystein's hand and pumped it, squeezing hard. "I don't know when I'll be back, but until then, enjoy, huh?"

"Least I won't have to put up with morning sunlight," said the other with a wink. "Take care of yourself."

"I will." He made sure Sam was secure on his shoulder. "So long."

"Oh, wait!"

"What?"

"I almost forgot—there was a copy here today, a Captain Pilsner—"

"Paulson?" His cheeks went cold.

"Right. Said it looked like you needed police protection again, and he wanted to re-inspect the layout, for the surveillance cameras and all."

He relaxed. "I'm sort of pressed for time—do me a favor?"

"Do you have to ask?"

"Give him a call, tell him I won't need the protection because I won't be here."

"Sure thing." He laughed. "You know, when he started

looking over your bedroom, I had to lock Sam out. Kept going for his ankles."

Again Feighan froze. "What was he doing in there?"

"Sam?"

"Paulson. What was he—"

"What he said was—" Greystein frowned. "—he said he wanted to see if he could put sensors under the carpet; being something of an electronics expert myself, I told him what a waste of time that would be, but—"

"Do me another favor?"

Greystein spread his hands. "At your service."

"When you speak to him, do not—repeat, do not—tell him where I'm going. I'm beginning to trust Sam's instincts, and—"

"You think Paulson—"

"Who knows? But let's not take the chance. So don't let him know you know where I am, all right? And I really got to go, so—"

"Enjoy, okay?"

Freighan shrugged. "'Bye."

PING

Sam bounced up and down as they materialized; he seemed to like Flinging.

Feighan looked around. The Director's reception room dwarfed his entire penthouse. Spotlit *objets d'art* hung on the walls and mounted pedestals around the perimeter. He padded across thick grey rugs, passing to the left of the three-meter tall fountain. *And they complain about a tight budget?*

The Director rated a human secretary, who looked up as Feighan drew near. His displeasure at having to wait late for a Flinger manifested itself in a scowl.

"May I help you?" From his intonation, he thought it distastefully necessary to be civil. Relations between the teleports and the unTalented bureaucracy might crackle with acrimony, but had not yet deteriorated into open warfare.

"McGill Feighan." Claws dug into his collarbone. "Sam, stop hissing." Gently, he rapped the Rhanghan snout with a finger. "He doesn't like you, either," he said. Before the secretary could absorb that, he went on. "I'm here to pick up a transfer notice for Mary O'Higgins—is it ready?"

The secretary said nothing. With a curt nod, he lifted a

heavy white envelope from the corner of the desk. Holding it between thumb and forefinger, he extended it to Feighan as though he didn't want his hand to get close to the Flinger's. "Will there by anything else?" His tone said, *There'd better not be.*

"Nope."

"McGill!" Across the grey acre hurried Gina Maccari.

All he could think of was that he didn't dare think: she would read him. And the last thing he wanted was to be Minded by someone he did not trust. "Hi," he said brusquely.

"You were leaving." She stated both fact and hurt.

"Yeah." Shifting his weight from one foot to the other, he tried to mask his thoughts by inventorying the contents of his suitcase. "Following a lead."

She rubbed Sam's stomach. "I heard all about it—and I'm sorry."

That confused him. "For what?"

"For Nadia."

His knees almost gave way. "What do you mean?" His voice was hoarse.

"Look, I'm a telepath! I don't probe people, true, I respect their privacy, but for God's sakes, McGill, I should have known she had it in for you . . ." She shook her head, tossing the short black hair that should have been washed that morning. "Maybe I did . . . I told you, I had a feeling that she had an ulterior motive—"

"In the cafeteria?" Relief washed over him; she hadn't heard *everything.*

"Last week, right."

It seemed much longer than a mere ten days ago . . . an entire romance had blossomed, withered, and rotted in those two hundred forty hours . . . and Maccari could have foresoothed some of the pain. "But you didn't, ah . . . ?" He touched his fingers to his temple.

"Investigate?" She waited for his nod. "No, I— all right, I'll admit it. I was angry with you, and—"

"I am sorry about that dunking."

"Not that!" Pursing her lips, she stared at the ceiling and blew air past her teeth. "You know, for a brilliant Flinger, you can be awfully dumb about people. Women, I mean . . . all right, at the time, I was, um . . . aggrieved? But once I dried off, it was *funny*—what I was mad about, McGill Feighan, was that from then on you dodged me."

He winced. "But I thought—"

"That's your whole problem—you *thought*. Next time, ask." She folded her arms and glared at him.

Something fluttered in his chest; recognizing it, he narrowed his eyes and reminded himself that she could be on two payrolls, too. And even if she weren't, she was a telepath, and— the fluttering stopped. "All right," he said. "Next time, I will ask."

She cocked her head. "What's with the cactus? I thought you were going to Delurc."

He stepped back, half-raising his hands like he would to fend off an attacker. "Jesus, stay out of my head, will you? And where I'm going is supposed to be a secret."

"Sorry."

"Yeah, I'll bet."

She blinked, and half-turned away. "You better get going."

"Yeah."

Suddenly she turned back and hugged him. "Take care of yourself."

She felt so good it had to be a trap. "I will," he said, releasing her with more reluctance than he wanted to feel. "You, too."

"Well—" She cleared her throat. "I've delayed you long enough, so—" She stood on tiptoe and pecked his cheek, then patted Sam on his headplate. "G'bye." Whirling, she rushed away.

He stood a moment longer, held by a sudden wistful sense that, in going to Delurc, he diverged from the path his life should take through the future. The door out of the reception room whispered shut. Mentally, he kicked himself. Then—

PING

Time had worn the tiles smooth, time and many moving bodies, but they still gleamed whitely. Mildew darkened their grout, and soured the cool, damp air that filled the dome. He raised his eyes to the clear walls. Around them swirled the ocean of Delurc. Great shapes glided in it, intercepting the sunlight that drifted down through the water. He shivered, partly from chill, but more from the gut-born fear that the transparent shell could not, would not, support all the water pressing down on it. Which was ridiculous. The dome had stood for three centuries without a single leak. The builders of the Flinger Network had raised it—and they built well.

"Greetings!" The voice boomed out of the head-high light fixtures that circled the wall. A panel to his right retracted, revealing a glassed-in walkway. "Please proceed through the door to the Customs area."

Post-Fling weariness thickened into a fog of *déjà vu*—for he had come to Delurc some months before, during a bout of brief madness. He wondered if they remembered him, then knew that they must. The Delu forgot nothing. Embarrassment crimsoned his cheeks: on his last visit he'd acted like a fool, shouting and screaming and blathering idiocy . . .

The walls reflected his tunic, catching its brilliance, cupping it, shimmering it around and around like a tail-chasing comet. Seaweed fondled the base of the dome, and through the waving stems darted tiny fish of a billion colors.

Before he passed out of the Flop Booth, he donned his oxygen mask, and inhaled heavily to test it. Satisfied that Sam's worked as well, he moved into the corridor. The door whisked shut behind him.

Within fifteen meters, the walkway fanned out like a river delta. A line of air-tight glass cubicles crossed the room at its widest point; the sign above one stated "Terrans" in subdued blue neon. Uncomfortably aware that he was the only being in the atrium, he approached the booth.

In it sat a human female whom he had seen the last time. Apparently middle-aged, but so fat that his estimate was a guess at best, she had skin whiter than her teeth, and lank blonde hair. She wore a metal cap; wires ran from its peak to gaskets in the ceiling of her booth. Outside, gills pumping and all eight fins treading water, a large fish wore a similar cap linked to hers. "Passchips," she said through her microphone. Robots spoke more vivaciously.

He pulled the plastic-sealed wafers from his pants pocket and slid them across the counter, through the mini-lock set in the glass for that purpose. She removed them from her side with shriveled, blue-nailed hands. The Customs area was chilly—12 or 13 degrees—but her fingers looked even colder. They moved stiffly, mechanically, to drop the two passchips into the reader that would interpret the alignments of their visa-molecules and warp others to record their arrival on Delurc. He wondered if the Delu were taking proper care of her.

Travelers and other Flingers told tales about those who translated for the Delu. He could not separate truth from rumor; too many stories conflicted on too many points. It seemed certain that, cap-linked to a fishbeing, an extra-Delu became its appendage. All agreed that the translators had no volition, that the link-wires were really puppet strings. But darker accounts had spread as well: that the Delu kidnaped unwary wanderers, and pressed them into service; that a being once encapped lost all desire for freedom and all capacity for thought; that those who died in service became zombies who served even after the flesh had rotted off their bones . . . he shivered.

"Nature and purpose of visit," said the frost-hoarsened voice at last.

"I'm a Flinger on loan to the extra-Delu City Consortium."

"The reptile?"

"My ward." *Are they going to try to keep Sam out?*

Overhead, the controller changed from cucumber green to sunset yellow. The translator's mouth opened and closed soundlessly.

"Is there a problem?" Feighan asked.

"Permission granted," she said abruptly. Her countertop spit up their passchips; she nudged them back into the lock. "Proceed to Transients' Quartering Offices." Her left arm lifted in a series of jerks and pointed down the hallway.

"Thank you." His mask muffled his voice. He reclaimed the chips, hoisted his bag and moved away, still wondering. Sam, silent, clutched his hair.

A hundred meters down, a similar line of booths blocked the passageway; signs in thirty languages labeled them as "Transients' Quartering Offices." At congested times, they would channel the pedestrian stream like spillways on a dam. Now, his footsteps rang sharply in the emptiness. Feeling conspicuous and self-conscious, he hurried to the one marked "Terran."

Within, an opaque-eyed boy of six or seven rode a high stool. Above his purplish-black skin gleamed the chrome of his cap; on him, it seemed a prince's crown.

"Hi," said Feighan. "The lady at Customs told me to come here."

"Name." His voice was as lifeless as the woman's.

"McGill Feighan."

"Wait." The tiny speaker set into the wall crackled absently.

He watched the fish that controlled the child. The Academy had exposed him to the Delu language, not expecting him to learn it, for no extra-Delu had ever achieved more than the ability to ask a few halting questions, but with the idea that attempting to grasp its structure would broaden his mind, and force insight into the creatures' alienness.

The language flowed on three main levels and a host of minor ones. Concepts—I, you; this reef, that fish—were conveyed semi-telepathically, with the listener "seeing" what the speaker referred to. Music delineated the relationships between concepts: a rising trill could suggest ascending to the surface, for example, while a single note protracted as its volume swelled then suddenly cut off, meant "to eat." Moods, and states of being, explained themselves visually, through color-shifts on the beings' skins. Then, for what Terrans would call "non-verbal communication," the Delu had eight fins, the set of which they could alter; three watery dimensions in which to strike poses; the speed at which their gills pumped . . . all of which is to say that, although he watched the black boy's puppet master, though he saw its colors change and sensed even through the dome the sound of its song, he couldn't make out a word it was saying.

But he wasn't alone. Only the squidfolk of nNocelphi had ever mastered more of the language than "Hello."

The boy's immobility broke: "McGill Feighan has been assigned to Spoke One, Wheel Twelve, Dome Twenty-six." His eyes closed.

"Thank you," said Feighan, uneasily aware that every translator in the room was studying him. "Where is that?"

The full lips parted. "Follow the signs."

"Ah . . ." The child so much resembled a statue in a wax museum that the Flinger's skin crawled. "How can I find Mary O'Higgins?"

The boy's left arm lifted itself like the fat woman's had: slowly, in a series of stiff and awkward jerks. "Address inquiries to the servant in the Information Booth."

Turning his head, he looked to the right, where squatted another row of booths beneath lighted "DATA" signs. "Yeah, ah . . . thanks."

At once the slim arm dropped, and hung limply by the boy's side. The unblemished face remained empty; the eyelids, shut.

Geez, he thought, heading for the Information Desk, *spooky.*

Kid acts like a servo-mech off the junk heap... as did the elderly Chinese man who informed Feighan that O'Higgins resided in Spoke One, Wheel Twelve, Dome Twenty-six. *Huh,* he thought, walking away, *either they're completely insensitive, or they know I'm replacing her.*

Sam chittered on his shoulder while he strode the curved-roof corridors. Reddish-orange light bathed the tiles. It ruddied the reptile's complexion, and bothered the human's eyes. A dull precursor to pain throbbed at the back of his skull. He blinked again and again.

"Fwah! Turang!" The voice was deep, gravelly. "Yuh, you, Turang Flinger."

He stopped and retraced his steps to a translation booth standing alone at the side of the hall. On a raised platform within crouched an Edbargian, a twelve-legged being with a meter-wide, tortoiselike shell and a flamingo's neck. Its bald, human-sized head ended in a daggerish beak. "Yuh," it said again. The bass notes rumbled the glass. "Welcome, Turang Flinger."

He looked outside the hall to the controlling Delu. Its mottled grey skin lay against some twenty meters of corridor wall; its orange-tinted gills pumped in an idle but complex rhythm. "What can I do for you?"

"Sull me dreams. One hundred points a night. Is a vury good price, all done in the convenience of your own dome. Guaranteed is the prosus agunst all side uffects. Nowhure will one find a butter, more ruputable dealer. What do you say, Turang Flinger?"

"Thanks, but..." Tired and ill at ease, he wasn't ready to sell his dreams to the first buyer. "I don't think so."

The creature hoisted its carapace an inch, and dropped it again: an Edbargian shrug. "You change your mind, you look for the Gambler."

"Right, I will." And he strolled on, wondering why that alien had displayed more liveliness, more animation, than his own people had.

When the corridor intersected another, glowing signs on its walls directed him to the right. The halls were almost empty, though far ahead, diminished by distance, scuttled something that could have been an Actuni. At least it looked like a mobile cactus... his footsteps echoed off the chill walls. He shivered. And wished he had not seen the alien.

In a few more meters, an airlock admitted him to Spoke One. The light seemed yellower there, less alien to his irritated eyes. A wallsign read: "Terrans and others conditioned to Terra-normal atmosphere may remove masks." He did, and wiped the sweat off his nose. Then he freed Sam's snout. The saurian indulged in an orgy of tongue-flicking.

Extra-Delu City—that compendium of tunnels and domes laid across the reefs by the construction crews of the Flinger Network—would look, from overhead, like a series of concentric rings joined by four spokes that met at the central dome Feighan had just left. Every alien on the planet lived in extra-Delu City, even those fishbeings who could have survived in the ocean. The Delu liked their eeties in one place.

A bit farther on, Spoke One passed through the narrower corridor of Wheel One; he peered down its curve and saw that doorways lined its walls. Apparently each wheel sprouted domes of its own. He hoped that Wheel Twelve, Dome Twenty-six would be clearly marked.

Except for the alloys of the light fixtures, the FNC builders had used perfectly transparent materials—at the Delu's insistence. Beyond the arched walls of the corridor, the water darkened as the sun set. Thirty-meter shapes parted the sea's shadows, as Delu finned and flashed and— "frolicked" would have been an appropriate word, if it didn't contradict everything the adult Delu represented. Perhaps the most humorless race man had encountered, they personified cold logic. Even their pursuit of dreams, which some xenosapiologists had equated with a desire for pleasure, was, on second glance, more like research. The Delu needed random associations and psychological distortions precisely because the rest of the universe was subject to them, and they were not. To understand the marketplace as thoroughly as the bottom line demanded, they had to explore the tangled undersides of those alien minds.

Feighan shivered again. Though vaguely conscious that a mid-sized Delu with a deformed fin was scrutinizing him, he was more concerned with incipient claustro-aqua-phobia. Thirty meters of water pressed down on the arch, and he could not stop visualizing the consequences of a leak. Water would spurt, not drip. Spurt at such force that the pinprick would widen and widen till suddenly the roof would collapse and the ocean would crush everything with its chill.

Don't be silly, he told himself. *The FNC's construction*

crews don't screw up like that. For three hundred years these archways had resisted tides and currents and the forces of the sea, bearing their loads with well-wrought equanimity. No collapse could occur...and even if it did, the contractors had installed, at every Spoke-Wheel intersection, barometrically-controlled doors that would clamp shut at the slightest increase in air pressure. The massiveness of the fail-safe soothed him.

Another half-hour of marching brought him to Wheel Twelve. The signs curved him to his right, to dome Twenty-six. As transparent as the rest of extra-Delu City, it covered roughly eighty square meters of tiled floor. It held a pallet, a chest of drawers, a chair and desk combination, a toilet, and a sink. On the pallet lay a woman, hand over her eyes. The pressure door stood open.

He cleared his throat. "Hello? Are you Mary O'Higgins?"

"No visitors, dammit," she said. "Go away."

"I'm not a visitor, I'm your relief." Sam hissed; Feighan stroked his headbone. "May I come in?"

Sitting up, she rubbed her bloodshot brown eyes. Grey-lined black hair tumbled onto her shoulders; wrinkles channeled the corners of her eyes and mouth. Her jaw thrust out pugnaciously. "Relief?" She extended an arm behind herself and leaned back on it.

"McGill Feighan, from the New York Flinger Building." As he stepped to the foot of her mattress, he dug into his suitcase for the Director's letter. "They told me to give you this, and to send you home."

"You're shitting me." She reached up for the envelope, bending forward while he stooped over. "Lemme see."

He'd looked down her blouse before he knew what he was doing, then with a guilty start twitched his gaze to her face.

She gave him a half-smile, and snapped her fingers. "The envelope, please?"

"Sorry. Here you go." He surrendered it, and glanced around while she tore it open. The room depressed him, but Sam scampered down his shirtfront to explore it. Which wasn't difficult, given its barrenness. "Did you know I was coming?"

"Not a word of it, but thanks be to God you did. Why? Were they saying that they would notify me?" Paper crackled as she folded the letter and smoothed it between reverent hands.

"No, but it looks like you sent all your stuff home."

"All what stuff?"

"Furniture, decorations..." No Flinger lived in such emptiness, even on temporary duty. Moving was too easy. "Books, video-display center—you know."

Her laugh bit harsher than sandpaper. "Contraband, you mean."

"Pardon?" He blinked, and stooped to pick up Sam when the Rhanghan tugged on his pants leg.

"Cute little thing, it is—your pet?"

"My ward. He's a Rhanghan, from Throngorn II."

She peered closer. "Sure and it is—my apologies. I'd never seen an infant before. About the contraband—"

"Yes?"

"What you see is what you're allowed. Our hosts don't believe in material possessions. Re-arrange it as you like, but don't add a thing, or they'll take it away."

"Neat trick." He chuckled. "They wouldn't even fit in here."

"No, it's their servants they send. Just as their servants will paw through your clothes, and take 'for safe-keeping,' they say, any color or cut that's illegal."

"Illegal?"

"McGill—" She sighed. "You're a handsome lad with a fine Irish name, and under other circumstances I'd be wetting my pants with the eagerness to bend your ear, but to tell you the God's honest truth, I won't spend a minute more here than I have to. Talk to the man in 25—" She pointed across the Wheel. "—he knows everything. Look me up in New York on your return."

As she disappeared, her Talent tugged at Feighan's, then released it.

"Hmph." Leaving his suitcase, he jerked open the desk to see if she'd left anything in its plastic drawers. She hadn't. The room's emptiness reverberated in each of them, and the light's yellow tinge made it all seem sickly.

Sam spat suddenly; his claws scratched the tiles.

Feighan whirled.

Over his now-open suitcase bent a slender, purple-feathered being with two stilt-like legs and a pair of delicate hands that sprouted from the inside of its wide wings. It was a Rehmal, an intelligent avian whose world was a full-fledged member of the Network. And it was sorting through his pants.

"Hey!"

It ignored him.

"What the hell are you doing?"

It didn't even twitch its marble-sized eyes.

The irritation and fatigue that had simmered in him for hours abruptly boiled over. He balled his fist. "Get out of there you—"

"Don't bother," said a voice from the doorway.

"Huh?" He looked up, instantly resenting the amused smile of the rumpled, obese Terran who leaned against the wall. "Who are you?"

"Harry Sherman." Waddling into the room, the middle-aged man extended a meaty hand. "And you are—"

"Oh." For a flustered moment he couldn't move. Here was the one person Walking Mule had told him to cultivate, and he'd already snarled at him. But who'd have expected a newsman respected throughout the Network to be so casual? "Sorry." As confusion submerged bad manners, he stammered. "McGill Feighan, Mr. Sherman. I'm Mary O'Higgins' replacement. Excuse me, but—"

"Thought she had another three months. And call me Harry." He squatted carefully to stare at Sam. "Hah! A baby Rhanghan, didn't know there were any outside of the caves. How'd you get him?" He held out a steady finger to Sam. "Hi there, kid."

While the reptile stroked the proffered finger curiously, Feighan said, "It's a long story, but yes, she had another three months. I'm afraid something came up. She did tell me to talk to you, though . . . so could you please tell me why the Rehmal is frisking my case?"

Sherman straightened. "Looking for illegal colors, I'd guess." He patted the forest green tunic that draped his paunch. In the orange light it looked ghastly. "Like this—one shade brighter and they'd confiscate it. Oops." He nodded to the Rehmal. "They don't like sky-blue, either."

Feighan turned just as the avian slipped a pair of azure socks into a drawstring sack. "Hey!"

"Don't bother," advised Sherman. "She's a zombie—can't hear you, or talk to you, either. All wireless servants do is obey their masters."

"Wireless?"

"Uncapped—before her controller told her to take it off, it

gave her a string of orders, ending with one to get back to station and recap herself. Right now, she's about as aware as a robot."

"But she's stealing my clothes!" His anger sparked into new life; he took a step towards the birdbeing.

Strong fingers hooked onto his belt. "Don't," said Sherman. "You'll get arrested." He jabbed a meaningful thumb at the Delu hovering just above them. Mid-sized, it had a deformed fin.

"Geez..." The warning—and the surveillance—cooled his temper. He moved away, relieved to see that the Rehmal had left him some clothes, at least. "Thanks...I'm usually not so hot under the collar, but ah...these lights are getting to me, I guess. I've got a lot to learn about this world...speaking of which, maybe you'd know. Where would I go for information about an alien that visited here, oh, twenty-one years ago?"

"Eleven years before my time, otherwise you'd come to me." Making a face, he tugged on his jowls as he thought. "Your best bet, I'm afraid, is ask the datadesk at the intersection. It probably won't have the answer, but it'll tell you who does."

"Great!" Delighted it would be that easy, he could not restrain his impatience. The need to know surged so strongly in him that he said, "Let me just check with it—can you watch Sam?"

"Sure."

"Thanks." He hurried into the Wheel and half-trotted to its crossing with Spoke One. In the booth, an Aronya ground its massive jowls. He approached. "Do you speak Terran?"

Two meters tall at the shoulder, the bovine-like creature swished its tail. "Sommme." Its green tongue lolled out.

From his pants pocket he took a hologram of the gastropod. "This being visited Delurc twenty-some years ago, Terran time, and I'd like to find out who it talked to."

Moist orange eyes focused on his face. "What is your point balance?"

"Ah..." He shrugged. "I don't know."

"Your nammme?"

"McGill Feighan."

"Wait." The suns of its pupils rolled into eclipse behind its lids. Outside, the Delu controller shifted from grey to black.

Then the Aronya wheezed, "Negative five."

"Pardon?"

"Your point balance is negative five, MmmGill Feighan. Mmmake five thousand five points, then return to repeat your question."

"Damn!" Disappointment sizzled across his soul. *I forgot nothing's free here . . . they musta charged for telling me where O'Higgins lived, too.* "How do I make five thousand and five points, then?"

Placidly, it blinked. "Mmmake one thousand, then ask."

With an effort, he controlled his ire. "But—"

"Good-bye." And it closed its fire bright eyes with the firmness of nightfall.

As his pivoted on his heel, Feighan thought he could guess why Mary O'Higgins had so disliked Delurc.

* * *

Clenched hands hidden behind his back, Milford Hommroummy faced a glass-walled tank taller than he. It nearly filled the vault carved from the heart of Kilimanjaro. It was filled with blue and gold gases that intermingled yet did not mix. They composed his immediate superior, Gryll.

"You have ordered me to capture McGill Feighan alive and unharmed, but he has fled my area of operation. I request permission to pursue him to Delurc, and to enlist the aid of the branch office on the reefs."

The speaker mounted on the pressure chamber gave a sixty-cycle hum. After a moment, Gryll said, "Permission granted. Use as base small rocket fleet two A.U. out from planet. Liaison will contact you; code-named Gimpy. Will assist. Offer quid-pro-quo."

Hommroummy scuffed the scarlet carpet with his toe. "What sort of quid-pro-quo?"

"Delurc Branch powerful; members have prestige and authority. Yet influence of Far Being Retzglaran also powerful—and Retzglaran's beasts hold upper hand now. Assist Gimpy in upsetting balance."

Hommroummy's thick eyebrows arched. "A revolution?"

"Minimum acceptable achievement is control of Auditor's Council Board of Examiners. Unmonitored Delu make very creative accountants; are essential to Organization's prosperity. Go. Succeed." A curtain slipped out of the wall to screen the tank.

Hommroummy left the room at once. In the chill stone corridor, he paused. He let out his breath in a long, slow sigh. He wiped his sweaty palms on a handkerchief. He looked old . . . and frightened.

· Chapter VII ·

When Feighan returned to Dome Twenty-six, Harry Sherman was sitting cross-legged on the floor, wrinkled pants pulled halfway up his shins. He wore no socks. In the deep red light, he looked like an amiable gargoyle. He had made a pendulum of his ruby ring and a length of thread, and he dangled that in front of Sam. On each slow swing it tapped the saurian's snout; Sam would cover his nose with his paws and spit/hiss good-naturedly. Then he would lunge. While Feighan watched, he caught the ring with his teeth, and bit through the string. Sherman chuckled.

"Having fun?" The asperity in his voice startled the Flinger. He wondered where it had come from.

The other glanced over his shoulder. Corpulence threatened his tunic-seams. "To tell the truth," he said, "I am. Something wrong?"

He bit back a snappish reply. "Ah . . . I'm just in a bad mood."

"They wouldn't answer, huh?"

He snorted. "I have to have five thousand points, first—and it'll cost me a thousand more to learn how to earn them."

"It's a mercenary world, all right." He rolled Sam over and tickled his leathery stomach plate, until the infant, pushing at the fingers, released the ring. Sherman pocketed it. "You can't let it get on your nerves, though."

"I know." He crossed to the desk and rested a haunch on its edge. His heel drummed against its tubular plastic leg. "I'm usually not this grouchy . . . maybe I just need a good night's sleep. Or a punch-field, I don't know."

Sherman studied him with a different kind of interest. "Are you sensitive to telepathy?"

"Not that I know of. Why?"

"People with a sort of micro-Talent for Minding react badly here. There's so much telepathy in the area that they start picking it up—but they've never had training in how to block it. So it's there, constantly, in the backs of their heads, like radio static. That's why I wondered—"

"I don't think that's it."

"The Delu, then?"

"Maybe." The fishbeings were as likely to have irritated him as anything.

"They do view data-sharing—or even small talk—from a different perspective . . . Let me tell you a story."

"About what?" Feighan was listening to his stomach as well as to his neighbor, and his stomach said it was time for dinner.

"You do know I'm a newsbroker?"

Feighan had to smile. "Yeah, Harry, I think I might have heard that somewhere before."

"Oh? You a subscriber?"

"For a year, now."

"Then I hope this doesn't scare you off." He picked up Sam and began to stroke his sides. "Eight or nine years ago, I had about ten thousand points in working capital. Investment opportunity pieces by high-graded brokers were the big wants, then; the sharers couldn't get enough of them. I had a reliability index of close to 99.5%, and a contact here touting a short-term sure thing. My mouth *watered*."

"Money in the bank, huh?" Idly, he pulled out the center desk drawer. Reddish shadows shifted in its emptiness.

"It's Network legend that Delu never lie," said the fat man, "so I bought the data and shipped it home express." He grimaced. "I advised something on the order of 1.2 million data-sharers that BemGems, Inc., had just discovered the richest lode of Syra-quartz ever, and that it would float a common stock issue soon to raise money to develop the mine. I allowed as how it might be a good buy . . ." With a wry headshake, he clucked his tongue.

"Wait," said Feighan, suddenly realizing what had to come next. "Don't tell me, your mine finally opened on the day they introduced synthetic Syra-quartz."

"Not my mine." Glumness settled over his coarse features. Scratching under his armpit, he said, "My *readers'* mine. I got hit with eighty-seven thousand accuracy gripes, and that was thirty months after the piece flashed the terminals. My reliability rating dropped two percent; the only thing that saved it from an utter flush was that the AccBoard found I had, at least, warned that this strike—and any new sources of supply—would lower the wholesale price of the jewel. Lost half a million subscribers anyway. Took me years to recover. Which in a roundabout way makes my point: the fish told me nothing but the truth. It merely neglected to mention the rest of the truth."

"That's unethical!"

"On Earth it would be." He sighed. "Mores aren't the same here, McGill. We had a contract that stated quite clearly that the advice the fish gave did not take into account probable, possible, or potential technological developments that might render said advice obsolete." He frowned. "God bless, do I remember that clause—to this day I read it in my nightmares . . ."

"But still," said Feighan, "you paid for advice on a good investment for your readers' money, and he gave you bad advice."

"She. And that's not the way they see it here. She asked for ten thousand points, and guaranteed a *short*-term sure thing. No more. I asked for a high rate of return coupled with reasonable safety. Well, for the short term, I got what I wanted—hell, the issue hit 37 and an eighth a month after going on the Board at 5. Some of my readers made a killing . . . the problem was, it took eighteen more months for the mine to open." He shrugged off the weight of his memories. "It was my fault for not taking the Delu perspective into proper account. You have to do that to survive here."

"I don't know," said Feighan slowly, "it just seems—"

"Bloodthirsty?" He spread his wide hands. "That it is . . . but that's the way it is."

"Speaking of the way—"

"Yes?"

"Which way to the nearest restaurant?"

Sherman's eyes popped open, then twinkled. Laughing, he pointed straight up. "About ten light years due north. You eat in your room."

Feighan looked around. "There's no stove, no refrigerator—"

"Did you miss dinner?"

"Yes, I did."

The fat man clucked sadly, sympathetically. "Then you'll have to wait for the breakfast serving—but at least it's delivered."

"Huh?"

"True, right to your door." Setting Sam down, he rose, and smoothed wrinkles out of his scarlet tunic. "One of the small amenities of life in extra-Delu City."

"What's it cost?"

"That depends on how much you eat. A small portion's five points, medium is twenty-five, and large is one hundred twenty-five." After an appraising glance at Feighan's figure, he said, "I'd advise the medium."

"But I don't have any points."

"Actually, you do—or will. The Delu are paying your salary, in points of course, and you make how many FNC's a day?"

"Thirty," he replied.

"There you go, then. The exchange rate's twelve points a fancy—so you're making 360 a day. The room's free, as is the air—the fish believe that the right to space and breath are inalienable—so if Sam's meals aren't too expensive, you might turn a small profit." He glanced speculatively at the light fixture. "I have to go; I have an important appointment." Spinning out the door without another word, he dove into his own dome.

Feighan shook his head, then picked up the Rhanghan and scratched his skullbone. "Damn, Sam," he sighed. "This is a strange place. Wish I could Fling home for a snack..." But he couldn't. Standing orders said Flingers stayed on station for the duration of their tours—and no properly indoctrinated Flinger would ever disobey standing orders without good cause. *Last thing I want,* he thought, *is for them to find out I never got brainwashed...*

The saurian's four eyelids drifted down; he breathed in raspy little snuffles.

"You're going to sleep on me, huh?" Feighan whispered. He started to lift his hand.

Sam grabbed it, and pulled it back to the top of his head.

Feighan chuckled. "Okay, kid, whatever you say..." Through the transparent walls he watched Sherman. The newsbroker went to his pallet, stripped it of its blanket, and reached underneath it for something which he palmed. Then he flapped the blanket open and let it settle across his separated desk and chair to form a small, thigh-high tent. Dropping to his hands and knees, he crawled inside.

"Weird place to have an appointment."

The blanket bulged at the sides; feet flashed in and out of view. It looked like two people wrestling in there...a few minutes later, Sherman stood up, and threw off the blanket. Moving stiffly, he crossed the room and lay face-down on the pallet. He seemed to fall instantly asleep, because he didn't fidget once.

"Why didn't he just say so?" Feighan asked Sam.

The Rhanghan's questing hand dabbled in the light-bands of the energy tunic. They fascinated the infant, but his fingers were cold on the human's skin.

"Hey, kid, stop it, huh?" Playfully, he puffed air into Sam's face, and laughed as the magenta tongue flickered out.

In the corridor, a shadow rippled past. He eyed it for a moment, then decided his tired eyes were playing tricks on him. *I oughta go to bed.* But his hunger outweighed his fatigue, so he prowled the room. Bored and restless, he searched every square centimeter for...he didn't know for what. It was just something to do, a way to kill time.

Unexpectedly, it paid off: O'Higgins had taped her work schedule to the backside of the desk. He squinted through the reddening light, and scowled at the strain on his eyes. *Let's see, I'm due to report at...30:30. Great.*

He stepped to his suitcase and searched for his travel alarm, hoping that its dimwitted chip would at least be familiar with Delu chronology. He lifted the last pair of pants, then rocked back on his heels thoughtfully. *Coulda sworn I packed it...* From his memory flicked an image of the cubical clock nestled in the corner of his top dresser drawer. *Dammit!*

His Talent flexed as he considered his options: do without, or find a local clock store. Again, Flinging back for his own was impossible. Doing without would be impractical. He decided to wake Sherman up and ask for directions to the nearest store with clocks in stock.

"C'mon, Sam," he told his equally tired ward. "Let's go bother Harry."

The infant didn't move.

"C'mon, kid." He jerked his head towards the doorway.

Sam held out his arms to be picked up.

"Oh, all right..." Cradling the saurian, Feighan tickled him under the chin. Then he crossed the Wheel, shoes scraping on the smooth tile, and went up to the pallet. The newsbroker lay flat on his stomach. His elbows looked wrongly cocked. "Ah . . . Harry? Harry? . . . Are you awake? . . . Hey, Harry—" He squatted to touch Sherman's shoulder. "—wake—" He drew his hand back. His fingertips had poked plastic, not flesh.

The body was a mannequin.

"Jesus God!" Standing straight again, unconsciously shielding Sam from any danger, he spun on his heel and scanned the room. Except that Sherman had a computer-desk, and had dropped the blanket in the middle of the floor, the dome was identical to his. Even in the somber lighting all looked normal. And the newsbroker was nowhere to be seen. *Oh Christ, I'll bet he works for Hommroummy.*

He almost ran, then, but remembered that Walking Mule had vouched for Sherman—and besides, he was curious. *I saw Harry come in here, so he musta done the dummy, which means he'll be back and I can ask about—* *hmph* *—that 30:30 business and the clock store.*

Still cradling Sam, he settled into the straight-backed desk chair (wondering as he did so how that frail piece of furniture had not collapsed under the newsbroker).

The dome, mirrored by outside darkness, held reflections of its occupants by their heels, and threatened to drop them. Slowly, the hairs on the back of his neck stiffened; he shot a nervous glance over his shoulder. He was being watched. Goose-pimples puckered his skin. He stared at the clearness of the arch until his eyes ached. Nothing. No faces, no snouts . . . *didja think they'd press right up against it? They don't need to; it's light in here and dark out there; I'm spotlit like a man on a stage* . . . He snorted. *I'm the lead in a play and nobody'll show me the rest of the script, won't let me walk into the wings, can't see or hear or smell the audience* . . . Despite his tension, he yawned. Stroking Sam's bellyplate until the reptile sprawled limply and fell asleep, he struggled to stay awake himself.

And failed.

So he dreamed.

Water, waves, watchers . . . and overhead a desert sun. He dog-paddled frantically, trying to keep his mouth above water, but every grasping breath sucked brine into his lungs, and the audience lining the rails of the cruise ship applauded as he sputtered.

"Throw me a rope!"

"No!" they said in unison.

Piranha prodded his legs, nipping at his knees with teeth as sharp as cactus spikes. He screamed for help; choking, he flailed his feet, driving them away while the audience cheered.

"Please, a rope!"

"No!"

A fin cut the water, a triangular omen that left almond-eyed eddies in its wake, and the spectators shouted, "Shark! Shark!" and he yelled, "I see, I see, please help!"

"NO!"

So he floated alone and motionless, knowing limb twitches would draw the predator, and the waves washed the sockets of his eyes with salt, and a fin scraped his spine, and pilot fish probed his groin for parasites.

He floated alone and motionless.

It was the hardest thing he had ever done.

Then with a swirl the shark disappeared. Free now to save himself, he started to swim for shore, but the audience gasped as a great black whale—

"Wake up," boomed a worried voice. An insistent hand shook his shoulder. "Come on, McGill, wake up— hush, Sam, it's all right, I'm just trying to—"

Jackknifing out of his slouch, he hugged himself. Sweat ran down his chest. "Harry. Sorry. I dozed off. I was waiting for you, and . . ."

"You were screaming your head off." The fat man sat on the edge of his pallet, squashing it flat. "Bad dream?"

He trembled.

"I get them myself now and then."

"I'll be okay . . . but, ah . . . there were a couple of things I wanted to ask." He inhaled, then shuddered it out. "I'm supposed to be at work tomorrow at '30:30.' I don't even know what that means, much less how to get up before then."

The newsman grinned. "At the 1-12 datadesk—where this Wheel intersects Spoke One—probably the same place you asked the 5000-point question—tell the puppet you wanted to be called . . . how much time do you need to get ready for work?"

He shrugged. "I don't know . . . hey, wait a minute. You're you, now." He looked around, groggy and still dazed by his nightmare. "I mean, when I came in, it wasn't you on the bed, it was— you know, the—"

"You do dream vividly, don't you?"

"No, this was before—"

"Let's talk about that some other time. What's important is that you get enough rest before work—remember, Delurc's day is only twenty-two hours long, and that's going to wipe you out until you get used to it."

Made uncomfortably aware that he had no right to pry into his neighbor's secrets, Feighan let Sherman change the subject back to time. "I need, say, ten minutes to wash up, fifteen to eat breakfast—what's that in Delu terms?"

"About a *troom* and a quarter. The day here has sixty-four trooms, each of which has sixty-four *twees*. The Delu use base-eight notation, though, so they call them each 'one hundred.' '30:30' is actually the twenty-fourth troom and the twenty-fourth twee. An easy guide is that a troom's about twenty minutes, and a twee's nineteen seconds."

"So, ah. . ." He juggled the numbers in his head. "That troom and a quarter you said I'd need equals like '1:20,' but with a few minutes safety factor it's 1:30, and that would make a . . . a 29:00 wake-up call?"

"Base-eight, McGill—that's 27:00. Just tell the puppet to call you then, and to feed you at 27:40. I warn you, though, it'll cost, let's see, a point and a half for the service."

Feighan frowned. "Do you know any place that's open where I could buy an alarm clock?"

Sherman cocked his head in amusement, then snapped his fingers. "That's right, they're not allowed to brief you, are they? You can't buy a clock here—hell, there aren't any stores at all. Of any kind. You'd have to get one custom-made off world, and even then they'd take it away from you."

The Flinger slapped his thigh angrily. "I knew I packed it!"

"A travel alarm, huh? You'll get it back when you leave, don't worry."

"But why'd they take it?"

"It violates the code—or at least, that's what they'd tell you if you asked."

"A clock?"

"Remember to take the Delu perspective into account."

"But how does it apply to a clock?"

"They'd rather sell you the time of day." Sherman chuckled. "And since it's their planet . . . fortunately, they have this ethic about giving the sucker an even break—see the lights?" He pointed to the ceiling.

His gaze followed the finger. "Yeah, sure—they're hard to miss. So?"

"The color tinge comes from a variable monochrome component, and that VMC's in every fixture in extra-Delu City. It goes through the entire visible spectrum once a day. You got here yesterday in the early red—now, you'll notice, we're starting over in the deep violet. The VMC shifts an angstrom a twee, so unless you're color blind, you can use the lights as rough clocks."

Flabbergasted, the Flinger dropped his forehead onto his crossed arms. "But how can you tell 30:30 from 31:00? You've got to be a spectrograph to see a thirty angstrom frequency shift."

"The Delu can do it." Sherman shrugged. "And they prefer us to live up to their standards, rather than living down to ours."

"Madness!"

"Well put."

Cramped and bad-tempered, Feighan stretched. Then he yawned and, as he recognized the extent of his fatigue, became embarrassed. He had been an inconsiderate guest. "Hey, I'm sorry, I didn't mean to impose on you this late—"

"I keep GMT," Sherman assured him. "Have to, so my article-chips get back by 6:00 EST every day. My bedtime's a long way off. And it's been a while since I last had somebody interesting to talk to—with all due respect, your predecessor was not what I'd call convivial."

Curiosity overwhelmed tiredness. He turned the chair around, and straddled it. On the desktop, Sam rolled onto his stomach and gave a raspy little snore. "About your stand-in—"

"Not now, McGill."

Following Sherman's upward gaze, he realized the newsbroker wouldn't discuss the topic if he could be overheard. So instead he said, with a gesture to the sterile furnishings, "They sure don't want anybody to get comfortable here."

"Precisely."

"But why?"

"The Delu don't like having aliens around—in fact, the only reason they allow us in is because their treaty with the FNC says they have to."

"We were forced down their throats, huh?"

"McGill, their throats are so large we could glide down side by side with room to spare."

Feighan had to laugh. "I can believe it. But what have they got against aliens?"

"Who knows? Jealousy, maybe, because they're too big to Fling and we're not? It's not a privacy fetish, or else they'd have made the City opaque . . . they claim that aliens disrupt their society, their culture, but they won't get more specific except for cash in advance, and so far, nobody's been that interested. I was thinking of investing in the answer myself, but I couldn't find a good market for it. For a one-hundred word statement on the matter, they want twenty thousand points—twenty-five thousand US—and I'll tell you, I couldn't sell that report to enough people to recoup my costs. Some government or foundation's going to have to buy it, someday."

Feighan suppressed a yawn, and tousled his hair with his fingers. "What gets me is that they joined the Network even though they felt this way."

The newsbroker folded his hands on his belly and rocked slowly back and forth. "It's not that simple," he said, picking his words with obvious care. "Not all of them feel that way. It's too early in the morning to go into all the details, but suffice it to say that extra-Delu residents are chips in a political poker game. See, this culture's changing, growing, evolving—and there are factions struggling to control the engines and vectors of change. It all gets back, eventually, to the buying and selling of information."

The Flinger was more tired than ever, so he shied away from conversational depths and instead began, "Speaking of information—" He yawned widely.

"I charge less, so go ahead."

He scratched behind his right ear. "I feel sort of dumb asking this, but I can't find the light switch in my room."

Sherman hooted, and slapped his beefy thigh. "I sure wish I could sell the FNC a guidechip on Delurc, since I'm teaching all you New York Flingers for free anyway . . . There is no light switch."

"Central control, then? I have to ask that it be turned off?"

"It doesn't *get* turned off, McGill. Ever."

"I haven't slept with the lights on in years!"

"Get used to it." He opened his hands to the violet haze that enveloped them. "You can't escape it."

"But why? More of the visitor-discouragement tactics?"

"Probably, though there's no way to prove it." He slapped

his open palm on the pallet. "For all I know, they're just curious about aliens. Maybe we're a hobby to them, so they put us on display like goldfish in a bowl." For the first time, sourness tinged his deep voice, and pulled down the corners of his lips. "Which definitely cramps your style, if you're unfortunate enough to have a lover here."

"Unfortunate?" It was the last word Feighan would have used, though he still could not bring himself to think of Liang. "How can having a lover be unfortunate?"

Sherman swept an arm to the curving sheets of glass that separated his dome from the wheel. "Can you imagine how frustrating it is to be sitting here, a handspan away from someone you'd like to crawl all over, while you know you're visible to anybody who walks by? Forget about the fish, that's like leaving the holo-vee on, but to have a stranger five meters away, beyond a clear wall and an open door? No, sir." He shook his head sadly. "I haven't yet found a woman exhibitionistic enough to join me in the sack in public, as it were—and if I did, I doubt if I'd be able to rise to the occasion. That's what I mean by unfortunate. Get used to celibacy."

Feighan couldn't help being warmed by Sherman's implicit compliment. The truth was that he'd never truly experienced non-celibacy...He yawned again, in part to change the subject. "I'm exhausted...any ideas what time it is?"

Sherman glanced at the light fixture. "Call it, ah, the third troom. That's close enough, anyway—you have a little under seven hours to sleep."

"Then I have to go." He rose, and stumbled away from the chair. "Thanks again for all your help; I'd have been lost without it."

"No problem. I'll see you tomorrow."

With a sleepy wave, the Flinger scooped up Sam and crossed the hall to his own room. Briefly, he thought of disrobing, but when he plopped into the chair, he was too tired even to pull off his boots. Besides, he couldn't shake the conviction that he was being watched. Despite the violet light, he felt exposed.

He peered into the surrounding domes. Most were empty. Harry Sherman sat at his desk, murmuring into his computer. Next door, a young man slept. Down the hall, a middle-aged woman raised binoculars to her eyes.

He'd sleep with his clothes on. The tunic wouldn't wrinkle...

What he couldn't put off, though, was using the toilet. He

turned his back on the nosy woman— *how come she can have binoculars when I can't keep a clock?* —but having to unzip in the middle of the room, unsheltered and visible to anyone with the right perspective, made him so anxious that nothing happened.

He'd had the same trouble in junior high, before the Academy, when he couldn't use the urinals during gym class. A doctor had called it a common occurrence, the "shy bladder syndrome," and knowing that it was widespread enough to have a name made him feel less of a freak. It didn't, however, provide a lot in the way of solutions...

"Later," he muttered. "If I wait long enough, I'm gonna go no matter how shy it is."

Then he fluffed his lumpy pillow and crawled between the scratchy blankets. No sheets. The previous residents of the room had hollowed out the center of the pallet with their weight; he slipped into their mold but was too tall for the fit to be comfortable. Besides, they had sloughed odors off on the rough fabric, and he could smell them all: O'Higgins, and below her a faint yet masculine stench, and behind that a non-human rankness... and the lights burned in his reddened eyes. Beside him rose Sam's reassuring snore.

"Damn," he said softly, as he wriggled for a position which wouldn't bring on a stiff neck or worse, "I don't know about this place..."

*　　*　　*

In the morning a birdy twitter-tweet broke through a dream washed in bleak grey. He opened his eyes to a pair of stilt-like legs supporting a slender, feathered frame. "Huh?" he mumbled.

"Wake up call, Mr. Feighan." The Rehmal was the one who had frisked his luggage the day before. It trilled a snatch of Reveille. "It is 27:00."

"Oh, yeah." He sat up and yawned immensely. A dash of green gave character to the blue light. The Rehmal pigeon-bobbed its way back into the wheel. Feighan arose, and headed for the toilet.

By the time he'd washed and finger combed his hair, the Rehmal had returned with a covered plastic tray and a small plastic box. Its purple feathers iridesced darkly. Lowering the box to the floor, it set the platter on the desk and lifted the lid. "Medium?" it whistled.

"Fine," said Feighan, sliding the chair back.

Again it whistled, "Medium?"

He stopped. "Ah . . . yes. Uh-huh. Medium."

One of the words triggered a response in the birdbeing, though he had no idea which. *Next time I'll say 'em one by one* . . . The Rehmal whisked the middle-sized plate off the tray and onto the desk, then replaced the lid. Without even a glance in his direction, it clicked to the door and into the hallway, balancing its burden on an outstretched hand.

"Hey, wait," he said, when he eyed the plate. "You forgot the silverwa—" But he reached the door too late. The Rehmal had disappeared. *Probably wouldn't have come back even if I could have found it* . . .

So he returned to the hard-seated chair and confronted breakfast: a brown oblong about fifteen centimeters long, five centimeters wide, and two deep. Its surface shimmered slightly, as though it had been fried in oil. He sniffed, but smelled nothing. Gingerly, he picked it up with his fingers, and nibbled off a crisp corner. In texture it resembled black bread. Stale black bread.

"And it doesn't taste much better, either." He forced the first mouthful down his throat and stared without appetite at the remainder of the food bar. Suddenly it seemed much too large. "Hope they did better by you, Sam."

But the Rhanghan squatted on the tiles, glumly regarding a roach-sized brown oblong.

As he sipped the flat, tasteless water, Feighan wondered if he dared Fling back to Earth for his meals. It would save him money—*like thirty bucks a shot,* he realized—make mealtimes more pleasant, and keep him from feeling quite so isolated . . . *but leave me incredibly exhausted, maybe alienate the Delu if they noticed, and screw me good if the NAC found out* . . .

Still, he considered it. He was pretty sure he could fast-talk the NAC, but he could not afford to insult his hosts, even if they were trying to starve him. He needed information that they had about the gastropod and the Far Being Retzglaran, and although he did not understand their mores, he suspected they would deny him answers if they resented or disliked him. *Or raise the price higher'n I afford* . . .

What clinched it was that he could not escape the physical

consequences. The standard ninety-six Flings in twenty-four hours drained him; a regular nine days on, one off shift left him ready to cry with fatigue on the last night . . . Here he lost two hours a day, so adding extra Flings, two extra interstellar Flings, would demolish him.

Leaden with resignation, he lifted breakfast and began to gnaw. If that was what Delurc offered Terrans to eat, that was what he would eat . . . at least until he could take it no more.

Gotta ask Harry how he got so fat on this stuff!

When he had finally choked down the last of it, he looked up. The newsbroker was pacing the perimeter of his dome, and checking the light fixtures once a lap. Feighan waved across; Sherman pantomimed permission to enter. For a fat man, he moved gracefully.

Sam at his heels, Feighan went in. "Morning, Harry."

Sherman stopped walking, but his eyes kept darting to the lights. "It's more like night for me, but how are you today anyway?"

"I wanted to ask you about the food—"

"Not very appetizing?"

"That's a mild way of putting it. Is it always this bad?"

Sherman's features sagged into melancholy. "It's always that *meal*. Three times a day, seven days a week . . . the kitchens of extra-Delu City don't cook anything else."

"I don't understand—I mean, that was a taste bud away from inedibility—they trying to kill us?"

"Just discourage us."

"More of that, huh?" Hand on his stomach, he groaned. "It's just lying there resisting my digestive juices . . ."

"Heartburn *is* epidemic here," said the newsbroker solemnly.

"Then why do you stay?" He could not understand it. Sherman had the money to live where and how he wanted, yet he had chosen this cold, cheerless planet as his headquarters. "You could have an incredible place in New York, or Shanghai—why do you put up with this?"

The other gave him a level stare that went on and on till he said, "McGill, this is the info hub of the Network. If anything important happens anywhere important—" He made a sound half-amused, half-disgusted. "—they've already heard about it here. Working out of eD City gives me a six- to twelve-hour jump on the competition, and in this business, that's how you stay on top."

"But—"

Sherman pointed to the gradually greening lights. "It's about time for you to get to work, isn't it?"

"I'll take your word for it." With a wave, he left—but not before he had tried to commit the exact color of the lights to memory.

* * *

Flinging from Delurc, he discovered that morning, bored him as much as Flinging from Earth ever had. Only the steady diminishing of the pressure made it at all worthwhile. As on Terra, he sat in a small room overlooking a large one; the major difference was that in New York, his cubical booth had white walls and ceiling, while on Delurc, his dome was transparent. The desktop still doubled as a computer screen offering destination information and depature times—but in Delu chronology, of course. Every twenty-five twees he had to teleport a traveler or a load of cargo. Four Flings a troom, twenty-four trooms (in base ten) a day.

"Sam, my friend," he said, halfway through his first shift, "I have a feeling that I'm going to like this place less and less as time goes on."

The child, still much too young to speak, regarded Feighan with dark-eyed impassivity. Politeness seemed instinctive in him: not till his guardian stopped speaking did he turn away. Having already explored the cramped enclosure, he snouted the wall to stare into the lightening waters. Seaweed tendrils slapped the glass in slow motion; at first he recoiled from them, but quickly came to learn that they did not hurt.

And while the small saurian made faces at the creatures of the ocean bottom, Feighan Flung for twelve straight trooms, four times a troom. At the end he arose, arched the stiffness out of his back, and cracked his knuckles. "Sam," he said tiredly, "let's go check out the city, see if there's anything to do that's halfway interesting."

It was just past mid-day; the fluorescents slathered them with mustard-yellow. Feighan adjusted their oxygen masks, and they strolled into the cluster of domes that formed the hub of eD City. Through the noon-bright waters overhead glided huge shapes that cast shadows like storm clouds. One had a deformed fin. A prickling came across Feighan's mind. He resented them all. He despised them. Each and every one.

Breath raspy in his mask, Sam on his shoulder, he looked around. A few domes away, a flock of Rehmal formed a ragged line and moved a shipment of cargo out of a Flop Booth bucket-brigade style. The sheets of glass and the intervening waters blurred their figures; he felt an impressionist painting had come to life.

Otherwise the city was still. Only his footsteps rang in the corridors. The servants in their booths waited like museum exhibits: immobile, unneeded, and faintly unreal. Ventilators whispered cool, damp air so redolent of mildew that it pierced his mask. A few sapients sat in untitled offices, but they didn't look up as he passed. Nowhere did he spot anyplace designed to amuse or relax. And there were, indeed, no stores.

Swiftly, the central city palled on him. He left it within half an hour for the oxygen-breathers' section, where at least he could remove his mask and inhale in comfort. Sam chittered in his ear while he turned off Spoke One to wander through the wheels.

Again, the majority of domes lay empty and unused—especially those close to the core. It angered him more as he walked further; the Delu could certainly have assigned him to one of those, and spared him that half-hour hike to and from work. That they had not was extra evidence of their animosity.

Time dyed the lights' yellow orange; he strolled along laser-straight spokes and ever-larger wheels. Each was identical to every other, and his sense of direction began to fail. When he looked around he could find not a single landmark to distinguish the locale from anyplace else in eD City. There were no statues, no parks (or benches, either), no historical plaques . . . in all his roamings during those twelve off-trooms, only one thing pleased him: Iona T. Reed had been transferred to Delurc, and her quarters were as sparsely furnished as his.

"Hi," he said through her open door.

"Who—" She blinked, and her face gelled with dark hostility. *"You."*

"Yeah, it's me. I saw you through the wall—what brought you here?" Entering, he bent so Sam could hop onto her desk. "This is the Rhangan, from the egg?"

"I remember." Her eyes slitted. "I've been named Terran Ambassador."

"Congratulations!" Looking at her with new respect, he decided she must have been more competent than he had thought. "That's quite a promotion."

"It is a punishment," she snapped. "If not the end of my career."

"Ah—" He swallowed hard in embarrassment. "Geez, I'm sorry to hear that." Her gaze burned through him and he had to back away. "You were punished because of Sam?"

She picked the child off the empty desktop and set him on the floor, then inspected her fingers for filth. "I am quite busy. Good day."

"Yeah." He nodded, absorbing the rebuff. "Okay. See you around."

Outside, he shrugged, and began to head back to his booth. Soon it would be time to report for his second shift, *though I don't know,* he thought, dragging his feet, *sure isn't easy to work here. If I didn't need a clue to the Far Being . . .* It seemed almost a betrayal of his species to work for a race so disdainful of humanity. He glanced up, and briefly caught the eye of a ten-meter long Delu. He dropped his gaze at once.

Half an hour later, the gaping Booth door beckoned. He closed it behind himself, sat and Flung, nibbled on dinner when it was delivered, sat and Flung . . . until twelve more trooms had elapsed, forty-eight more Flings all told, and Wardens Duty and Need freed him until 30:30 the next morning.

"Let's go home, kid."

Sam hauled himself up Feighan's pants leg and grasped his belt. With a final hiss for the still-waving seaweed, he nuzzled his face into the Flinger's side and wagged his tail as if to say, "I'm on, let's go."

Evening had dimmed the sea. The lights, though deep into the red, seemed brighter in contrast. Too tired to teleport again, even the short distance to his room, he trudged up the long bleak spoke. The twenty-two hour days were already wearing him down. The last alien planet he had lived on, Throngorn II, had had forty-hour days which he had thought were enervating, but Delurc was worse. *Probably 'cause T II gave me a lot more time for sleep, huh?*

"Hey, Tewan," lisped a high-pitched voice from the booth he was passing. "Would you wike to eawn ten points?"

His sore eyes swung up to focus on an orange and purple face. His blasé reaction to an Othci was not feigned—during training he had visited their swamp world, Othcar. "Sorry," he told the limbless creature, "I didn't hear you."

Confined to a large aquarium, it squirmed, and rippled its ten-meter length into a new coil. Its four fangs gleamed blackly as it eased its capped head over the edge of the tank. "I asked," it said with some severity, "would you wike to eawn ten points?"

"Doing what?"

"Taking a fwee-association test—onwy five questions."

Ten points? Ah, hell . . . He propped a shoulder against the cubicle's outer wall. "Sure, but make it quick."

"Just say the fiwst wowd that comes into you' mind: as-pawagus."

"Lentils."

"Baggage."

"Harridan."

"Typewita."

"Obsolete."

"Sex."

"Love."

"Hate."

"Die."

"Vewy good." Its tripartite tongue lashed like a bullwhip out of control. "You' account has been cwedited with ten points, and we thank you vewy much."

"You're welcome," he said. "Hey, can I ask you a question?"

"State it, and we'll state the pwice of the answer."

He blinked, then decided that costing it out could not hurt. "Why is it that the Terran, ah, translators I meet seem stiff and lifeless, but the Terran-speaking extraterrestrials don't?"

The Othci rolled its large brown eyes for a moment, then responded, "Five hundwed points for a weply."

"Forget it." He sighed. "I don't want the answer that badly."

"Fou' hundwed."

"Uh-uh."

"Thwee-fifty, and that's my wowest offe'."

"Not a chance. Nice talking to you." He waved, and set off home.

So the Delu would bargain. It was a useful bit of information to have acquired—for free, yet—though he winced to think that he might have bargained up his fee for taking the test. Funny nobody had mentioned to him that their prices were negotiable. *Ah, well,* he thought, as he strode into his wheel, *live and learn . . .*

Outside Dome Twenty-six he hesitated, and glanced into Sherman's place. The newsman, in a purple tunic a scintilla flashier than a Rehmal's feathers, sat pensively at his computer-desk. Feighan cleared his throat. "Busy, Harry?"

"Huh? Oh, McGill—no, come on in." He half-rose, but settled back before the gesture became an action. "Another question?"

"Yeah—about local prices." He set Sam on the floor and let the reptile scamper over to the other Terran. "Are they fixed or flexible?"

"It varies." He motioned the Flinger to the pallet, and made Sam comfortable on his own lap before he continued.

"It's very much a free enterprise, supply-and-demand economy here. Offer a fish a chance to make a buck, he'll name the highest price he thinks you're willing to pay. Sometimes he'll cut it if you turn it down; sometimes he won't. Depends on the merchandise."

"Well, what isn't negotiable?"

"Standard services—wake-up calls, meals, things like that—the price is set on them, and you can talk your head off without getting a better deal. Damn, I for—" He checked the redness of the lights, then relaxed. "It's the one of the kind of deals where you can bargain."

"What about services they buy?" He told Sherman about the test. "Could I have held out for more?"

The newsbroker frowned. "Do you know who controlled the Othci?"

"No, I can't tell them apart—why?"

"Because . . ." Squinting at the ceiling, he measured out his words. "I've never heard of it's happening before, that's all. But—" He stopped.

"What?" The newsman's uneasiness infected him, displacing his fatigue.

"Nothing, really . . . they just seem to be showing a lot of interest in you."

Feighan wondered to himself if Sherman were jealous.

"But about your question—if they wanted you in particular to take that test, then yes, you could have gotten more. As you could have if they'd needed the answers in a real hurry."

"What about dreams?"

Sherman cocked his head to one side. "Selling them?"

"Yes."

"If you take my advice—" Avoiding Feighan's eyes, he

scratched Sam under the jaw. "—you'll leave the dream dealers alone."

"But I've got to find the gastropod, so I need all those points!"

"Not that way, you don't."

"They'll pay hundreds a night, though."

"One-fifteen tops, if you're really tough with them." He looked like a Trappist prophet: burdened with foreknowledge, but sworn to silence. "Don't do it, McGill."

Feighan did not know whether to draw back or plunge ahead. "Why, Harry? You've got to give me a reason."

Sherman's jowls drooped. "I probably shouldn't have said a thing, but..." Carefully shifting the Rhanghan off his lap, he stood, and laid one hand on either side of his belly. "I've been here eleven years, and seen maybe a thousand people who sold the Delu their dreams. They came here to do it, most of them, so I didn't get to know them before they started. Once they did start, though..." Coming close to Feighan, he lowered his voice. "Look, this isn't the kind of thing I could put in a chipflash, because I don't have the hard proof, but these people, they act like they've lost something the rest of us still have. It's subtle, intangible. Their creativity, call it, or... a spark, you know? Whatever it was that made them uniquely alive. Their souls?" Sweat glistened on his palms; he rubbed them up and down his tunic. "I shouldn't be saying this; they could be listening... but don't do it. I'd hate to see you become a, a *zombie*."

"The real zombies are those translators," said Feighan, wondering what had worried the older man. So what if somebody overheard? "I don't know what they get paid, but it can't be worth it."

Sherman looked hastily at the ceiling. "You mean you don't know about them?"

"What's to know?"

He dropped his voice still lower. "To begin with, they're not paid, or even hired, for that matter. They're drafted—forced to serve."

"Enslaved?" he asked in loud surprise.

"Ssh!" He spun like a top, face lifted in alarm. "Not so loud... 'enslaved' isn't 100% accurate, but—"

"Why does the FNC let them do it?" Just outside the dome, a skin glowed bright green, then faded. Wondering if their entire conversation were illegal, he pointed it out to the newsman.

Sherman nodded, and fell into a soft whisper. "It's punishment." At the question raised by the Flinger's eyebrows, he said, "If you violate the Delu civil code—and there must be ten million ways of doing it—you're fined. Major crimes rate major fines. When your point balance drops below negative one thousand, you're sentenced to a term as a translator."

"But that's involuntary servitude!"

"McGill, the Network Charter says any indigenous legal system—"

"—right," he said, remembering his Network History courses at the Academy, "'shall be extended to all alien visitors and residents in the same degree to which it is applied to natives.'"

"Exactly."

"What if you refuse to be a translator?"

"Then—" He rubbed the sole of his shoe on the tiles; it made a subdued, gritty rasping. "—they kill you."

"Damn . . . So what do you do, work off your debt as a translator?"

"Exactly. One hundred points a day until the fine is paid."

"That could take a while."

"It's been known to." He checked the lights, and seemed reassured that they were still deep red.

"What if you agree to leave, instead?"

"They won't let you. I don't know how they'd stop a Flinger, but for the rest of us mortals . . . let me tell you a story. A friend of mine—" He stopped, and became very attentive to the interlocking of his hands.

"What happened to your friend?" prodded Feighan.

"She . . ." With a grace surprising for his bulk, he went to the wall and looked out. Darkness made the glass a mirror in which he could see only himself, but to himself he could recall, hoarsely, "She was a whistler. I mean, she liked to whistle. And she did it well, too, not like some people who only know one off-key tune. She was good. All kinds of music—Bach, modern, 20th Century whatchamacallit—"

"Rock'n'roll?"

"That's it. All kinds, and all of it . . . magnificent. The thing is, though, it's illegal here. The Delu say it, uh, interferes with their navigational systems. So they fined her. She apologized, didn't know the law, the whole bit—but she whistled like I breathe. I mean, it was second nature to her. Instinct, almost. The only time she could keep from doing it was when she concentrated on not doing it. When something absorbed her attention, though . . ." Shutting his eyes, he raised his fingers to his temples and massaged them.

Outside, skin signals flared and flickered like St. Elmo's fire. "Harry, I think we've got company."

"I don't care! This they can listen to—it's not like they haven't heard it before."

"What happened?" he asked quietly.

"They fined her again. And again. More each time, because to repeat a violation is to commit a larger crime. The last fine was for close to a hundred thousand points. And of course she didn't have it, and that was right after I'd spent all my money on the BemGem data, and so . . ." Spreading his fingers on the wall, he pressed his forehead to the coolness of the glass.

"Harry, if you'd rather not—"

"No! You've got to know . . . She became a translator. For three years she sat in a booth, wired up to a fish that—" He swallowed hard. "By the time she'd worked off her fine, she'd become a different person. Cold. Lifeless. She had huge brown eyes; before, I could fall into them like a sky-diver . . . but afterwards, they were mud puddles. I mean, nothing. And they'd taken all her music. She didn't have a note left in her." He paused for a long moment, then said, softly, "Not a damn note."

Feighan let a respectful silence gather before asking, "You loved her?"

"You noticed, huh?" Forcing a chuckle, he moved away from the wall, but kept his back turned while his fingers wiped things off his cheeks.

"I'd have to be blind, deaf, and dumb *not* to have noticed. Where is she now?"

He pivoted to face the Flinger; his shoulders stiffened as though he were afraid of what was behind him. "Which?"

"The girl you loved."

"Here." He tapped the rolls of fat over his chest. "The girl I loved is here, in my heart and my memory. What she became . . . I don't know where that person is . . . I don't want to know . . ."

"Funny," said Feighan slowly, "you're so cynical about

everything else, I hadn't expected you to be this sentimental about a woman."

"I'm not," Sherman said with some bitterness, "now."

"Oh."

"Look at all those damn fish out there, waiting for me to—" He caught himself, and threw an impatient eye at the lights. Their deep waning red announced the approach of midnight. The newsbroker lowered himself into his deskchair; it creaked. "So. Do you have love trouble?"

"Uh-huh." He picked up Sam, and with a cautious finger nailscraped the reptile's spine in the areas where the fins grew out of the skin. "Well . . . I don't know if it's trouble, exactly, just that, ah . . ." Nibbling on his lower lip, he wished he were as facile with words as with his Talent. "I'm socially retarded, you know?"

"You sure picked the right world to come to."

"Huh?"

"Never mind, you'll see for yourself. You were saying?"

"Oh, ah . . . back when I should have been discovering girls, I was involved with . . . other things. So now—" He peeled a large patch of flaky skin; Sam wriggled in apparent satisfaction. "—now I find there's this incredible game going on between men and women. I want to get into it, but I don't know the rules. That's already gotten me in trouble. But I have a feeling that at my age, it's bad form to ask what the rules are."

Sherman fingered his middle chin. "What's the basic problem?"

"How do you, ah . . ." He blushed, and bent closer to the shedding Rhanghan. "How do you tell love from lust?"

Sherman cleared his throat, and laid his hands on his knees. Even in the cool air, sweat stuck his tunic to his chest. "That is a difficult one . . . you want the romantic answer, or the coarse one?"

He would not look up. "Why not both?"

"All right, both it is. Romantic first: if you can't bear to be parted from her, if she's with a more beautiful woman but you have eyes only for her, if her least little gesture or touch or glance sends you into transports of joy—that's love."

"Is it?" he asked dubiously, thinking of Nadia, thinking, *My God, I loved her!*

"In my book it's infatuation, which is something completely different, although it sometimes turns into love."

"That's three you've got to tell apart, then."

"Not really," chuckled Sherman, "because infatuation, if it isn't love, is almost always lust."

"Then what's the coarse answer?" he asked in something akin to resignation.

"Lock yourself in a bedroom with her, and go at it for a month straight. Don't even put your clothes on in between, just sit on the bed and talk or whatever. At the end of the month, move to a different city, go out—and to bed with—as many women as you can for another month. If, at the end of that second month, you find you'd rather be with the first woman after all—then that's probably love."

"I see what you meant about coarse."

"Hey, the problem with love is that it's intertwined with sex—and to be sure—to be positive—that what you feel for someone really is love, you've got to burn off all your sexual desires, at least temporarily. When you're completely sated, what's left is how you feel about her."

He squirmed. "But what if she were to do the same thing— I mean, make the same test?"

"Do I hear a double standard?"

"No, it's...I..." Again he regretted his verbal clumsiness. What he wanted to say was, *But if she's the kind who could have all those men, how could I have been attracted to her? She'd be, I dunno, probably not a tramp, but* . . . "Maybe," he said, "maybe you do hear a double standard . . . or maybe I couldn't take your test. I mean, I don't know if I could go to bed with one woman just to see if I were in love with another. You know what I mean?"

Sherman nodded, and a small glint of pleasure, or approval, lit up his eye. "I do, McGill, I do. I know exactly what you mean." Lifting his fist, he coughed into it. His jowls wobbled. "I heard about a possible job for you—I'll get the details, and let you know as soon as I can. And for now—" His hand hovered in mock threat. "—off with you. I have a living to make, and my chip goes out at 40:73."

"Sure thing, Harry. Sorry I took so much of your time."

"Don't be silly! I enjoyed it."

"Thanks. I'll see you tomorrow." He trudged into the hall. The day had tired him, and his belt said he was losing weight again. He pondered that all the way down to the 1-12 Datadesk, where he arranged his wake-up call and breakfast time. When he returned, still testing the slack in his waistband, the wheel floor reared up before him.

He came to an abrupt halt.

It rippled away, traveling like the hump in a cracked whip.

"Jesus!" He staggered back, instinctively checking the arch for signs of collapse. It was fine. And the tile floor was not even marked.

Heart still thumping, he caught his breath, and shuddered as the moment of panic passed. Then he frowned.

Inside Sherman's dome, a mannequin lay on the pallet.

Feighan snapped his fingers in sudden comprehension. "A fiber optic suit!" He hurried forward, hoping to catch the newsbroker, but the wheel floors were flat. Sherman had disappeared—again.

Walking back, Feighan resisted fear. *Walking Mule said he was okay! Said he'd had run-ins with The Organization, too* . . . but it bothered him, a lot. He did not like having a neighbor who prowled the corridors wrapped in manufactured invisibility. Not when Feighan had good reason to fear for his own safety.

He realized, as he stepped inside his dome, that he was also hurt. If the newsbroker were not Feighan's enemy—if he were, indeed, the Flinger's friend—then he had not taken him into his confidence. He had said he was going to write an article, not . . . Feighan scowled. *Just what the hell* is *Harry doing?*

"Hey, Sam." Sahaang had said the infant was an instinctive bodyguard who could sense if anyone meant to harm Feighan, and that seemed true. He had attacked Liang, and did eye the Delu servants with obvious suspicion. "Come here, Sam."

The child came over, swishing his tail.

Feighan jerked a thumb at Sherman's room. "What do you think, kid?"

Unblinking eyes met his gaze, then broke contact to study the other dome. After a moment he swung his snout back, unperturbed, at ease. Reaching out a small hand, he patted the back of Feighan's wrist. It was a peaceful, soothing gesture.

"You figure he's okay, huh?"

Cocking his head, Sam swept his tail from side to side.

"Well, if you vouch for him . . ." Yet his unease would not pass. Sherman might not be trying to harm him, but he certainly was not leveling with him. He glanced across at the mannequin, and shook his head.

* * *

Five planets orbited the sun. Beyond the third, six rockets flared, heading inward, toward Delurc. In the flagship's main cabin sat Milford Hommroummy. He sat on the floor, for the cabin was bare. Stars gleamed through its transparent walls, which could maintain internal pressures up to a thousand kilograms per square centimeter: Gryll used that cabin on its tours of inspection. The only fixture, a communications ceiling, had a two-meter by three-meter screen, a speaker, and a microphone.

A young boy's face filled the screen. His eyes were dead brown; his skin, purplish-black. Mechanically he said, "What are Feighan's weaknesses?"

Hommroummy thought a moment, then looked up. "He is immature. He loses his temper easily, and when he does, he stops thinking. If you can goad him—"

"We can. We have. What else?"

"He lives in the moment. He learns too little from the past, and does not plan for the future."

"Yet he is considered sapient?"

"He has wealth and Talent. His future is assured; he can afford to be impulsive. But he does not think ahead, and can be trapped through a succession of attractive lures."

"Other vulnerabilities?"

Hommroummy smiled. "He is obsessed with two things: the Far Being Retzglaran, and the female of his species. The former runs deeper; the latter, more strongly."

"Ah." The boy's head bobbed. "Yes, that is good. That is very good. We have just the bait. However, you will have to remove him from the trap."

"With pleasure," said Hommroummy. "With pleasure."

· Chapter VIII ·

By his third day on Delurc, McGill Feighan was lonely and depressed. Between shifts that day, he moped around the core of eD City, looking for someone to talk to. The spoke was deserted; he stared out the wall. A school of blue and gold fish slalomed through the weeds.

Behind him a door closed. As he turned, a tall, hook-nosed man bumped into him. Sam hissed.

"'Scuze," said the stranger. Though off-balance, he tried to brush past.

"That's okay." Feighan righted him. "Hey—do you have a minute?"

"No." He whisked away.

An hour later, a scar-chested Timili delivered the same rebuff, as did a second human that night, when the Flinger walked wearily home. *Whatsa matter?* It was nice that they respected his privacy, but they did not have to do it so abrasively. He stepped into his dome and dropped onto his pallet. *They got something against Flingers?* He sniffed his armpits. A little stale, perhaps, but certainly not offensive...

It surprised him. He would have thought that since there were so few aliens on Delurc, all of them confined to the domes on the reefs, a small-town mentality would have taken hold. After all, when one has nothing to do but to mind his neighbors' business...

Bewildered, he took to watching the passersby as he roamed the spokes and wheels. And began to understand.

They all hurried; they all buffered themselves with tense preoccupation. They pursed their lips and avoided eye contact. It was as though each hunted a buried treasure and suspected the others of racing to find it first.

117

By the fifth day, he had stopped making overtures to friendship. He filled the lonely hours with Sam and Sherman, instead.

Sam, for all his swift intelligence, was still a child, and the games he loved to play distracted the Flinger only because his ward took joy in them. It warmed Feighan to have someone respond to him favorably and uncritically; the child projected so much happiness that it enveloped Feighan like a weather field, and insulated him from the indifference of the City.

He pulled Sam's tail. "Gotcha!"

Sam stuttered a wheezy hiss and clashed his teeth like castanets while he waved his snout in the air.

"Don't you love that laugh, Harry?"

The older man shook his head. "Sounds like faulty brakes."

"That's why you never pay any attention to him, right?"

Sherman drew back his tickling fingers. "Well . . ."

"Uh-huh."

When time really weighed heavy, when the very lights seemed to slow their spin through the spectrum, he'd wander. Up a spoke, around an entire wheel, he'd walk, and pause, and peer for differences. There were none, except for the air in the various sectors. ED City was stamped from a mold that showed no signs of wearing out. And every alien ignored every other.

The only breaks in the monotony of his restless explorations came when the occasional translator hailed him. One would invite him to take a test, another to explain a point of Earthlore, a third to read a passage from Terran literature. They seemed curious about his planet and its people, and were willing to pay for it.

But not enough, which became a problem. The points accumulated slowly. Terribly slowly. Five here, twenty there . . . he needed over five thousand to learn about the gastropod, but at the rate he was earning them, he would have to leave Delurc before he had gathered anywhere near enough.

On this ninth morning, he ran into Harry Sherman at the 1-12 Datadesk. "Good morning," he said, nodding to the cow-faced Aronya.

Sherman, who had clearly been up all night, eyed him without fondness. "You really think so?"

"Don't give me a hard time, Harry, I'm not in the mood for it." He regretted his tone at once. *Pressure's built up again.* Like he'd told Maccari in that cafeteria long ago and far away—

he felt a sudden yearning for its stale, syrupy coffee—Flinging was also a compulsion. An itchiness accumulated within; only teleporting could vent that diffuse frustration.

Flingers called it "the pressure," and hated it, for it haunted them. Even on Delurc, where the dwarf days sapped his stamina, he woke up taut, ballooned by his outthrusting Talent. And that made him irritable. "Sorry, Harry."

"Got the Delurc blues, huh?"

"You're not exactly smiling to split your cheeks yourself."

The newsbroker shrugged, and wiped his palms on his wrinkled mauve tunic. His voice rasped with fatigue. "My visa's up for renewal, and the local authorities are red-taping it."

"Why?"

"Ah, who knows?" He waved a hand smelling of mildew. "I go through this every year. I apply, nothing happens. I inquire, they say they have a few more questions." Displeasure creased his face. "They want an audited accuracy rating, a statistical profile of my readership, substantiable credit references . . . what it boils down to, every year, is 'Tell us, Sherman, how we profit by your presence here.' That's really all they care about."

"How do you answer that one?"

"With difficulty." He forced a smile that vanished at once. "I really have only three things to say to them: First, that I'm a steady customer for their information; second, that I sometimes have data to sell them; and third, that I'm doing good PR for their image as the best brains in the galaxy." He sighed. "And they reply, 'So? Others would do the same as well, if not better,' and I just don't have a good come-back for that."

"Hmph," said Feighan. "Is this a factional thing, too?"

Alarm in his eyes, Sherman jerked his head. "Sh!" he whispered, motioning Feighan away from the big-eared Aronya. "Do me a favor—if I'm within a klick of you, don't mention factions. They'll bounce me out of here if they think I'm investigating them."

Grumpy with unbled pressure, he took perverse satisfaction out of asking, "But you are, aren't you?"

The ruddiness drained from Sherman's cheeks. "No," he said firmly, though he did not meet Feighan's gaze. A bead of sweat rolled down the trunk of his neck, and disappeared into his tunic. "No. I am not researching anything of the kind. I am a simple newsbroker."

"Oh, sure, Harry. Anything you say, Harry."

The great bulk untensed. "Despite the sarcasm, thanks." He bent down to scratch Sam between the ears. "So what's gloomed you out today?"

"Ah . . . I'm forty-eight hundred points short of what I need," said Feighan ruefully, "and I won't be able to get enough before I leave." He snorted. "Place is getting to me—only reason I'm here is to learn about the gastropod—but if my tour ends before I have the points, I'm gone anyway."

"What do you have, eighty more days?"

"Uh-huh."

"That's sixty points a day . . ." He stood, grunting a bit, and pulled down his tunic. "They'll pay overtime for extra Flings."

Feighan scowled. "No way. Ninety-six in twenty-two hours is killing me—I feel like I'm dating a vampire. Maybe you've noticed, I *walk* to work?"

"Thought that was for the exercise."

"Funny." He let Sam crawl up his wrist to perch on his shoulder. "I'm thinking about dreaming again."

Sherman snapped his fingers. "Think about your girl friend, instead." He reached into his hip pocket for a long envelope. "I forgot this came in today."

"What is it?" He held it in his hand and eyed it curiously.

"It's a letter for you, from the Maccari woman, the one you told me about the other day."

A memory-wisp of Maccari's smile spread warmth all through him. He wished he could lean across a table and talk to her again—till he remembered he might not be able to trust her. "How'd you get it?"

"Um . . ." The newsman tried to look innocent. And failed. "I decided to meddle a bit—when I sent in my chip the day before yesterday, I added a note for her saying that if she wanted to write you, she could route the letter through my computers, and I'd print it out for you here. Which I did." Hastily, he said, "But I didn't read it. Honest."

Feighan turned the envelope over in his hand, pinched a corner of it, and ran the pinching fingers along the envelope's edge as if to sharpen the crease. "I, ah . . . thanks. I didn't . . . I mean—"

Sherman broke in. "It's okay, don't worry about it. And if you want to reply to her the same way, drop in and use my terminal. The letter'll get to her tomorrow."

"Harry, you're incredible!"

The fat man blushed. "What's the good of having a private line to Earth if you can't act high and mighty and let your friends use it once in a while?"

He shook Sherman's hand. "Thanks a lot."

"You're welcome."

"Hey," said the Flinger, "something's been puzzling me since I got here."

"What's that?"

"Why can't I convert dollars into Fancies, then convert them into points to buy the information I want?"

"Well, you could—" At Feighan's surprise, he smiled. "—if you could find a fish who wanted to sell points for FNC's. You can look around if you like, but I've never heard of it. Even if you got lucky, you'd get raped on the exchange rate."

"But why—I mean, you do it all the time, without any trouble, right?"

Sherman raised his eyebrows. "You mean my operating expenses and buy-money?"

"Yeah, don't you—"

"Nope. I finance my local operations completely out of what I earn from selling the Delu information."

"But you can exchange money anywhere else in the Network!"

"And it's legal here, too, but..." Thoughtful, Sherman squeezed a fold of neck skin and rolled it between his fingers. "Look: the Delu don't want FNC's—they have no use for them. I mean, what can a fish buy in the way of material goods? The way they figure it, for them to offer unlimited exchange privileges, Fancies to points, would encourage inflation—they'd have to 'create' the points to sell, which would expand the money supply too quickly. So." He paused for a breath. "You following this?"

"Sort of; we covered some of this in IntroEcon."

"Good. Like I said before, you might be able to sell some Fancies here—but not at the official rate of twelve points per Fancy. One for twelve, maybe..."

"One hundred eighty bucks a point? That's robbery!"

"It's supply and demand, McGill. They're flooded with FNC's from their consulting work, and they don't need that many to repay the FNC loans."

"I thought those were supposed to have been paid back two hundred years ago."

"The Delu," said Sherman dryly, "held out for better terms."

"That figures . . ."

"Admittedly, they do hire off-world contractors to come in and expand eD City once in a while, and of course, they hire dreamers. Then they're constantly buying information from all over. It seems like they'd need more Network currency, but . . . I don't know, they're the economic experts, and if they say their system works—"

"—then it works." Feighan forced a laugh. His Talent reminded him that it wanted to be used.

"To put it mildly. Hey, I've got to get to work—" He slapped his forehead. "I'm dumb today. That job I was telling you about? Go talk to the translator at Datadesk 1-19. Even if you don't qualify, you'll enjoy it." His hands cut mirrored curves through the air. "*So* good-looking you want to cry . . . and she talks normally, too. It's worth the trip."

"Spoke One and Wheel 19, huh?"

"That's the one." He patted Sam on the head, then let his hand drop lightly to Feighan's shoulder. "And I've got to run— see you later."

He waved good-bye with Gina's letter, then turned to walk in the opposite direction. *What the hell, I can take the pressure a while longer.* He steadied Sam, who seemed about to slip off his shoulder. "Wake up, kid."

Sleepy, the Rhanghan snake-lashed his tongue, but tasted nothing of interest. Claws considerately retracted, he tightened his grip and dozed off again.

Once Feighan was sure he was headed outward, he ripped open the envelope. He didn't know what to expect. As he rubbed the lightweight paper that Sherman's computer preferred, it struck him that this was the first correspondence he'd ever had with a woman other than his mother. And she—he didn't want to think about her. Those memories hurt.

He unfolded Maccari's letter.

"Dear McGill,

I received a note from Harry Sherman today, in which he said that you are having trouble adjusting to life on Delurc, and that you would probably appreciate a letter from a friend.

The Talented always find it difficult to make themselves at home. Certainly I have discovered this, and you have, too. It is because the average person is not only afraid of that which is different, but is even more afraid of that which is almost the same. And so the Talented are rejected.

In a way, though, it might be somewhat easier for a Talented one to adapt to a society on an alien planet—for there, at..."

He ran his devouring eyes down the blocks of square-faced print. Curiously, they disappointed him.

In length, the letter would have pleased almost anybody—three single-spaced pages, it was—but its tone...impersonal. Essayish.

She spoke of many things—ethics and restaurants and the loneliness of the Talented—but though she probed her essence to show what she meant, she kept an ultimate, unifying portion of herself private. By shining too strong a light on the parts of her being, she left the whole in shadow. The Maccari of the letter was the Maccari of life—less that last, animating spark.

Damn, he thought, folding it back into its envelope, which he pocketed with care against wrinkling, *she coulda said, 'I miss you,' or*...yet the fact that she'd even tried to ease his loneliness lightened his step. That concern for her distant friends was one of the things that made her worth knowing.

He rounded the corner of Wheel 19, and stopped, stunned. There in the booth, as festooned with wires as an old oak tree with Spanish moss, sat the most beautiful woman he'd ever seen. *No*, second *most beautiful*, he corrected mentally. *Nadia was first, and always will be*...

Short blonde hair framed blue eyes as big as a baby's fists, but their size made her beauty all the rarer. Soulful, expressive, their depths trapped wistfulness and humor and intelligence. Her pert nose and full red lips invited lingering gazes; he could study that face with a magnifying glass and not find a flaw. And the rest of her! From her neck to where the booth hid her hips, her body flowed like a river, with a narrow waist and high firm breasts, and sleek arms that tapered into fingers as long and slender as willow branches. Her smooth, tanned skin looked like the softest thing on Delurc.

She turned her head towards his gape, and smiled. "Hi." Her voice caressed his ears with husky richness. Her eyelids fluttered. "You're McGill Feighan, aren't you?"

He cleared his throat. "Yes, yes...I am."

"The old female wanted to speak to you."

"Who?"

"The old female." Gracefully, she gestured with her left hand to the ceiling, beyond which hovered a hulking black presence. It blinked an abstract greeting pattern of green and orange spirals. "My controller."

"Oh . . ." He leaned his elbows on the counter, and propped his chin in his hands. "What does she want?"

"To hire you, I think." She smiled again and her teeth flashed with a brilliance greater than his tunic's. "But isn't it time for you to be at work?"

Yes! pulsed his Talent, but he hardened himself against its stridency. Unwilling to leave, he glanced at the light fixture. Though he still couldn't read its frequency displacements accurately, the color did seem the shade of almost green it had been the last time he's reported to the Booth. He nearly asked her what time it was—but remembered he couldn't afford the answer. Instead, he asked, "What's your name?"

"Taranya." She ducked her head and peered through the golden haze of her lashes.

She delighted him, and puzzled him too. "Will you be here tomorrow?"

Like mercury she flowed into another attitude, and sprawled luxuriously along the counter. "From 34:00 to 67:00—why don't you come on up and see me?"

"I will." He stepped away. "I will." Walking backwards, he realized he looked like an idiot. "Come on, Sam, we're late."

And she waved good-bye . . .

Hurrying down the long Spoke to the Fling Booth, he wondered where she'd come from, and what she could possibly have done to merit her punishment. Maybe she hummed? Paper crackled in his pocket as he swung his arms. For a brief instant, as if he were overlaying their portraits, he compared and contrasted Taranya with Gina. The New York Minder came out a distant second.

*   *   *

The first Fling of the day provided instant relief. *God, I needed that!* He leaned back in his chair, no longer feeling he'd go out of his skin if he stayed immobile a moment longer.

Outsiders wondered why people with such a skill would

work one day in ten, much less their actual nine. Flingers shrugged and said, "We have to." The outsiders then wanted to know, "Don't you have a union or something to protect you, get you decent working conditions? And the Flingers would roar with laughter. Though the five consortia of Earth did need all the revenue their teleports could generate, Flingers worked because if they didn't, they'd go nuts. Of course, the fact that all but two of Terra's were brainwashed might have had a little to do with that . . .

So he sat at his console, bored unto stupefaction, barely aware of his functioning, growing more tired with each Fling—yet more at peace, as well. The light would blink, the cargo's destination would flare across the screen, the clock would downcount—and his hunger to *do it* would mount until it peaked when the clock flamed 0.

PING

And he'd exhale in contentment, a little more fatigued, a little more relaxed . . . ninety-six times a day, nine days out of ten.

Between Flings that day, he tried to compose a letter to Maccari. Communicating through an interface bothered him, though; the machine blocked the things he wished he could pour into her liquid brown eyes. It was like talking through a closed window. *Ah, tell her about Sam . . .*

"Sam's putting on weight pretty steadily, and at times he moves so quick you wonder how he could possibly be anything but a machine, a spurt of electrons or something. Honest to God, the other day we're walking down this corridor—or I am; he rides on my shoulder a lot—and from the other direction comes this fat old Terran man with a silly-looking dog. Really. It's from Unjni, a planet that's not even in the Network, and it's got six legs, orange skin, and hair only on its belly. I thought dogs weren't allowed here because they disturb the fish, or so the Delu say, but I found out later this Nvele had had its vocal cords removed so it couldn't bark—or oink, whatever it does.

Anyway. There I am, walking along, minding my own business—this guy comes abreast of me and we sorta nod—and the Nvele goes for my ankle. Well, I didn't even see it happen, because Sam started to move at the same time the Nvele spread its lips sideways—and truly, the *instant* those fangs touched my skin, Sam was chewing on its throat.

I have never seen such a surprised animal in all my life. It musta jumped six feet straight up into the air, with Sam hanging on all the way up. The owner didn't know what the hell to do—he was bowing and apologizing to me while trying to hold onto the Nvele's leash and pull Sam off at the same time without tearing out ol' Orangeskin's throat... When I saw what the problem was, I just said, 'Leggo, Sam,' and he did.''

He flung another load to Earth, then paused to reflect. His brows furrowed at a sudden, incredulous thought. Staring at nothing, he counted on his fingers. To double-check, he queried the console, but it wanted to charge for the data. He made do with his estimate:

"It just hit me—Sam's not even three weeks old yet! He acts so much older, so... independent—and besides, so much has happened since he hatched that it feels like he's always been around. To me, he's more than a pet—"

Frowning, he told the console, "Erase that last sentence." Then he lifted the Rhanghan into his lap. "Sorry, Sam; I didn't mean it like it sounded. I, ah..." Carefully, he scratched between the attentive eyes, shielded behind their transparent inner lids. They seemed to peer straight through him to the truth.

"Damn," he said softly, fleetingly sick of himself. He pushed the feeling away before it seized mastery of his mood.

"Twee twenty in one," said the console.

"Right..." The two crate-bearing dreamers in the Booth said they were ready; when the O flashed he sent them back to Shanghai. Then he stroked the gleaming scales on Sam's flank, enjoying their pebbly warmth. "I didn't know, kid... I'm sorry. I'll try to do better."

"Sir?" the console asked.

"Nothing. Ah... hard-copy that letter for me. I'm calling it quits for the moment."

"That'll be one point, sir."

He gave a weary sighchuckle. *What a planet!* "Oh, all right."

When the draft chattered out, he reminded himself to rewrite it and to read it into Sherman's computer later that evening. *It oughta hold her for a while, though. Same kind of letter she wrote me, not as long maybe, but it sure is funnier . . . all of a sudden I see why hers was so distant. It's not easy, saying something meaningful to one special person . . .* He almost read his again, but folded it into his pocket. His failure to get beneath the superficial would only depress him further, *and I'm depressed enough as it is.*

After work that night, as they sat in a bubble of light tinged macabre red, Sherman gave him a heavy package. "Open it," he said. It unwrapped into a bound paper edition of *The Complete Works of William Shakespeare*. "You want to know about love, this is what you ought to be reading."

It felt softened by many perusals; he stroked its wrinkled spine. "Geez, a real book—where'd you get it?"

"I brought it with me when I came. I don't know why, but they never confiscated it."

It fell open; he squinted at the page chance had chosen. "What language is this?"

"The original Elizabethan."

"Never heard of it—I thought Shakespeare was English?"

"That's the way they talked in England then," he said with genuine dismay. "Didn't they teach you *anything* in school?"

"Not really." He hated to display his ignorance in front of the older man. "What do you recommend? I mean, in this book?"

Sherman chewed on a thumbnail while he thought. "Try the sonnets, see if they do anything for you—see if he's expressing emotions you're familiar with—or read some of the plays. *Romeo and Juliet*—"

"We did that one in school." He flipped through the volume for the start of it; the pages breathed mildew on him. "It didn't look anything like this, though. What are all these names on the left here?"

The newsman spat out a bit of nail and stared at him. "Do you mean you read a novelization?"

"Yeah—I mean, it was written just like a book—'he said,' and 'she said,' and all that." Suddenly he despised the Flinger Academy for having mal-educated him. They'd made him look stupid. "All they care about is the Talent, you know? The school's just 'cause of the law. They—" He stopped himself. "What's this 'Exeunt omnes' mean?"

"'All exit,'" said the older man. "Try it anyway, maybe you'll like it."

Feighan couldn't prevent himself from shrugging. "If you

say so . . . better than staring out the walls."

Sherman chuckled. "Anything is."

"I saw that girl today," he said, making no effort to conceal the fact that he was changing the subject. "You were right— she is gorgeous."

"I just wish her controller were the same," said Sherman glumly. He reached down to roll Sam onto his back and scratch his stomach plate, which was beginning to harden. Before long it would be natural armor, but now it itched.

The Rhanghan stuttered his wheezing pleasure, and nuzzled his muzzle against the newsbroker's wrist. With each sharp exhalation, his tongue flickered and snapped.

"Is the old female giving you problems?" asked Feighan.

"To put it mildly. She's a decision point in the social order, and has absolute authority to regulate the number of eedies permitted in. She's the one who's hassling me over my visa."

"Still no progress on it?"

"Progress in less than a day?" He raised his eyes to the crimson lights. "Hey, I'm not as young or resilient as you, and I've got to get to bed."

"How can you sleep with them on?" Feighan rose to his feet.

Yawning himself, he scooped up the sprawling Sam.

"Ten years here sort of gets you used to it." Sherman grunted. "I'll see you in the morning, all right?"

"Sure." Book in one hand, Rhanghan in the other, he crossed the wheel and draped himself across the hard, thin pallet, where he tried to make sense of the way he felt and the way the world worked.

Comprehending the archaic language took so much of his attention that he noted only peripherally the unnatural attitude of the shape on Sherman's pallet, and the bulky ripple headed towards the Spoke.

Eventually, sleep pushed his face onto the pages.

And dreams came on burgling feet to steal his peace of mind. Mist washed the walls and filled the domes and he, for once, had privacy. The absent eyes were a lifted weight; relaxed, he rode a couch and reveled in a day no fish would watch.

Swirled in fog, a face took form: large and round, with hanging jowls and a sunburst smile. "McGill," the man boomed, "McGill, hello!"

"Harry, hi," he said, extending a hand, which the broker seized too gladly.

"Let me sit at your side," and his arm wrapped around mute shoulders, which his fingers caressed.

"Ah, Harry—" said the Flinger.

"Ah, love," said the man.

And McGill's heart trembled as he lifted his face for the lingering kiss and his clothes were gone, lost in the mist along with Sherman's, and a great white whale of a hand sweated on his rigid self, while he searched the softness of the other for his hardness, and finding it, worshipped it with his eyes, then parted his lips as the clouds burned away and a million fish thrashed on the dome flashing, "Do it, do it, do it!"

A whistle blasted away the dream.

Sherman's face dwindled, still leering.

"Get up, Mr. Feighan, get up!"

He jackknifed up, feeling the last throb and sticky splash in his groin. For an instant he loathed himself—he'd *liked* that kiss, that touch—but the instant faded in the light of perspective. A dream is spun by a mind's twin tasks: to find a pattern in all it perceives, and to process and store its perceptions. At day's end, half sorts its heaping basket; the other must weave those random facts into a spuriously coherent reality.

That was the answer—he spent long hours with Sherman, but they didn't fill his huge loneliness. Only a woman could, so the need remained, to become a motif in a nightmare tapestry. He rubbed his eyes, wondering how he could act normally around the newsman later...

The Rehmal servant stood a careful one-and-a-half meters away, and again said, "Get up, Mr. Feighan, get up!"

He glared at the avian. "It's my day off; go away!"

"We do regret the inconvenience." It whistled a minor-key run. "But circumstances have caused a temporary shortage of teleports, and a surplus of priority shipments." It chirped without emphasis, as though it were simply reading a message. "Your off time must be postponed for four more days; you will, however, be paid a ten percent premium today."

Angered and exhausted, he bent forward till his forehead rested on his raised knees. "Do I have a choice?"

"None."

"All right..."

"Are you up, Mr. Feighan?"

"Yes."

It seemed to relax. "Breakfast will be served in forty twees."

Groaning, the Flinger pushed himself to his feet, and staggered to the toilet. In the corridor outside passed a couple arm-in-arm, but he didn't give them a second glance. Nor did they peek in. The artificial culture of extra-Delu City governed them. Each greedy eedie raised a wall around himself to hide his secret—his chance for wealth—from the others there for the same prize. By refusing to *see* the rest, one could shirk the duty to share. Selective blindness worked; the wall opaqued in both directions. At least to the point of unshying his bladder.

He stripped, threw his stained shorts at the dirty clothes pile, and jabbed the controls of the shower. *Am I—? No, uh-uh. Didn't mean a thing. Stress.* But he wished he could bury his self-doubt in a woman, anyway.

The Delu forbade sonic—or even electric—shavers because, they said, they emitted disturbing vibrations. He lathered soapsuds on his cheeks and reached for what was permitted: a razor. He cut himself just as the Rehmal returned. A dot of blood bulged on his right cheek. The servant gasped, snatching a piece of toilet paper from the roll, and ran to dab his cheek.

"Hey," he said, pushing the bird away, "what's the matter with you? It's breakfast time."

Its arm shot out; he ducked. A wing slapped his right cheek, then his left. He tried to back away, but a talon caught his belt and jerked him forward. The arm reached towards him again.

Rhanghan anger hissed like pipe-freed steam, and the Rehmal squealed in pain. Frantic, it pulled at the flurry of green meanness raking its arm.

"Sam!" said Feighan. "Let go!"

Thud the saurian dropped to the floor, still raging at the assault on his guardian. Electric blue Rehmal blood spattered the crown of his head. His tail curled upright; its scorpion end hung over his spine.

"It's okay, Sam," said Feighan soothingly.

"Is that a mature being?" chirped the Rehmal.

"I'm sorry—he's just a baby; he doesn't—"

"It is exonerated." Despite the furious reptile and the blue ooze seeping out of its arm, the Rehmal again extended the ball of toilet paper. This time, Feighan remained motionless. Softly, it brushed his cut cheek. Then the bird scurried away, hand to arm.

Shaking his head, Feighan ate breakfast and hurried off to work—the long way, past Datadesk 1-19. "Hi," he said, waving to Taranya as he passed.

Her smile could have melted a glacier. "Hi! Come see me after your first shift."

He practically skipped the rest of the way to the Fling Booth.

Time crawled. It dragged. It dug in its heels. Scoffing at Einsteinian laws, it decided to pass at one-twentieth its normal speed.

And for once, Flinging didn't relieve the pressure. In fact, at first it seemed to increase it. He couldn't sit still in his chair. His Talent peaked long before the clock read 0. Ozoney shocks of restlessness jolted his body again and again.

He was well into his sixteenth Fling before he realized that it wasn't Talent-pressure that fidgeted so mercilessly within, but . . . *damn*, he thought in surprise, *it's Taranya!* He was so eager to see her again that even his Talent gave her priority.

The rest of the shift passed, somehow. He stayed at the console that long, at least, but before the screen had blanked out the details of his final Fling, he was already at the datadesk.

"Hi." He donned a mask of cheery cool. "You asked me to come back."

She leaned forward. Like a magician forcing the card he has chosen, she made him focus on her breasts: their fullness, their smoothness behind the dragon's head brooch that pinned her blouse closed. "Yes, I did." She purred. "And I'm glad you did."

He caught his breath and tried not to stare down her cleavage. "What, ah, what did you want?"

"The old female would like to hire you."

Involuntarily he looked up, past the mustard-yellow lights to the dark shadow that spread across the ceiling. "What for?"

"As a Conversationalist." Cautiously she reached to touch Sam, who nictitated as her fingers padded on his skull plate. "She'll pay sixty-five points a day. She's researching Talents."

Feighan frowned. "I—"

"Oh, say you will!"

"I have a job."

"This would be between shifts only."

65 times 80-some days is 5200 . . . no safety margin. "Make it seventy a day."

"It's a deal!" She clapped her hands like a birthday child.

"Oh, it will be nice to work together . . . I am looking forward to it so much."

"How about starting by explaining what this is all about?"

Her eyelids drooped and her jaw jutted forward: a near-sighted professor peering up at his class. "The old female is constructing, in physical rather than psychical terms, a model of reality that will account for a Flinger's Talent, for his apparent random access to any point in space. To do this she needs to know a Flinger well, to interview him thoroughly, to . . . to sense his responses to the life-stimuli of Delurc."

"I thought Knxalad of Mrxelpha had already come up with that kind of model."

She sniffed. "Knxalad purveys pseudo-science, and knows it. His so-called 'theory' is no more than a semantic band-aid slapped onto a gaping wound in the structure of theoretical physics."

He stared fascinated at her; he'd never seen anyone don and doff so many disparate personalities. Sexsym, naif, acerbic old expert . . . he couldn't think of a thing to say that would appeal to all of her. "The Academy didn't tell us—"

"This might interest you. The old female contends that the notion of symmetric necessity demands that there be temporal analogues to teleports; individuals who have random access to any point in time. With your help, she believes she might develop some of the mathematics necessary to prove this."

He held his hands out, palms up. "Fine by me. Whatever I can do—"

The switch clicked facially; she changed direction. "I understand a friend of yours has just arrived here."

"Who's that?"

She tossed her head like a jilted lover; her jaw clenched. "Gina Maccari," she spat.

For an instant it meant nothing; he couldn't associate the Minder's stocky cheeriness with the chill of Delurc. "Gina Maccari?" Then he goggled. "Gina? Here? What for?" He felt like a desert-lost traveler hearing of an oasis.

Insulted righteousness melted into a wink. "Five points for that answer."

"No, thanks, I'll ask her myself."

"As you like," she said indifferently. "Do you know that the Delu are immortal?"

"They can't die?"

Extending a spread-fingered hand, she waggled it from side to side. "They *don't* die, unless— What does it feel like when you Fling?"

He was slow to answer because the best phrases didn't exist. "Ol' Knxalad got that right, at least. Sort of."

"Ah? Are your siblings Talented?"

"I have no brothers or sisters."

"Neither do I . . ." Her eyes dropped. "The old female ate all her brothers and sisters."

He coughed down his start. "Ate?"

"In the nursery of the reefs, she remembers . . ." Her head rolled loosely on her shoulders. "Come here, McGill, let me touch your temples, let me show you what I see."

Cautiously, he bent forward. The smooth softness of her fingers traced circles beside his eyes, circles that, as the stroking continued and his thoughts cleared away like wind-broomed smoke, became eyes themselves, eyes into another being's mind and memory.

Darkness. And warm jostling. No songs, no shades, just the seeing. "I. I. I," she projected for the others to see, while each of them 'pathed the same to her and to each other. Darkness. And warm jostling.

Then the spurt! The squeeze and the whoosh and the swirl and the slam! into salty water so blinding bright, so burning brilliant, that its currents had no impact, her tumbling had no upset. "I. I. I," she projected automatically, knowing who she was though not a single other thing, not even how to differentiate herself from the others who shouted, "I. I. I."

Dazzle up, dark down, bobbing and tossing in her tininess while all around great monstrous shapes feasted on her kin, sped through the cloud of fertilized eggs jaws agape, drinking in intelligence, sucking up sentience . . . the seeing lessened as voices choked off . . . she bobbed and tossed and tumbled in eddies and once a mighty tail slapped her, threw her almost to the flaming surface . . .

The current dragged her through the reef. Dizzy with fright and light and motion, she oozed stickiness. The water washed her against a rock; her adhesive integument stuck her fast. Contact bruised the walls of her cell, and she hemorrhaged micro-milliliters of protein that triggered her chromosomes into initiating processes that sprouted roots.

By morning she'd sunk fibrous feet deep into the sandy soil

of the reef, and was stemming rapidly towards the surface.

The fingers pulled away. "Well?" she asked.

He shook his head to dim the remembered glare of light on water, seen from beneath. "Fascinating . . . how could she remember her birth?"

"The same way you did."

"The—?" *Hah! While she showed me hers, she peeked at mine* . . . "So what happens next?"

"Tomorrow," she said. "Tomorrow."

"The time's up already?" He couldn't believe it, and had to check the lights. They glowed appropriately orange.

She nodded. "Tomorrow."

"You bet." And he walked away, Sam in tow. It pleased him immensely that they liked each other.

* * *

He found Gina that evening, before he'd even started looking for her. The Delu had assigned her the dome next to his, and he couldn't mistake her open stance as he walked down the wheel. Fine black hair gleaming luxuriously, she stood in the middle of her room, turning on one heel as she studied her quarters with a newcomer's wonder. The mirror effect seemed to awe her. An oxygen mask and mini-tank dangled from her hand.

He stuck his head through her doorway. "Gina—hi!"

"McGill!" Pleasure splashed across her face and she bounced towards him, spreading her arms. "God, it's good to see you."

"Good to see you again, too," he said. Impelled by a feeling he obeyed without understanding, he thrust out his hand. As they shook he wondered about it, because he would have liked her softness against him, her breath warm and friendly on his ear. But . . . he wasn't a hugger, and he didn't trust her, and in the half-instant that he had to consider the matter, he'd thought it better to avoid the embrace.

"It's nice to see a friendly face," he said, even as hurt tightened her cheeks. Blushing, he looked away. *Geez, am I ever going to learn how to play this game?* "Ah, what brings you here?"

She dropped his hand and retreated a meaningful two steps. "They needed a telepath," she said. "I volunteered."

"Oh, no!" He foresaw her misery and felt responsible. "Aw, Gina, you shouldn't have!"

"Why not?" She gestured at the bare room and the battered furniture. "I mean, living conditions don't look exactly plush, but McGill—you know what I'm like. I've been trying to get off-Terra for years, and I finally did it! Congratulate me."

"If you say so—congrats. But—"

"No!" Her tone had sharpened more than she'd wanted. "Sorry—I'm overtired—I was too excited to sleep last night."

"You didn't mention this in your letter."

"I didn't know!" she exclaimed. "They didn't tell me until yesterday afternoon. Walking Mule came up—"

"Walking Mule?" What did a Senior Flinger have to do with Minders?

"This is NAC business—he said there's so much traffic between Terra and Delurc that the NAC needed a telepath on the spot, and he said he preferred one who . . . er, who could get along with you," she said in a rush.

"Am I that difficult?" The light sparkled in her hair like rubies on velvet.

"You can be," she said mysteriously. "Anyway, I'm *delighted* to be here. McGill, you don't know what it's like for a Minder—you Flingers get to toss yourselves all around the galaxy while you're training, but we get locked up. From the day my change-ringer found me to the day I graduated, I lived like a thousand klicks from nowhere. So this—" She spread her hands to indicate the walls, the wheels, the entire planet. "—this is heaven! Just the chance to experience something new . . ." Trailing off, she nibbled her lower lip and stared at him. "You don't understand, do you?"

"Uh-uh. I'd like to, but . . . what can I say?" He slid a hand under Sam's belly and picked up the Rhanghan to display him. "See how big he's getting?"

"He's huge!" Leaning forward, she touched his nose with the tip of her finger. "Hi, Sam—I didn't recognize you."

The Rhanghan remembered a friend. He stretched out his arms to her, and clutched at her fingers.

"Can I hold him?"

"Sure." He passed Sam over, feeling a strange twinge at the way she cuddled him and held him close. *Jealousy? Why should I be jealous of Sam?* "The thing that really surprises me," he said, "is that the Delu are telepathic themselves. I can't figure why they imported an extra Minder."

"Apparently—" Carrying Sam, she moved to her pallet, and sat on it, the Rhanghan in her lap. "—it's something to do with the messages getting garbled. I guess the Minders here can't really communicate with the receiving Minders back home." She chuckled. "Let me tell you, McGill, trying to figure out what a Delu is really saying is like . . . like seeing a snowball in a blizzard. They are just so *powerful*! But . . . undisciplined. I mean, in our sense of the word. From what I know of the Delu language, it's the way they talk to each other, letting all sorts of peripheral images and impressions leak out around the words they speak, coloring them—but when you're Minding a business message from a salesman to his home office, you only confuse things. A sales manager doesn't need to know how many fish the message-sending Minder had for breakfast that morning, the key of its latest song, anything like that. So they sent me out to try to clarify the situation. I have to convince the Delu to purify the messages they relay, and chop out what's extraneous." She cocked her head and looked up at him. "Who is she?"

Feighan gulped. "P-pardon?"

"The one you're so hot for that your ache keeps surfacing even while *I'm* talking."

He sighed. He'd forgotten about this aspect of Gina's character. "She's a translator and the most—I mean, no offense or anything—the most incredibly gorgeous woman . . . *and* she's the only Terran translator here who talks like a living human being, you know?"

"You have it bad."

"Well . . ."

"And you're really uncomfortable about talking it over with me, aren't you?"

He nodded. "Uh-huh. I mean . . . you're a Minder, you know how I'm feeling even when you don't probe because it pops right out of my thoughts, so you know how I feel about this woman, but . . . but I keep thinking that at one point and it wasn't all that long ago, you were in— I mean, ah, you were sorta attracted to me, and I figure that that probably isn't all gone—that you still feel sorta, you know—" His cheeks burned so badly he was afraid they'd boil his eyeballs. "It's really hard to talk when your mouth's full of foot, you know?"

She laughed, but said, "It's okay, I don't hold it against you."

"Thanks. I get flustered when I talk about— about— ah, about me and women. Especially when I'm talking with another woman, and a woman who, ah, you know . . . it's not you, it's me—I couldn't talk with anyone about, I mean any woman, especially a woman . . . ah, forget it, okay?"

"Sure." For a moment she chewed her index fingernail. "Look, if it'll ease your mind any, after you left, I, er, managed to occupy my time."

"Huh?"

"What I mean to say is, I don't want you to think that I'm jealous of you and your feelings for this translator. I don't want you so much that I hope you're unhappy elsewhere. Honest, I don't. I like you, McGill." She leaned forward to touch his wrist with her sincerity. "As a friend, that is. But as a lover . . . no." Her eyes widened. "Oof! Boy, did you react to *that*. But my point is, I'm happy you're in love with someone else—because I'm not in love with you."

"I'm not in love," he managed to say. "Just, ah . . . attracted, that's all."

She stood and studied him. "You're strange, you know that? I can feel your relief like a clean wind—but it's all mixed with gloom."

Feeling like a friend had just shown him the door, he hid in nonchalance. "Sorry."

"It's okay. Look. Let us be friends, okay?" She extended her hand. "Close—good—best—platonic friends. All right?"

He took the hand and shook it. "All right," he said, after a hard swallow or two. "Sounds, ah, good."

From her wry smile, he knew that she knew that he was tremendously, curiously disappointed.

But at least she hadn't picked from his mind anything about Nadia.

* * *

Hommroummy lay on the bare metal floor, hands pillowing his head. He still looked elegant. He spoke to the boy in the ceiling screen. "It seems as though the Far Being Retzglaran has intervened."

"Statistically speaking," said the boy, "it could be coincidence."

Hommroummy waved a hand. "Nonsense. At great cost we have cut Feighan off from his base of support, and isolated him on a planet inhospitable to his kind, but to what end?" He ticked the points off on a manicured finger. "He brings a bodyguard, makes friends with the best-informed Terran on the planet, is joined by a first-rate telepath, and is attracted to the one servant on the reefs whom we cannot purchase. That is rather more than coincidence, Gimpy. That is the Far Being Retzglaran."

"We have managed to rent the translator—"

"For a mere five twees—and at an exorbitant price."

"She claims to be using it for a research project."

"Again I smell the Far Being." He closed his eyes and thought a moment. "Our only choice is to isolate Feighan even more. You are affecting him?"

"Of course."

"Then warp him. Irrationality will drive his human friends off. Work on his temper; provoke him to violence. As for the lizard—"

"It dies soon, Hommroummy."

"Very good." He frowned briefly, then clicked his fingers. "Something else I would suggest: give the newsbroker, *gratis*, data that verify the incompetence of the old female."

"It lacks subtlety."

"True—but it will indebt him to you. And when we need his help—"

"Ah." The boy grinned.

"Exactly." Hommroummy closed his eyes again. "Now go. I must sleep."

· Chapter IX ·

The next morning, anticipation churned in him. As soon as his first shift ended, he made straight for Datadesk 1-19. In the yellow light the spoke seemed endless. He knew he shouldn't teleport—he'd been Flinging too often and resting too little—but his time with Taranya was limited, and he did not want to lose a second of it: *To hell with the consequences*, he decided.

PING

"Hi." He stifled a yawn and leaned on the counter. "How are you today?"

"Just fine, now that you're here. Hello, Sam. Where were you born, McGill?"

His eyelids hung as heavily as iron shades; it was all he could do to keep them up. "Cleveland, Ohio, in the United States of America, Sol III."

"Does living in two dimensions heighten the territorial impulse?"

"Pardon?" Thick with fatigue, his mind couldn't begin to decode that question.

She pressed a finger against his nose. "Who taught you to read?"

"My change-ringer." Even through his exhaustion, the twists and turns of their conversation mystified him. "A retired Flinger named Jose Schwedeker. Why?"

"Can you wiggle your ears?"

Quit trying to figure it out; just relax and let it flow. "No."

"Do you like to swim?"

"Ah . . ." He shrugged, and stretched sleepily. "I used to—when I was a kid at summer camp I did the mile swim and took lifesaving courses—but lately . . . I don't know, I guess I haven't had the time."

She lowered her voice to whisper conspiratorily, "The old female is shocked! She doesn't see how anyone could leave the water behind."

"Ask her—" He grinned. "—when's the last time she took a five-mile hike?"

"Oh, that's different. But she remembers the two dimensions. Here. Let me share." She held out her hands head-high, and massaged the area around his temples as she had the day before. Again his own personality dissipated when he tapped the old female's memories.

Bud on a reed, sun burning bright, flashes off the water far below . . . rotsmell tainted the air as the reef shook the sea off its back. The pod that penned her restless tossings withered in the blazing sun . . . she swelled and it dried, flaking and crumbling dustily, until at last a fevered foot rippled a hole into the humid, salty air.

"I. I. I," she projected, while the others beamed their own self-images into her head, "I. I. I."

Clutching the stem with her tiny claws, she heaved this way and that, splitting, then shredding and shredding the papery pod. The wind whipped away its crumbs, and almost her, too, but she clung tight. In the light. The scorching light.

Instinct bowed her neck and opened her mouth. Broadcasting, "I. I. I," she nibbled on the succulent stalk and relished its acrid sap. It sharpened her teeth and nourished her muscles. Her beady eyes watched the brown-stained waves recede.

An insect hummed by her head. She paused in her feeding to watch it, to hear it, to envy it its freedom and its song.

Slowly she ate her way to the water, even as the water fled her coming.

Hot lights. Warm darks. Rising drones of multiplying insects. The stalk thickened towards the base but she grew, too, so she descended unslowed. All the while projecting, "I. I. I."

Lips brushed his forehead as the fingers eased away. "Back to work, McGill," she breathed.

"Oh, no!" he groaned. "It can't be that time already."

"Sorry." Her hand touched his chest, and pushed him away. "Tomorrow."

"Wait," he said desperately, as she began to slip into a statue's stasis.

"Yes?"

"I, ah . . ." The blood stormed into his cheeks. He looked

away, up; outside flashed a mid-sized Delu with a deformed fin. "What would it cost to free you?"

Laughing, she stroked her wires like a grande dame her pearls. "More than you can afford."

"No, I'm serious. I'd like to free you." His voice undercut him with its trembling, but the idea was right, and true, so he said it again. "To free you."

She pressed his hand between the warmth of her palms. "Thank you. But the fine I couldn't pay totaled twelve thousand points."

His heart sank. "You're right. I can't . . . twelve thousand! How did you—?" He looked at her questioningly.

She shook her head. "I can't say. Now go. You'll be late for work."

*   *   *

Halfway down the hall, a familiar voice called, "Yuh, Turang Flinghuh—hear you want to spring the girl."

He turned to the tortoise-shelled Edbargian translator. "How'd you know?"

"The news is on the markut alrudy—did you think we were slow, or what?"

"No, I just . . . never thought about it at all, really."

It tweaked its hooked beak in a gesture of exasperation. "Wull, if you're going to live here, you ought to think about it. But before you do, we've got a proposition for you."

He glanced at the lights to see if he had time to tarry. He did. "What's the proposition?"

"My controller—the gambler—will pay that translator's fine."

The flat statement drove the air out of his lungs. For a minute he couldn't breathe, or even think. "I—God, that's great! I—" Suspicion, irritated by his naivete, reminded him. "What does the gambler want in exchange?"

It nodded approvingly. "You're learning. But it doesn't want turribly much—this is a sporting world, you know, and he was thinking that—" It gestured towards Sam, who fixed it with a nictitating eye. "—your putt might—"

"He's not my pet! He's my, ah, ward."

"Putt, ward, mistress, whatuver you say. What the gambler was thinking, though is that thure could be one hulluva contust between your thing thure and a young *pwodee*."

"What?" As he recoiled, a Delu settled on the dome overhead. It was the same one he had noticed above Datadesk 1-19.

"A fight. They're about the same size, and pretty evunly matched, on paper at least. We heard about the incident with the Nvulu. So . . . if you want to take that dubt off that woman's head, just say yus."

He visualized himself ringside at a prize fight. An image of a referee raising Sam's hand in victory floated across his mind. Quickening excitement jettisoned logic; all he could think was: "And then he'll free her?"

It lifted one of its twelve legs, which it scratched with the scythe of its nose. "She's serving time for a large dubt. The gambler gurantees to pay that dubt the instant the fight is over, win or lose."

The deal sounded tailored to his needs. He wanted badly to shake on it at once, but vestigial wariness forced him first to ask: "Can I see a pwodee before I agree?"

"Of course." It pointed to the place where the wall curved into the floor. "Thure's an adult in that patch of weed—the bluish-green thing with the snappers."

Feighan bent over to peer through the glass. Mud clouded the water, and through it tumbled ribbons of algae. He squinted past his reflection; a sea-shadowed tangle of limbs caught his eye. He stiffened.

The dark-shelled pwodee was all pincers. He counted six, seven, eight . . . six were small, more like taloned feet than real weapons, and they clustered beneath its armored oval body. The other two looked vicious. Serrated triangles of chitin, they opened and closed in the rhythm of the currents, ballerina graceful till they caught a rock. They tasted it. Then crushed it into pebbles.

Obsession withdrew like clouds before a wind, and the light of sanity shone down. He saw those claws in his mind; his gut froze. They advanced in slow-motion, advanced and outspread, then swung— narrowed— trapped Sam's fragile neck. Bones cracked and popped. The knowing eyes darkened. He shuddered. "I—"

"What?" said the translator sharply.

The scene in his head burst like a window does when a rock comes through it. "I . . ." He trailed off into confusion. He tried to remember what he'd pictured, but the shards on the floor of his mind drew together to form a new vision, more vivid, more compelling. *"Hi there," breathed Taranya. Supine on a long soft couch, she beckoned him with a crooked finger.*

"Wull?"

The fantasy faded into a diffused throb of longing. He had to have her. He looked at Sam. "Can you take it?"

The Rhanghan focused his attention on the pwodee. He made a leisurely nictitation. The blades of his spine twitched upright; his tail swept the tiles. Jaws parted, he threw his tongue at the glass, and hissed with contempt.

Feighan let out his breath, and grinned. "Guess that'll do for an answer." Straightening, he turned to the Edbargian. "Would the fight be under water?"

"No. The pwodee is amphibious; the fight will be in the two dimunsions."

"Huh?"

"On dry land."

"Fine." He nodded decisively. "When and where?"

"Whun you gut off work this evuning. Return here and we will have uverything ruddy."

"Great!" He beamed down at Sam. He knew how quick Sam darted, how swift and smart and deadly; the fight was as good as over. Taranya would be his! And that evoked such a high-soaring joy that he swooped the Rhangan into his arms. "Ah, you're great, ol' buddy!"

Sam merely blinked, and made himself comfortable. Then he glanced at the lights.

Feighan checked, too, then looked askance at his ward. "How'd you know it was time for work?"

Sam patted him on the chin.

"All right, off we go—"

PING

But once he was in the Fling Booth, keeping his mind on his job proved difficult. He couldn't sit still. He chuckled over nothing. And he demanded a Fling count so many times that the console began flashing it automatically.

For once, he didn't even feel his fatigue. It lay sullen in a corner but hope so filled him that there wasn't room for much else. *God she's pretty.* He couldn't wait. *She's gonna be so happy . . . wonder if she'll let me— no, can't ask that, I mean, gratitude's one thing, but to come out and say, 'Hey, how* *about we find someplace private and *harrumph*, uh-uh, that's a shitty way to do it . . . but I wonder if she'll let me . . .*

Halfway through the shift, Maccari dropped by with some schedule changes. Darkness smudged her undereyes, and she yawned into his smile. "Boy, you're feeling good." She leaned against the wall and soaked up his mood for a moment. "What happened? I can tell it's that girl, but—"

He told her.

Her good humor dried like rain on a griddle. She dropped into the chair he'd vacated. "McGill, you're risking Sam's life!"

"Naw." He shook his head. "Not a chance. Sam's—"

"—still just a baby!"

He swallowed. "If you'd seen him go after that Nvele—"

"Now you're feeling uneasy, aren't you?" Her grimace bared her teeth.

Defensive against rising doubt, he said, "Dammit, it's not fair to Mind me!"

"You're right, it's not." Her shoulders sagged. "But why did you agree?"

"Because, ah—" He stopped, and scratched his temple. The answer was there, on his tongue, in his throat, but he couldn't—a minute earlier he could have explained the whole thing, laid it out, traced the reasons, but now—but now he couldn't. The relationships escaped him. The perspective was lost. Puzzled, he blinked. "I don't know—I just, ah . . . I just did, that's all."

She closed her eyes, and appeared to concentrate on something behind them. "There's wrongness here, McGill." She looked around, then up—and suspicion tightened her lips. "You might have been 'influenced,'" she said. "Can you call it off?"

A sick sense of doom swirled through him, and he sat on his console. "I— I don't think so. They're pretty tough about enforcing contracts here."

She bit her lip. "Then you'll have to go through with it."

"Sam— Sam'll win. Sure he will."

"You're not as confident as you try to sound." She regarded them glumly. "What time is this happening?"

"74:30 tonight, after I get off work." Suddenly it seemed much too soon. "Why?"

"I want to be there."

He looked down at his ward, who was busily untying Maccari's shoelaces. "Hear that, Sam?" He tried to recapture his earlier certainty. "You're going to have a cheering section."

"Hardly that."

Her tone chilled him, but he cajoled, "You know what I meant."

"Yes," she said. "I'll wait for you outside."

"Thanks."

"You get off when, in a couple of trooms? I'll find Harry Sherman, too. He should be there."

When the appointed hour came, the Edbargian directed the three Terrans and the Rhanghan to a small dome adjoining a miniature, sand-floored arena. There waited a young pwodee. Now that air could carry sound, the castanets of its claws clicked a deadly rhythm. Sam bared his fangs but made no move to leave Feighan's arms. Instead, he shifted position and looked up at his guardian, as if to say, "Just give me the word."

And Feighan did. He bent over, set the reptile before the tunnel leading to the arena, and swatted him gently on the tail. "Go get him!"

Sam blasted down the tunnel.

The pwodee's feet kicked sand as it pivoted to meet the Rhanghan's hissing charge. Its right claw jabbed out and snapped! Sam yelped, then backed away. A drop of blood smeared the side of his snout.

"Stop it, McGill," said Maccari.

"I can't," he said, though he wanted to with all his heart. "I've got a contract."

Tail swishing the sand smooth, Sam circled the crustacean. He kept his hands up like a boxer guarding his face, with his jaws parted and his small teeth ready to slash. The pwodee stayed in one place, turning only to keep the other in view. Its six minor claws stayed close to its body, protecting its belly.

"C'mon, Sam," muttered Sherman. "Make me rich."

"You have a bet down?" asked Feighan.

"Even odds, but I put a thousand points on him, so— c'mon, Sam."

Why didn't I think of that? Woulda gotten me that much closer to the gastropod . . . damn.

More and more Delu swam into position overhead. Skintalk spattered the dome like paints off a dropped palette; occasionally a harsh grating resonated as a careless spectator scraped the glass. In the corridor outside, too, a small crowd gathered—

mostly reticent, arm-folded Terrans, though a twelve-legged marsupial from Rii-edsch stood right up front.

Sam lunged. The pwodee's claw flashed out, flashed open. Maccari gasped. Saw teeth sped for the reptile's throat. "No," she whispered.

At the last instant the Rhanghan ducked. Carried by momentum, the pincer rushed past, exposing its arm. Sam twisted his neck and bit up, hard. The pwodee spasmed, for the first time making a noise. It sounded like the whine of a kicked dog.

Sam's jaw muscles bulged. Crustacean blood smeared copper on his cheeks. Clearly he wanted to chew right through, but even as he intensified the pressure the pwodee hammered its other claw down on his head.

He fell and lay still.

Feighan thought his heart would stop.

Tucking its injured arm under its belly, the pwodee inched its good pincer towards Sam's throat.

"Sam!" shouted Feighan.

The Rhanghan wriggled alive and snapped! Saurian teeth crashed through chitin. With a muffled hiss he found his feet. While his tail lashed out, sweeping the pwodee off its claws, the leverage he exerted threw the beast onto its back. Then, releasing the crushed limb, he sprang for the pwodee's soft blue belly, and bit it again and again. Blood spurted over his skull plate. Raking his midlegs up and down the creature's groin, he pinned its head with his hands and beat its skull against the floor. For a long minute the room resounded with Sam's angry hisses. Gradually, the pwodee ceased struggling. And died.

Sherman exhaled his relief. "He did it!" He dried his palms on his tunic.

Feighan sagged against the wall. "Uh-huh..." He wiped sweat off his forehead and looked at Maccari. "Well?"

She shrugged. "You figured it right, I guess—but I'm still not happy about it, McGill. If that thing had been a little stronger—"

"I was thinking the same thing myself. But it wasn't. And Sam won."

The door connecting their dome with the arena opened. Feighan squatted on his haunches and whistled through it, "Here, Sam. It's over. Leggo, come on in."

The Rhanghan climbed off his prey, and pawed the bloody

sand with his rear legs. Before turning towards the exit, he paused to tail-slap the corpse. Then, fatigue bowing his shoulders, he trudged into the observation dome and waited at Feighan's feet. Leaning against one boot for support, he stunk of saurian sweat and crustacean gore.

"Jeez, you were good, Sam." With his handkerchief he wiped the mess from his ward's muzzle. "Are you okay? Looks like . . ." Sam's head jerked away from his touch. "Hold still, I have to— ah, yes. Just a small cut. Not bad at all. Let me just dab up the blood . . . easy, easy . . . I know just how you feel; I once had to hold still for your mother while she pulled frindrin thorns from my butt . . ." The urge to crush the Rhanghan in a tremendous hug almost overwhelmed him. Gratitude welled up in him; he had to blink and duck his face to hide the moistness of his eyes. "Thank you," he whispered, "thank you very, very much."

All four eyelids nictitating, Sam touched his snout to Feighan's nose, then clung to his upper arm and laid his muzzle on the human's shoulder.

They lingered by the arena for a while longer, as if their elation would shrivel were it removed from the scene of the triumph. They chatted with each other, though the people outside dispersed without a word, while Sam's breathing slowed and his heart beat eased and his muscle tension gradually softened. Then he fell asleep.

"Poor thing," said Maccari, as she pried him off Feighan's biceps. "You should take him home and put him to bed."

His eyebrows flickered.

"I felt that." She struggled to repress a laugh, but failed. "All right, I'll take him home so you can pick up your girlfriend and put her—"

"Now, now," he said, sputtering on a giggle.

"I'll go with you, McGill," said Sherman.

"Thanks." Together they set out, down the spoke to the Edbargian's booth, and the Flinger, though his mind was elsewhere, asked, "How's the visa thing going?"

"I think they're weakening," he said gloomily, "or they were before this. But they're weird beings, and I'm not sure how the old female's going to react when my friend steals her favorite translator."

"You think she'd hold it against you?" His own jubilation made that seem impossible.

"Who can say? There's a chance . . ." He jammed his hands

into his pockets and walked along, head lowering, watching the tips of his shoes. "I'd really hate to have to leave this place."

"You're kidding."

"Are you serious?" He glanced at Feighan. "Sure you are, you're a Flinger. But look: no place in the Network has a comparable information flow. Admittedly, on other worlds it's easier to gather your data, but here, it's reliable. Guaranteed, even."

"In Delu terms," said Feighan. All around them, the cycle slid into the infra-red; for a few precious minutes they could splash through pure white fluorescence.

"There's that," conceded the broker, "but hey! Every word they utter is true; the danger lies in drawing your own conclusions."

He rubbed his eyes. "You'd *really* rather live here than somewhere else?"

"I'd really rather *work* here," he said. "At least until they amend the data-'change rules. One of the factions—"

"Which you're not investigating?"

"Right." Sherman smiled at his friend's sarcasm. "So I won't say anything more. I'd like to stay. It wouldn't ruin my business if I had to set up shop somewhere else, though. To tell the truth, someday I will—but . . . dammit, McGill, I don't like the idea of being thrown out. It's not leaving that bothers me so much as *having* to leave. Know what I mean?"

"Sort of. I mean, yeah, I guess I do. I've never had that problem, though, so I can't really empathize." *Or feel glum, either—not on a day like today!*

"Here's your gambler's puppet."

The Edbargian laid its flamingo neck on the counter and looked up. "Come to colluct your prize, uh?"

"You know it," said Feighan, grinning widely.

"The mobile servants are bringing her—ah, here thuy come." He nodded down the spoke behind them.

Sherman turned; Feighan spun. Lumbering towards them came an eight-legged Aronya, a wide, squat being with flame-red hair and a back as broad as a dining room table. Across it lay the translator, swaddled in blue. A gold-feathered Rehmal accompanied them to insure her balance.

"She's still asleep," said the hook-beaked translator. "Quite common in a detached servant."

"When will she wake up?"

"Oh, a couple of trooms, maybe more, maybe luss. Depunds on her mutabolism, if you know what I mean."

As the Aronya drew level with them, Sherman sighed. "She is gorgeous, McGill, especially in that blue robe. You're to be complimented."

He blushed. "For what?" He stopped his hand from tousling her honey hair.

"For arranging her release—that's next to impossible—and also for the obvious."

"The obvious isn't definite, yet," he said. It was all he could do to keep from scooping her up in his arms.

"It will be when she hears what you've done."

"That might be some time, juntlemun," said the Edbargian. To the Rehmal it said, "Okay, take her away."

"Oh, are you delivering her to my room?"

The translator laughed. "Hardly. We're returning her to her booth."

His jaw dropped. "What for?" His fists reflexively clenched. The Aronya shouldered past him, orange eyes blazing.

"She's under arrust."

"What for?" Within him, disbelief and anger fought for mastery.

"A vury large dubt."

He pounded on the countertop. "The gambler paid that!"

"No," said the Edbargian, wagging its bald head. "The gambler paid the dubt for which she had bun suntunced. This is another dubt, a bigger one."

Teeth gritted, he said. "He promised to free her!"

"He did." Its carapace bounced in a shrug. "From the first dubt. That was just dumonstrated to you by the Aronya and the Ruhmal, who brought her here for your inspuction. It's not the gambler's fault if she had incurred another dubt."

Furiously angry, Feighan leaned across the counter, reaching into the booth to grab the beak-faced turtle and throttle its skinny neck and— Sherman caught him in a neat full nelson. "Don't," snapped the newsbroker. "There's an immense fine for assaulting a translator. Don't even think of it."

Face pressed into the countertop, he said, "But the girl—"

"You were suckered, McGill."

"But he promised."

"You didn't investigate enough." Sherman dragged him five meters from the booth, then released him. "Look, McGill, that's how Delurc works—you made an agreement with the gambler, and you both lived up to your ends of the bargain. The thing is, the gambler hadn't told you the whole truth—I warned you that they were like that, remember?"

"But I've got to do something!" He eyed the fat man, wondering if he could break around him. The newsdealer balanced easily, warningly, on the balls of his feet. "I can't just—"

"Nothing you can do."

"But she—"

"Uh-uh. Not a thing. Unless you want to send Sam back into the arena."

Hmm . . . and this time I could get a bet of my own down— Feighan's blood froze as he realized that he was actually contemplating that possibility—but before he could begin to loathe himself for his willingness to risk Sam's life a second time, the translator called.

"Don't bother. The chance has gone out of it; you couldn't gut a rematch no matter how much you bugged."

Hot anger settling into banked resentment, Feighan said, "I guess that solves that."

"Sure seems to."

He looked down the long, sterile spoke to where the Rehmal and the Aronya were unloading the translator into her booth. His heart hurt—*so near she was, I thought sure I could get to know her, to . . .* His head hurt from fatigue and worry and overwork. And his pride hurt, because he'd been outwitted by a gambler and used in the process. Suddenly he punched his fist into his palm. "Dammit!"

"Can't say as I blame you," said Sherman, throwing a heavy arm around his friend's shoulders and aiming him towards home. "But what can you do?"

A dark shape swirled over them, and they raised their heads. Pressing against the dome, it shifted its colors. Its fins flicked in eight different directions at eight different speeds. A faint series of runs and trills vibrated the interface between air and water. "It's the old female," said Feighan.

"Do you know what she's doing?"

He looked up again, and shook his head. "Haven't the faintest."

"Laughing," said the newsman sadly.

"Really?" If he'd had a harpoon, he would gladly have sunk it into her.

"Really."

"Dammit. And her. And this place." Angrily, he paced ahead of Sherman, squeezing the moisture out of his eyes, fighting to keep the emotion out of his voice. "Dammit, Harry, I hate this whole world."

* * *

He hated it even more an hour later, when Maccari slipped into his dome to say: "Don't trust Harry Sherman."

Astonished, he gaped at her. Sam ran to her leg and begged a lift. "But the kid loves him, and that's practically a seal of approval. Harry's—"

"Lying to you," she said. She kept her tone firm but soft, and gave only a single over-the-shoulder glance at the mannequin on Sherman's pallet. "Listen. I haven't probed him, and you know I won't, but when the two of you talk I can *feel* him lying."

"Dammit, dammit, dammit! I knew I shouldn't trust him, I knew it!" Then he looked up. And wondered if he could trust *her*. "How is Harry—"

"I don't know." Cradling Sam like she would a cat, she sat in the desk chair. "I just wanted to warn you."

"Aw, Christ." He rolled on his back and stared into the dark waters above. Ten meters up, a green glow showed for a moment, then faded. It was enough to light up a misshapen fin. "He acted like such a friend..."

"He is fond of you," she admitted. "I can feel that, too... but he's lying to you, so watch him."

He lay there in silence for a long time, while she baby-talked Sam and the Rhanghan wheezed sleepily. The pallet was hard beneath his shoulders; the lights violet in his eyes. He was angry with Sherman—and her, too, for scuttling a friendship—and with Walking Mule for misleading him, and the old female, and the gambler, and... gritting his teeth, he simmered to himself, and wished he had someone to talk to. But he didn't; there was no gentle ear into which he could pour his woes; no soothing, loving, listener... He clenched his fists, tautening the tendons of his arm until they stood out like cabled intentions. He wanted so badly to expend his rage that he imagined punching the wall— *no, break my hand* —the mattress— *no, awkward angle* —Maccari— *hey, no! I'm not*—

Shaken by his wild desire, he sat up slowly. Knowing he couldn't hurt her only made him more furious with her. He caught calculation in her eye and said, "Get out."

Her lip curled. "With pleasure."

"Now."

She set the drowsy Rhanghan on the floor and jerked to her feet. "I wouldn't spend another—" She broke off and pinched the bridge of her nose. Squinting past her thumb and forefinger, she said in a different tone, "McGill—"

"I said, get out." Irritated by her dawdling, he rose.

"No, no, the mood—"

"Revulsion."

"—it's not yours or mine, it's—" Vaguely, she waved her left hand at the night-shadowed ocean. "—it's coming from out there somewhere."

He had to restrain himself. "I don't care. It's mine, now. Get out."

"But—" From across the dome she looked at him, and let her left arm droop. "All right," she said. "All right, I'm going."

He stood immobile till the lights softened into lilac, resisting the heat of his hate yet warming himself in it as well. Towards the end he had to stoke it to maintain it; he had to review his plight, the slights, the lies . . . yet weariness cooled him, eventually, and then even the bleakest of images failed to rekindle him.

Exhausted, he limped over to his pallet and lay on it, sick with the ashes of rage. He wondered, briefly, if he were going insane.

Then he slept.

Poorly.

* * *

The fleet was a few hours out of Delurc. Milford Hommroummy was pacing. He slammed his heels against the metal floor, now and then looking up at the face of the screen. Finally he said, "What went wrong?"

"Both were stronger than expected."

"Gryll will hear of this."

"We convinced him to jeopardize the beast!"

"But not to attack the telepath," Hommroummy said with a sneer. "What about the newsbroker?"

The boy smiled. "That segment of the plan proceeded as desired."

"In other words, he took your data." His jaw muscles bulged. "But: Is. He. In. Your. Debt?"

The boy ducked his head. "Who can tell what an alien feels?"

Hommroummy pinched the bridge of his nose. "Do this, then," he said with a sigh. "Tell Sherman you have more information, but that you will not reveal it unless Feighan is there to hear it. Tell him to take Feighan to an isolated place— without Maccari!—and then . . ." Rubbing his jaw, he trailed off.

"Yes?"

Hommroummy completed three laps of the cabin before he stopped and spoke again. When he had finished, the boy was grinning.

And so was he.

· Chapter X ·

The next afternoon, grouchy and over-tired, he stumbled towards Datadesk 1-19. The siren and her song drew him down the long spoke. His shoes scraped the tile's mildewed grout. Deprived of targets, he berated himself for returning to the old female. Considering the way she'd mocked him the previous night, he should quit the job—*just not show up* . . . but he had to find out about the gastropod. *And it'd be nice to see Taranya again, too,* he thought.

The arch of the spoke ran ahead and down, shrinking with perspective as if succumbing to the weight it bore. His spirits felt heavier. Even lifting his feet seemed impossible.

She sat on the stool behind her counter and smiled as though the preceding day had never happened. Then her eyes glistened with empathy. "You're sad." She reached over to smooth his unruly hair.

The single gesture swept away all his ire. "I wanted to free you—I wanted it so much . . ." He cleared his throat. "What do you owe on this debt?"

"Eighteen thousand four hundred points." Her long, slender fingers touched his right cheek gratefully, then tapped a soft rhythm on the counter. "How many children do you have?"

That startled him into a double-take. "None!"

"What are you favorite colors?"

"Ah . . ." Puzzled, he cocked his head to look within himself. "I guess that depends on my mood . . ." He couldn't resist adding, as he gazed into her face again, "Right now, they're blue and blonde."

"Thank you." She batted her eyelashes and burlesqued coyness. "Have you ever traveled to the Hub?"

"Never—although I'm sure I will, one day."

"Close your eyes," she said softly, and touched his temples. Within seconds he was in the memory-trance, so deep into it that he could barely remember that he was a Terran Flinger named McGill Feighan, not—

—"I. I. I." She sat at the stump of her birthstalk, clashing her teeth together experimentally while she made shadow-pictures on the mud with the uppermost of her eight notched fins. The sun lathered her light-grey skin with warmth. All around her lay or sat or crawled her brothers and sisters, each broadcasting, "I. I. I."

After a while, hunger outweighed the allure of the shadow-shapes, and she flopped forward, propping herself up on her fins. The surf tumbled at her rear, but she trotted to the reef's highest point, the spot that had first emerged from the sea. A few of her siblings had had the same idea, and she came upon them digging in the muck. Above their heads hummed a cloud of insects that hung maddeningly out of range.

"I. I. I," she projected, knocking a brother over.

He—she?—rolled down the small slope, skin color-muttering with anger. The sun so outshone it that it appeared as a visual ripple, the kind that goes away when you blink.

Her fins churned the soft ground, scooping up sandy mud and splashing it to either side while she watched it closely. A long grey grub wriggled in the brilliant light; she pounced on it. Two siblings eyed her jealously, but the grub wasn't even an appetizer, much less a meal big enough to be shared. Inhaling it, she returned to her excavation, hunched over the hole she'd hollowed out, and—

—strong sharp teeth seized her tail.

She twisted, and arched her spine, but that failed to shake loose her assailant. The sun beat down, warming the blood smell, spicing it. She curled under her own belly, and clamped her teeth on his gillbuds. With a squawk he released her, and would have stumped away on his fins if he could have.

She would not let him go. Uncoiling, and flapping onto her stomach, she chewed. Hot blood gushed down her gullet. It was good. She closed her jaws all the way, ripping a great chunk of his flesh off his ribs. He sprawled east and she west, thrown backwards by her straining.

She would have launched herself upon him again—for she had swallowed the hunk of him whole—but he had already disappeared under a flock of their siblings, all anxious to feed off of him. A few on the fringe even dared a tentative nibble in her direction, but her fury drove them back.

When the crowd melted away, only gleaming bones lay scattered on the reefbed.

The scene imploded as though a picture tube had failed. Feighan's eyes snapped open on their own; his head jerked up.

"I'm sorry," she said, while she stroked the back of his right hand soothingly. "The transition was too abrupt."

"Is it over?"

"Yes . . . back to work, now."

"Oh, hey—can't we—"

A shadow swept across the oceans of her eyes. "I'm sorry, McGill. We can't. Good-bye."

Reluctantly, he backed away. "I'll see you tomorrow?"

She nodded, biting her lip. "Yes. Definitely. Tomorrow."

And through the whole second shift, he could think of nothing but that sadness in her eyes . . .

* * *

He dreamed, that night, of a cloudless sky in July at the shore, white sand dry and loose beneath his sandals, cool wind refreshing on his bare chest. Cacti grew tall and man-like on the dunes. The beachgoer's summer had tamed the waves. They rolled in three feet high, slapping down with metronomic regularity, then whispering to themselves as they retreated to regroup.

He dropped his gear and kicked off his sandals. Alone, he was, with seasonal restlessness daring him to test his body's limits. He sprinted for the surf, kicking up sand then water; he stopped when the sprint became a ludicrous slog. Then he dove, flat and long, skimming the wavetops, surfacing into a butterfly stroke that stretched his shoulders and brought him to gasping within two hundred meters.

And there, as he trod water and looked back to the people hugging the land, too fearful to venture more than waistdeep into their ancestral element, something bumped his knees, and lifted.

A great dark whale rose beneath him.

He sat on its back, crossed his legs, and said, "Hello."

It rolled up an eye the size of a basketball. "Hello." The words burbled through its blowhole. "Can I give you a ride?"

"Where are you going?"

"To see the sea, and see what scenes can be seen."

"Sounds good," he said, but...a kilometer or so out the whale unflicked its tail and dove! like a submarine plummeting from the bombs of a plane. "Hey! What are you doing?"

"The good stuff's on the bed. Let's dive!"

"I don't have gills!"

"Well, neither do I, you silly human. Hold your breath. We'll be up in half an hour."

And as he started to protest the gentle giant teeth closed on his ankle and pulled him down and the water went up and the sun burned bright and—

"McGill, McGill, wake up."

He raised his head, the coarse blankets falling off his sweaty shoulders. "Wha? Who?" Maccari's concerned face loomed into focus. He mumbled, "Gina, wha?"

Squinting, she rubbed her temples. "You were having a nightmare."

Her proximity steadied him like a friendly tree. "Did I scream?"

"That, too." Exhaustion pallored her cheeks and cut lines at the corners of her eyes. "Mostly it was in your head—and mine." She shivered.

"Damn, I'm sorry..." He drew a breath of cool, damp air, and let it out with a shudder. "I don't know what it is, I've been having more and more of these dreams...probably overwork, huh?"

She regarded him gravely. "Probably. But..."

"What?"

"Never mind. Can you get back to sleep, now?"

"Where's Sam?" Suddenly he needed to know that he was present, watchful.

"Right there." She pointed to the foot of his pallet. The Rhanghan lay alert on his belly, all eyelids up and tail swinging from side to side.

He relaxed, and lowered his head back to the pillow. "I'm sorry, Gina—but thanks for getting me out of it."

In the doorway she paused. "McGill, believe me, I did it for myself. I'll see you in the morning." And she was gone.

"Good night, Sam," he whispered.

The saurian flicked his tongue through the air and stretched out, snout on his folded hands. The light sparkled off his attentive eyes. He would see no harm came to his guardian.

So Feighan slept.

* * *

On his way to work the next morning, the Edbargian called out to him from its booth: "Yuh, Turang!"

Sam chittered at the alien, but Feighan asked, "Yes?"

"How about sulling us your dreams?"

"Uh-uh."

It scratched its nose. "One-fifty a night, couldn't find a butter price."

That is high. But he couldn't see surrendering part of his soul. "No, but thanks anyway."

"Two hundrud thun."

Its persistence amused him, and despite his bleak mood he laughed. "No."

"All right, but if you change your mind, you know whure to find us."

"That I do," he said, giving it a wave and strolling off.

* * *

As he'd been promised when he'd had to work that extra shift, he got the following day off. Tired and anti-social, he moped in his dome. Taranya appeared sadder every time he saw her. Sherman, even though he was trying to deceive the Flinger, seemed to blame him for his visa problem. Maccari hadn't spoken to him since the night of Sam's fight—except to drag him out of another nightmare, and she'd admitted she did that only because her Talent developed static when he had bad dreams. The one person who spent time with him was Sam—*and that's probably 'cause I'm paying for his food . . .* he thought in self-pity.

So it surprised him when Sherman stuck his head into the room. "Hey, McGill."

He didn't look up. "Yeah?"

"How about a picnic?"

"Uh-uh." He studied the back of his hand, pretending an interest in the tinge imposed by the yellow-green light. He did not trust Sherman any more, but liked him too much to say so. An awkward silence gathered. Feighan could not lift his eyes.

"C'mon."

"I said, no."

"What is it with you?"

"What is it with *you*?" he said, unable to contain himself. "I'm not the one who's going around lying to people! I'm not the one who leaves a plastic dummy on his pallet every night! What do you mean, what is it with me?"

Taken completely off-guard, the newsman rocked back on his heels. "Whew! You trying to ruin me? I thought we were friends."

"We were, till you started lying."

"About what?"

"You know."

Sherman scanned the surrounding waters. Then he sighed. "Look, McGill. It's not a safe topic—this is stuff it's dangerous to know, much less talk about. I haven't lied to hurt you, really. It's only been to keep us both out of trouble."

"I'm a big boy, Harry," he said bitterly. "I can stay out of trouble all by myself. Especially when I know who not to trust."

The newsman shifted his weight from one foot to the other. "I'll tell you what—come on the picnic, and I'll outline the situation for you."

"You mean that?" He cocked his head quizzically.

"Yes, I do. And for a fringe benefit, you can watch some baby Delu die."

His eyebrows arched. "Really?"

"Really."

"Well, if you put it like that . . ." He pushed himself to his feet. "Where are we going?"

"To the nursery. It's a stiff walk, so wear comfortable shoes. I've got what passes for food." He pointed across the wheel, to a basket in his doorway. "Believe it or not, that also holds a bottle of rather good wine."

"How'd you get that?"

"It was brought to me last night by one of the servants—remember that Rii-edsch that came by last night?"

"I didn't see any twelve-legged opossums."

"Maybe it was before you got home . . . anyway, it bowed, handed me the bottle, bowed again, and said, 'This is with the compliments of the Gambler.'"

"It's probably poisoned." Feighan scowled.

"Now, now . . . you're supposed to enjoy yourself today, not brood."

"I'll see what I can do . . . is Gina coming?"

"She's busy." He perused his young friend's face. "Look, McGill—she said she was busy, but I don't think that's it—I think, um . . ."

"What?" He had his own ideas on the subject, but wanted to have them confirmed.

"Never mind."

"No, I want to know."

Sherman clucked and rubbed his belly. "All right, if you insist. What I think it is, is, she doesn't want to be around you when you're like this. I mean, I can barely stand you—"

"What?"

"Temper, temper." Raising his hands placatingly, Sherman advanced like a conciliatory tank. "You've been in a lousy mood since the Gambler cheated you—and it's natural for you to be disappointed, or upset, or even furious—but, McGill, you're so goddam gloomy that when you enter a room you darken it. It's like you turn off the lights wherever you go— and that's the opinion of a man who is not notably sensitive to human moods. Think how you must be affecting Gina, with her telepathy. No wonder she's been avoiding you."

He grimaced, and looked out the wall. Sherman's reflection stared at him over his own shoulder. "I don't know," he said "Maybe you're right—"

"I am right, and you know it."

"All right, so you are, dammit. It's just . . . I mean, how am I supposed to feel, huh? How would you feel if—" He caught himself, but not before subjecting Sherman to painful memories. "Sorry, Harry. I'm lousy company, and I admit it. So why do you want to take me on a picnic?"

"You want the truth?"

"Uh-huh."

"I've got nothing better to do." He laughed at Feighan's crestfallen expression. "Besides, I thought it might cheer you up to watch baby Delu eating each other—as well as give you a slightly deeper insight into this weird planet. What do you say?"

"In your own inimitable words—got nothing better to do. I'll come."

"Good." He whistled to Sam. "Brought some goodies for him, too. Come on, Sam, I'll give you a ride. Up on my shoulder, now."

As Sherman had warned, the walk was long. Feighan couldn't even have saved them the trip—though he planned to spare them the return—because he'd never been to the nursery before, and could Fling only to places with which he was familiar. "Still getting hassled over your visa?"

"Still," he said glumly. "I had another interview this morning—the old female again—"

McGill's heart twinged as he thought of the woman through whom the old female would have spoken. "How is she?" he asked softly, though he'd seen her less than a day earlier.

"As fine as could be, given the circumstances," said the newsman, apparently knowing which "she" Feighan had meant. "Anyway, the way the old female talked, everything was vague and indefinite, but . . . she seemed to be hinting that if I confined my investigations to events that occur off Delurc, I might be able to stay."

"Did you agree?"

"Like I said, everything was indefinite . . . it was— we take this left into this wheel, then turn right at the next spoke. You did bring your oxygen mask?"

"Of course. Sam's, too."

"Okay, because this wheel's the last with good ol' O_2. Where was I? Oh, yes. It was the way she was questioning me, as though she were trying to pin me down into stating that I was neither a spy nor a cultural anthropologist . . . it bothered me, you know? I asked her three times what she meant, but she would not even name a *price* for the answer—and that's unheard-of. Something's up—something very big—and—" Dropping his voice, he looked nervously around. "I plan to find out what it is. We could be sitting on a coup." He shook his head. "If you hear anything—"

"You'll be the first to know," said the Flinger.

"Thanks. And this will about do it for the oxygen, so— masks on."

Feighan adjusted his own, then bent over to slip Sam's onto his muzzle. By the time he had strapped it tightly and fastened the bottle to the Rhanghan's thorax, Sherman had activated the air lock and the door opened. They stepped in together.

For another hour and a half they walked through the mildly poisonous atmosphere which sustained row after row of potted Lumbi, sapient plants from the planet Lumb. Four meters tall with a swollen crown and huge glossy leaves, they stretched into the distance as far as he could see. He marveled at their numbers until Sherman radioed that the Delu had imported them to research the nature of intelligence and the forms which it could take. Fully half the plants were wired into translator booths—not as punishment, but to aid them in communicating with the Delu. As it turned out, the Lumbi had come to research the Delu: they were trying to devise a theory, consistent with their biology, to explain how intelligence could appear in a fish . . .

The spoke ended in a staircase, a spiral affair spun of glass and steel. Sherman began to climb. The risers were higher than Sam could comfortably manage, so Feighan scooped him up and carried him. After thirty-three steps, they emerged into a thirty-meter high dome divided into eight sections by transparent panels. Sherman headed for the pie-slice that a dozen languages marked: "O_2." A cap-wearing Rii-edsch translator let them in.

Inside, they stripped off their masks and closed their bottles, then sighed with relief and rubbed their sore cheeks. Sam conscientiously imitated them, though Feighan doubted that his bony cheekplates hurt at all.

"So what's the story here?" asked Feighan.

"This is the observation dome; it's as close as the Delu allow aliens to get to their nursery." Sherman pointed to a rocky spit of land that jutted a few meters above the ocean's surface. "Those things squiggling around on it are baby Delu."

He wondered how many were playing shadow games. "Uh-huh. And—?"

"Look close—you'll see they're eating each other."

"Have any binoculars?"

"It's a magnifying wall. It only costs five points to adjust it to your vision; just tell the puppet what you want."

"Oh." He had the points to spare, so he gave his instructions. It focused for him. "How long do I have?"

"Fifty twees," said the marsupial. It squeaked, then licked the fur on its twelve legs.

He felt he was standing on the island. The infant Delu were bigger than Sam, and just as toothy. As promised, they were eating each other—and now that he observed the scene from a Terran point of view, he derived a great deal of satisfaction from it.

Even as he watched, three infants fell on a fourth. Two pinned it awkwardly while the third chewed off its head. Then all three tore into it, spitting out scales and bits of bone. They kept a wary distance between them, and their eyes swiveled nervously the entire time.

"You know," said Feighan, "I've re-lived the old female's memories of this, but I still can't figure out how they tolerate cannibalism."

"You've memory-swapped with her?" The newsman looked at him with new respect. "You're lucky; you're the only Terran I've heard of who's ever gotten the chance. As for cannibalism . . . it only happens at this stage of their lives, and to them, there's nothing wrong with it. What they figure would be wrong is if it didn't happen. The law is survival."

"But why is it necessary?"

"Because they've eaten the nursery bare of everything else."

"Yeah, but . . . this plant, animal, fish cycle makes no sense!"

"Blame it on the weather," the broker said wryly. "Delurc's almost completely under water—and it has no axial tilt. Its orbit is just elliptical enough to keep the temperature at the poles in the vicinity of 0° C. Wintertime, it drops to -2° or -5°—something like that, but not too cold—and in summer, the high hits 2° to 5°."

Impatiently, he cut in, "So what does that have to do with anything?"

"Everything." Like a lecturer at a podium, Sherman raised a finger. "All year round, warm, moist air from the tropics rises and heads for the poles, where it condenses. It snows like hell there in winter—I saw a figure once; it's something on the order of 400,000 cubic kilometers of water *before* it turns into snow—and that drops the sea level all around the world by two or three meters. In egg-laying season, though, or late fall, the water's at its highest. The reefs are barely submerged when the eggs hatch, and they break the surface almost at once. If you've memory-swapped, you know how quickly the babies clean off the reefs . . . after a while, all they have left are each other— and incredible hungers. So—" He shrugged.

"Competitiveness is bred into them, huh?"

"To put it mildly."

He peered through the magnifying wall again, and watched one larger than average baby stalking another. "Does this have anything to do with the factions?" Something tugged his Talent, then, and he closed his eyes in an attempt to identify it. It felt like . . . fingers clutching at the sleeve of your mind as you pass by. He spun around.

Except for the translator, the observation dome was empty.

"Harry?" The Rii-edsch glanced up. "Sam?" *Oh sweet Jesus, I've been set up again!*

Plastic clattered at his feet. Eyes alive and wild, he crouched to pick up the small grey box. As he turned it over in his hands, it spoke: "McGill Feighan?"

Surprised, he could say only, "Yes."

"Milford Hommroummy, here. Try not to Fling away: you're Anchored."

His hand fell involuntarily to his belt.

"And should you be thinking of Flinging a pebble or two through the Anchors, you should know that it wouldn't bother them at all: they're Delu, and rather large enough to survive what is, after all, merely a pinprick to them. And, of course, if you attempt to Fling to them, you'll have a spot of difficulty breathing at that depth . . . stay where you are. We're bringing in a landing craft to take you off-planet."

"I swear to God, I'll kill him."

"Who?" Hommroummy sounded puzzled.

"Harry Sherman! Who the hell—"

"He is not on my payroll," said Hommroummy. "I only wish he were."

"That's what you said about Nadia."

"Ah, but that time I lied."

"Then where the hell are they?" He'd never forgive himself if Sahaang's son were hurt on his account.

"I really couldn't say; my planetside assistant handled that aspect of it."

"You mean The Organization's here, on Delurc?"

"Do act your age, Feighan—The Organization is everywhere."

"But how do you think you can hold me? You know I won't go quietly."

"I believe that's our problem, not yours. But trust me—we shall hold you like a miser does a coin."

Squeezing the radio as if he could crush it, he stared out the window, and glared at the waves. Below the platform, a dark shape disturbed the waters. He told the marsupial translator, "Focus on that, will you?"

Hommroummy asked, "Are you speaking to me?"

"No." He peered through the readjusted wall—directly into huge eyes peering at him. He recognized the fish, though he wasn't sure how: it was the old female. "Can you contact her?"

"For a price," said the Rii-edsch.

"I'll pay—do it."

"Certainly." It cleared its throat, and in a higher, rather effeminate voice said, "Yes?"

"Am I speaking to the old female directly, or through a relay?"

"Your words are being relayed to her through my translator and through myself; her answers are returned likewise."

"Tell her—"

"You don't need to say that; I realize to whom you are talking."

He clenched his fists in frustration with the being's haughtiness. "Dammit, tell her I'm in danger! The Organization is trying to kidnap me."

"She knows."

"Well, I could use some help, here."

"You're unable to pay for it."

"She's just going to let me be taken?"

"Unless you earn two thousand points now and then, yes."

"To hell with this." He ran for the door—but it would not open. He whirled on the translator. "This is locked!"

The marsupial nodded. "It was ordered."

"By whom—the old female?"

"No," it said with scorn, "by another."

He leaned despairingly against the transparent walls of the airlock. It looked thin and fragile, but a material strong enough to withstand three centuries of wind and sea would laugh at any force he could apply. He tried it anyway: removing his belt, he accelerated the buckle into the glass at four kps. It blasted a fist-sized hole right through it—but nothing more.

Scurrying over to slap on a patch, the Rii-edsch said, "That'll cost you."

"Dammit!"

Striding back to the windowwall, he looked up at the sky. A dot of flame yellowed the blue. The landing vehicle was dropping for him already. It had to be incredibly old if it relied on chemical rockets—but trust The Organization, it would lift off as though it were brand new. Lift off with him in it and no way out, no way at all...

The radio crackled, "We shall send a small boat over to pick you up, Feighan."

"From where?" he asked absently.

"From that reef, of course."

He readjusted the focus on the wall and saw that, sure enough, the reef's surface was flat enough for the ship to land safely. Of course, the flamewash would burn away all the baby Delu, but what did he care about them? A kilometer beyond the reef cruised the Anchor.

Then he snapped his fingers. "Does the old female know that all those children will die?"

"Most usually do," said the translator.

"No, what I mean is, when that rocket lands, it will kill them all."

"Ah..." The puppet seemed nonplussed. The controller went away for a moment, leaving his toy blank-faced behind, and returned to say, "She hadn't realized."

He looked down. The whale-shape now swam in fast, tight circles, breaking the surface once a lap. Her dark bulk lifted out of the water, then slapped back down like a massive hand swatting a full sink. Water sprayed everywhere, darkening the reef with its mist. The wavelets reached up between the rocks, here and there pulling an infant away with them. "She seems excited."

"She's frantic," said the other dryly. "They are her children—her first in nearly twenty seasons."

"I thought so." He let a long moment go by, a moment during which the flame overhead brightened and sharpened. "You might tell her I could save her children."

"You can't save yourself!"

"Oh, I can now."

The marsupial's voice cracked: "She says to go ahead and save them."

"Sure—for a price."

The translator went schizophrenic. While its sharp-nosed face grinned and winked approvingly, the voice groaned, "You bargain at a time like this?"

"'When in Rome . . .'"

"She offers three thousand."

"I want a hundred thousand."

"Four, then."

"Uh-uh."

"The price you ask is ridiculously high."

"Her tough luck."

"She doesn't have the points available."

"A hundred thousand," he said firmly, though when he saw how much closer the landing vehicle had come, he began to get worried. He could save himself—but he had to start before the ship touched down.

"Five and a visa for your friend Harry Sherman."

"How long a visa?"

"One year."

"Ten."

"Dammit, all right!" it said, through its alter ego's grin and clapping paws. "Five thousand points and a ten-year visa for Sherman."

"It's a deal." He inhaled hugely and stared at the windtossed sea. It all depended on how close the Anchor was. Only one way to find out . . . he stared at the water, visualized 900 kilograms worth in a nice tight ball, felt how to take it from here to there, then—

PING

—nine hundred kilograms of water, with an angular momentum parallel to the ocean's surface and a velocity approaching two kilometers per second, materialized next to the nose of the descending vehicle. Smashing into its side, the water globe burst into steam as its speed flash-boiled it—but by then it had already delivered its hammer-blow.

The sudden force crushed the craft's nose, and threw the entire ship off balance. It pinwheeled, rockets burping long and short as the frantic pilot tried to save it, but he hit the controls a second too late. A gush of flame boosted it past the reef, then javelined it into the water. It exploded as it hit.

The radio crackled, "Damn your soul, Feighan."

"Shit! I thought you were on board."

"From now until you're mine, Feighan, I'm nowhere near you, nowhere you know where I am. But you will be mine."

"Fat— ah!" Hot plastic splashed his wrist as the radio melted. He dropped it.

"The old female thanks you," said the Rii-edsch.

"The question is, did she pay me?"

"Of course—we're all honest fish here."

"Fine, fine. Tell her I want—" *The girl*, he thought, but he knew he had nowhere near enough points, so instead:"—to know about the giant gastropod."

"You don't have enough points."

"She just paid me five thousand!"

"Ah, but you were two hundred twelve in debt before you even entered this room—and my charges for the wall and the liaison come to well over four hundred. You are still a bit short." At Feighan's curse, it hastily smoothed the fur on its chest. "However, sir, the door *is* unlocked."

He slammed it as he left.

*   *   *

Hands behind his back, Hommroummy paced the cabin. The dark young face grinned down. "Gryll will not be pleased," said the boy.

"Not when he learns where you dropped your Anchor!"

The grin faded into dismay. "How were we to know?"

"Oh, do shut up, Gimpy." Chewing on his lower lip, he paced some more. One lap. Five. Ten . . . On the twentieth he stopped. "There is a possible solution."

"Do tell."

"Feighan thinks he has defeated us, but knows we will try for him again. The stress must certainly have tired him; the tension of anticipating our next attack will tire him even more. It would be a good moment for you to goad him to the maximum."

"Why ever for?"

Hommroummy's scowl brought his thick eyebrows into a V. "I am unfamiliar with eedie life on the reefs, Gimpy, but I recall hearing about a very strict legal system. Goad Feighan into breaking the law and he is ours."

"Hommroummy, he's a Flinger! If we arrest him, he'll teleport out."

"No." He chuckled. "No, I rather think not. Flingers are indoctrinated, you see. Should he be arrested, he would serve out his sentence . . . in fact, he would burn out his brain were he to try to flee your jurisdiction." He chuckled again, more loudly, more happily. "Proceed, Gimpy. Goad him well."

· Chapter XI ·

Shaken and angry, Feighan materialized in his dome. Sherman, Maccari, and Sam were on the floor, playing with rings and strings. They did not notice him until he grabbed Sherman from behind and yanked him to his feet. "You bastard!" He spun the broker around and shoved him hard. "Nobody sets me up, you hear? Nobody!"

Sherman caught himself. Eyes slitted, he crouched slightly and balanced on the balls of his feet. He spread his arms a bit and stiffened his hands. "What's wrong with you?"

"Nothing that putting you into the sun won't cure. After all, you're the one who tried to feed his 'buddy' to The Organization. What'd they pay you for that?"

"Me? Set you up?" The newsman's eyes widened; he straightenèd. "Christ, Feighan, you Flung me and the kid back here so hard you broke the damn bottle of wine."

He opened his mouth, then closed it. Sherman wasn't going to admit his betrayal, not in front of witnesses. *To hell with him, then.* He concentrated— visualized—

"McGill, wait!"

He looked at Maccari. "Why?"

"Because he's telling the truth—he *didn't* set you up."

"Jesus Christ, woman! You told me not to trust him yourself—you told me he's been lying to me! Now—"

"McGill," said Sherman in a calmer voice. "Listen. I don't know what happened out there, but I took you there because my source had a hot story for me—about the old female—but he wanted you to hear it. That's what he said, at least."

He glanced over to Maccari.

"He's telling the truth, McGill." Her eyes were clear and steady.

He met her gaze head on. Hot with adrenalin, he clenched and unclenched his fists. He couldn't decide. It was all screwed up. She was a Minder; she could read Sherman—so if he trusted her, Sherman was okay. *But* do *I trust her?* he thought in anguish. *Jesus Christ, which side is she* on? *I thought Nadia—* Aloud he said, "I can't believe you. Every time I turn around, somebody's lying to me. Get out. Both of you. Now!"

Slowly she got to her feet, never once taking her eyes off his face. "You think I—"

"I don't know. If you're straight, I'm sorry. If you're not—" He saw Nadia's face, and the word FAILURE carved in human flesh.

She blanched. "Oh my God, McGill, did you—"

"Get out on your own or I'll throw you out!"

She seized Sherman's arm and led him away. At the doorway she paused. Over her shoulder, she said, "McGill, I—"

"Leave me the fuck alone!"

She did.

* * *

At work the next morning, Feighan was still seething. Mostly at himself, for having been so vehement the night before. His outburst had gained him nothing: if Sherman and Maccari had been on his side, he had alienated them; if they had been on Hommroummy's, he had warned them. *Stupid asshole*, he thought.

Overhead, a mid-size Delu twitched a deformed fin to keep the current from sweeping it out of its hover. Blue's last lengths muddied the green of the lights. He whipped a load of fully briefed economists back to New York, then watched the servants muscle in a pile of wooden boxes. *And dammit! I'm stuck here for ten more weeks!*

"Hey, McGill." Harry Sherman stood at the Booth door. "May I talk to you a minute?"

He fought down his anger. "Yeah. Come on in. About last night: I'm— I blew my top. I'm sorry."

"No problem. I understand."

"It's just—Jesus! There I am getting kidnaped, and the Delu float around twiddling their tails. They demand cash on the thumb to help me, then get mad when I do the same. What the hell kind of world is this? Don't they have any laws? And where were the damn police?"

The broker scowled. "The fish don't give a damn *what* one eedie does to another. They are not concerned with our fates. Hommroummy could spread-eagle you on the floor and flay you alive, and all they'd do is fine you for screaming in a pitch that offends their sensibilities. Or for bleeding where they can see it—the color upsets them."

"All right, all right, so their law stays out of our private feuds—but they're embezzling my account, Harry! And I don't see any police there, either. How could I be in debt? I earn sixty points a day from the old female, and my regular salary on top."

The reporter pulled at his pendulous lower lip. "Well, that does seem strange. Their accountants don't screw up often; it's too dangerous. When you see the old female, ask about it. If anybody mishandled your credit balance, he gets fined. I'll see you later, all right?"

But he continued to simmer, and it so disrupted his concentration that Maccari had to visit him. "McGill, I was just Minding with New York, and they say you're bringing them in high and fast." She consulted the sheet of paper in her hand. "Point eight centimeters up, with an angular momentum in the right direction, but three meters per second too slow—they have crates skidding across the Flop Booth at ten kph, and they don't like that a whole lot. Can you do something about it?"

Wearily, he raised a hand in silent acknowledgment. "I'm just pissed off."

"I know," she said pointedly. "Try to be less so, all right?"

He nodded, and resumed Flinging. His anger hadn't diminished, but, reminded of his responsibilities, he did manage to partition it off from his Talent. *Which is what being a professional is all about, I guess*, he thought grumpily. *Not letting your personal problems screw up your performance on the job.*

At the end of the shift, he teleported up to Datadesk 1-19, where Taranya, dark circles under her eyes, forced a fleeting smile and held out her hand. Fury dying down before her sadness, he stepped forward, grasped those cold fingers, and impulsively kissed her forehead. "You okay?" he whispered.

"Yes," she murmured, "now that you're here."

He'd rehearsed his demands a dozen times, but now that

the time had come to deliver them, the hot ire which was to have blazed in them had cooled. Clumsily, he began, "About yesterday—"

She stiffened. "Would you have allowed my children to die?"

"Would you have let them kidnap me?"

She closed her eyes. "I . . . I would have had to."

"Why?"

"That is an internal affair of Delurc, and is none of your business."

Taken aback, he gasped. "What? I almost get kidnaped and it's none of my business?"

"The kidnaping," she said, "is naturally of concern to you, but the reasons for my non-interference are . . . classified? No, that's the wrong concept." Her high forehead wrinkled in thought. "Perhaps 'taboo' most approximates our word."

That rekindled all his anger. "What the hell's going on here? I'm supposed to be working for you people, which means you're supposed to guarantee my safety, but one of your Flingers hides my friend and my ward, and one of your Anchors pins me down so The Organization can come get me, and somebody arranges for a crucial door to be locked . . . then it's none of my business?"

Her eyes moistened, but she looked past him, at the far wall. "It is not illegal for a Delu to conspire against an extra-Delu, no matter in whose employ is that extra-Delu. Do you comprehend?"

"No, dammit, I don't!" He slammed his fist onto the counter-top. "And I don't understand how I was two hundred some points in debt when I ought to've been a thousand or more to the good. You wanna explain that for me?"

Though her outstretched hands implored him to be sympathetic, she spoke with ice in her voice: "The records show that the day before yesterday you purchased information valued at two thousand five hundred points."

"That's crap!"

She lifted a perfect eyebrow. "Do you dispute the bill?"

"Damn straight I do—who claims he sold me the data?"

"That is none of your concern; the matter will be investigated."

"Again with that 'none of your concern'!" He ground his teeth together until a detached but observant part of his mind wondered if they'd crack off. "Lady, what the hell are you trying to do to me?"

"McGill," she said suddenly, "I'm not trying to hurt you! Believe me!" She seized his shoulders and drew him close. "McGill, I— I love you. I wouldn't hurt you for the world. Please. It's not me."

"Hey," he said, in a tone softened by surprise, "I know it's not *you*—it's her." He jerked a thumb upward, at the black bulk hovering above the dome. "I don't blame you, I don't. Okay?"

She sniffed back her tears. "Don't blame her, either— please? She—" Her manner changed at once, as if a new presence informed her. "She is not permitted to speak of these matters to unauthorized extra-Delu."

Disgusted, he shook his head. "I'll be seeing you."

"You don't wish to earn your fee today?"

"You mean I haven't?"

"Not in the least."

"All right." He begrudged her the cooperation, but he did need the points. He lowered his head and let the questing fingers find his temples. They circled, slowly, gently, rubbing away his anger and his frustration and his vision and his present and his being and . . .

"I. I. I," she piped thinly, as the water lapped at her belly. Reflected sunlight burned in her eyes. The lone survivor of her nursery, she had climbed the reef's highest point to elude the rising sea. Yet it licked at her fins, splashed on her tail. It would already have carried her away, if she hadn't held the rocks so tightly. "I. I. I—" A wave slapped her face, and gushed down her throat, choking her. She sputtered and coughed; blinded by the salt, she failed to see the next wave, a bigger one, which crashed down on her head and back. It numbed her. It broke her grip on the stones so that when the third wave came it could hoist her and spin her away while she wailed, "I. I. I."

The boom of a big bass drum resounded in her aural membranes; a soft-edged mind voice said: "Morpheanious the Weed-Weaver, I-father, child-father, I-teacher, child-teacher—" Colors flared and flickered across the spectrum. Her eyes, still smarting but growing accustomed to her new element, focused on the hugeness in her path.

"I. I. I," she projected plaintively.

Happy bronze glowed the bulk. "I—" *twwirrph* "—child. Morpheanious the Weed-Weaver—" *twwirrph* "—child-father. Morpheanious the Weed-Weaver—" *twwirrph* "—'I'-father."

Fins moving strangely in this new environment, sculling back and forth to hold her in place against the strength of the current, she chirped, "I—" *twwirrph* "—child?"

Twwirrph. And the great-tailed shape pushed a fish in her direction.

Eating it, she noticed that she, too, glowed happy bronze.

The scene and all its reality shrank, as though Feighan was looking through a telescope that retreated from his eye. He blinked. "Is it over?"

"Yes," she whispered, "for today." Her fingers caressed his cheeks, then one hand slid behind his neck and urged his face forward to her lips. "But tomorrow—"

"Oh, yes!" He leaned across the counter for another kiss, but she smiled and pulled away.

"Not today, McGill. Tomorrow. Go on, now. I'll see you then."

So it was back to work, but in a far better mood...

* * *

By evening, though, the embers of his anger had come to life again. He paced the bare floor of his quarters, heels clicking on the old cold tiles. Maccari sat on the pallet, watching him through her warm dark eyes, holding Sam on her lap and stroking the Rhanghan's sleek, bony head. Sam twisted his neck to position her fingers correctly. "Calm down," she said.

"Calm down?" He whirled to glare at her. "My God, The Organization's here to nail me again, the fish are conspiring against me, I save a whole damn nursery full of aquatic mini-computers for a mother who only values the entire school at five thousand points and a ten-year visa—I'm still short of what I need and don't see any way of getting it—and you tell me to calm down?"

Green pulsed through the fluorescents' red as a flickering Delu swam over the dome and took up station there.

"That gives me the creeps," he said, glancing up. "I get the feeling they're always watching me."

"They are," she said.

"Huh?"

"They are watching you—and discussing you among themselves."

He touched his throat. "Why me?"

"I don't know." Worry wrinkled her forehead and tightened her lips. "Of course it's not just you—they talk about every eedie now and then—but you crop in in their conversations more often than anybody."

Inside Feighan, alarm jangled with fury, but both yielded to a triumphant sense of vindication. He dropped to his knees and asked impatiently, "Well, what do they say?"

"I don't *know*." She groaned. Plainly, she'd been harassed by that same question herself. "I don't speak Delu. I wish I did, but..." She sagged back to the pallet to stare at the circling fish. "All I get are flashes and throbs of their telepathy—you know how their language works, and if I'm not concentrating on something else when they're talking nearby, I'll 'see' the alien they're discussing. I see too much of you."

"Thanks a lot."

"I meant *see*, McGill," she said in exasperation. "In my *head*. From them." She kicked a pointed foot at the ceiling. Almost to herself, she continued, "But the picture comes through wrong. I don't know if it's because they've only seen you through the domes, because their minds don't work the same, or because they've got it in for you—but the image of you they project is—" She made a face, and shrugged.

"What?"

When she answered, it was with reluctance. "Distorted, I guess. It's an overhead shot; you're foreshortened, your nose sticks way way out—" She mimed a Pinocchio with her right hand. "—and not only do you look a lot smaller, you look... dumb."

"That's a cartoon!"

She nodded. The water beyond the dome seemed to press down on them. "They use caricature like we use tone of voice; the distortions, I *think*, represent value judgments..."

"They have a real high opinion of me, don't they?" He glowered at the floor.

"They're pretty arrogant..." She sat up suddenly, and leaned forward. "I don't like it at all; it makes me nervous. You ought to get out of here, let the NAC send somebody else."

"I can't," he said, though he agreed with her.

"How many points do you need now?"

He juggled numbers in his head. "Six fifty or so, for the gastropod answer."

"You can get those easily."

"Plus nineteen thousand more for Taranya."

"Oh." She fell silent for a long time. "Listen . . . let me help."

The offer startled him, though he had known she was the kind to make it. "How?"

"I don't know . . . I'm getting a few points together myself, every day, out of my salary . . . I could probably eat one less meal a day, give you another twenty-five—" Lifting her head off the pillow, she eyed her waistline, then patted it. "Wouldn't hurt if I went on a diet anyway."

He was genuinely touched. "Hey, thanks, but—"

"And I could find somebody to buy my dreams."

"Uh-uh!"

She jerked as though burned. "Boy, you feel strongly about *that*."

"You bet." He crossed over to her. "It's not a good thing to do." Swiftly, he recounted some of Sherman's horror stories. "I couldn't stand to see that happen to you—especially if you were doing it for me."

"Why, McGill, I didn't know you cared."

He recoiled from her sarcasm. "That's not what I—"

"I know what you meant, silly—I was just teasing you."

"Oh." Strangely, that depressed him further. "I don't like this place."

"You're not alone."

He looked at her in astonishment. "You, too?"

Features downcast, she nodded.

"But you were so excited about coming here!"

"That was before I knew what it was like." She shuddered. "The sterility's bad enough, but I could get used to it—the Training Center was just as cold, just as . . ." She raised her hands to gesture at the walls. "Just as bleak. Visually, I mean. Emotionally, though, it was . . ." She closed her eyes and remembered rapture warmed her pale cheeks. "Ah, McGill, I don't think I have the words for it . . . There were a couple hundred of us, of all strengths and specialties, all of us trying so hard to keep our thoughts quiet and our 'ears' shut . . . but any time you were lonely or scared or hurt, the warmth came at you from everywhere . . . it was better than basking in sunshine, because sun is warm and strong and good, but it doesn't love . . . here, though . . ." Unconsciously, she wrapped her arms around herself and huddled into a small ball. "There's chatter, all the time, deliberately broadcast—do you know each of those fish keeps a running tally not only of his own score, but of five or ten thousand other Delu's point totals? And all the time they're broadcasting that, and what they want to buy, and what they want to sell, and the conceptual underpinning of their latest songs, and . . . it's so noisy," she whispered, "so terribly, terribly noisy . . . but it's cold noise. It's all slick, hard, sharp and different, so very scarey different . . . oh, I don't like it here, either, McGill . . ."

He knelt before her to wipe the single tear off her satin cheek. He ached to comfort her, to envelop her in his arms and murmur, "It's all right, everything'll be fine," in her ear. But she wouldn't want—

"Do it, please," she said.

"Every time I decide I know you, you surprise me," he said with feigned rue and real joy.

Ah, she felt good, with her head on his chest and her arms slowly sliding around him and her hair tickling his chin and her softnesses comforting to him . . . he breathed her soapscent and stroked her shoulder, saying, "It's okay, Gina. Don't worry, it's okay."

His tunic splashed color into her cheeks. She sniffed, and hugged him hard. Then she raised her face while her eyes gently, slowly, slid shut, and—

An indigo Rehmal strode into the room whistling, "The Gambler has sent me to offer you an exchange." It stopped when Sam, with a hiss, started towards it.

For an instant neither would release the other, but self-consciousness overcame need, and they parted, Feighan to rise, Maccari to sit up straight and dab at her shining eyes with a surreptitious hand.

Everything about the avian messenger irritated the Flinger: its unheralded entrance, its flutish condescension, even its haughty pose. The back of his neck warmed up; he demanded, "What's this about an exchange?"

"He asks, 'Do you want the translator?'"

"Ah—" He resented being put on the spot by a beak-faced zombie. He did, indeed, want Taranya—but after hugging

Marraci, he did not feel entitled to say so in front of her.

She helped him out of his quandary. "Yes," she said firmly, "he does." To him she added, "And I *know* you do."

"You're right." He told the avian, "Yes, I do."

"The Gambler has been able to arrange an even exchange."

"Oh?" Out of the corner of his eye, he noticed a Delu stop a fin's length away from the dome. A bent fin's length.

"The translator for her." It pointed to the Minder. "She will serve the remainder of the translator's sentence. If this is agreeable—"

From a well of raw hostility geysered: "No, dammit, it isn't!"

Maccari's smile rewarded him—not for the words, but for the fondness that had partially prompted them. Then she cocked her head and stared at him curiously.

"The Gambler thought you might say as much," continued the Rehmal, "so he authorized me to offer you, at this time, six hundred fifty points as well."

"Get out." Even to him, the disgust he felt seemed out of proportion to the provocation, yet he couldn't contain it. "Out!"

"But the Gambler—"

"Dammit!" His temper snapped like a frayed rope. While a part of him studied his overreaction with dispassionate interest, the rest of him shook in rage. He reached the Rehmal in two swift strides. "I told you to get out of here—" He seized the servant's wing and spun it around. "—and if you won't leave under your own power, then I'll goddam well throw you out!"

"Please, sir," it tweeted, "it is not wise—"

"OUT!" He pushed it towards the doorway, but it balked. He drew back his foot—knowing that he was out of control but unable to rein himself in—and kicked it. It flew into the wheel, trailing broken feathers.

A groan came from outside, then a familiar voice said, "Oh, you didn't do that!"

"Bet your butt I did, Harry." He shook his fist at the retreating avian. "Get lost, birdbrain!" To the newsman he said, "Come in."

"Why the hell did you kick a puppet?" Sherman leaned against the wheel's wall and massaged his red-tunicked belly. "I've told you, that's about the worst crime you can commit."

He stepped out of the doorway to let his friend enter. Already abashed, he said lamely, "It's not like attempted murder or anything."

"It is forbidden to assault a servant in the slightest." Sherman recited it as if by rote. "'For servants only do their masters' biddings, and deserve no blame for fealty.'" He reversed the desk chair and straddled it. "You're in for it now, McGill, and there isn't a thing in the world that can save you. Hiya Gina, Sam."

"But it wasn't his fault," Maccari said.

"What do you mean?"

"I mean, he kicked that bird because he lost his temper, but *that* happened because somebody reinforced all his emotions—telepathically, I mean."

"You're saying somebody made him kick the zombie?"

"No." She shook her head. "I mean somebody goaded him into violence."

"But no Delu would—" He stopped himself, and fingered his middle chin. "I take that back. There are a few who'd go to any lengths . . . McGill, you and Sam had better get back to New York City real quick—like right now."

"Uh-uh," said Feighan. "No, I'm not going to run from The Organization—I'm here to get an answer, and I will."

"But now *all* the Delu are against you—you broke the law, remember?"

"So what can they do to me?"

The newsbroker's pudgy fingers curled over the back of the chair, and squeezed until their knuckles whitened. "Fine you," he said curtly.

"And if I don't pay?"

"They deduct it from your credit balance automatically—you do recall that they keep the books?"

"Yeah, but if I haven't—" A tramping in the corridor drowned his words. He turned. A horde of aliens marched towards him: four Aronya, a green Rii-edsch, a brace of Rehmal, and six tentacled beings that otherwise resembled Terran gorillas. "What's this, a parade?"

Their eyes focused on him. Their hands/claws/tentacles opened and closed as though around his throat. Their teeth flashed and gleamed and glittered.

He retreated into the middle of his dome. "They don't look too friendly."

"Cops never do," said Sherman.

"Cops?" *They're not wearing badges*, he thought, and realized in the thinking how inane that was. His mental processes seemed distorted, clouded. He felt as insulated from what happened around him as if cotton gauze swaddled him.

Gina glanced sharply in his direction, then swiveled her head to peer through the dark waters outside. A mid-size Delu with a deformed fin floated twenty meters away. "Stay cool."

He wanted to tell her about the numbness infiltrating his brain, but couldn't get the words out.

The green Rii-edsch stepped in front of him. Apparently the leader, it drummed its twelve legs. Sam interposed himself with a hiss, but it ignored the Rhanghan. It wheezed: "You are under arrest. Do not attempt to resist us."

He surveyed the well-muscled assemblage one more time. Through disbelief as thick as custard, he said, "I'll go quietly." Then he turned to his friends. "Watch over Sam, will you please?" He scooped the saurian off the floor, stared into those too-knowing eyes, and hugged him. Then he passed him into Maccari's open arms. "Be good, Sam."

The Rhanghan waved good-bye.

Outside, Aronya-riding Rehmal boxed him in: one in front, one in back, and one on either side. Not a member of that grim company talked to him, not even when he shouldered away his disorientation and asked, "What happens next?"

They led him along the wheel to the spoke, then down the main thoroughfare in a silent, half-hour possession. The eedies they encountered looked away. In the heart of the great city, not far from his Fling Booth, they stopped, and directed him into a small room.

As soon as he went in, they locked its door from the hall. He shivered, then sneezed from the mustiness. The low dome barely allowed him to stand erect. The violet of early morning glowed on the tiles.

In separate domes abutting his sat heavily-wired translators, all staring at him. The one on the far left, a purple-feathered Rehmal with a cracked beak, asked, "Did you strike a servant?"

"I kicked him, yes." The Flinger's vision rippled; he blinked. "Am I on trial here, or what?"

A Timili from Throngorn, tall and lemur-like, said, "Did it strike you first?"

"No." He dropped his gaze in confusion.

"Then," said a blue-shelled, twelve-legged baseball fan from Cygnus XII, "surely it must have threatened your life or your points."

He got the feeling that the Cyg Twelvian was trying to help him, but he had to say, "No."

The judges rocked back. "No?" they all asked.

"No, but, you see," he said, "the servant acted real insulting, and ah . . ." He groped in his mind for the words Maccari had used. "Somebody else, a telepath, made me angrier than I would have been normally, got me madder and madder until I blew up, so . . . it wouldn't have happened if that Minder hadn't interfered like that."

The Timili leaned forward. "This is the woman Gina Maccari?"

"No, no," he said hastily, "somebody else."

"Who?" said the Cyg Twelvian.

"I don't know, just somebody else."

"Is he claiming," tweeted the Rehmal, "innocent by reason of insanity?"

"Sounds more like diminished capacity to me," said the Timili.

The baseball fan adjusted his Yankees' cap. "I think he's maintaining third-party provocation—perhaps even collusion between the injured party and the alleged telepath."

"Look," he said, "I don't know! I can't think straight; there's static in my head. There was then, too. And I'm sorry I did it."

For a long moment they looked at him in silence. Their pressures of their varied gazes squeezed him till he couldn't breathe.

The Timili said, "It appears as though you confess to violating Verse 12 of the 18th Stanza of the Song of Servants."

"Well, I . . ." He shook his head, not to deny the charge but to direct his attention at the proceedings. "I don't know that song."

"You don't have to," said the baseball fan. "We do."

The translators closed their eyes in unison, and slouched in their chairs as their controllers removed consciousness from their bodies. Overhead, massive shapes swirled through interlocking patterns, and flashed stroboscopic lights from all patches of their skins. Faint dissonant notes penetrated the dome. Then the limp bodies stirred, and the Rehmal chirped, "McGill Feighan, Terran Flinger, we find you guilty as charged."

"What does that mean?" He clenched his fists at his side; a trickle of sweat ran down the nape of his neck.

"It means," they said together, like a chorus in a Greek tragedy, "that you are sentenced to a fine of 24,450 points, payable immediately."

"But I don't have that much!"

"We know," they chanted.

"So how can I pay?"

"You can't."

A cold certainty grew within him. "Then what do you want me to do?"

"Join us."

His eyes widened. "You?"

"Us."

The door into the dome opened and a green Rehmal entered, holding in its hands a wiry cap. It proffered it to the captive Flinger.

"Wear it," intoned the judges.

"Uh-uh," he said, almost in panic.

"You must pay your fine."

"No way." He backed away from the cap-holder, who stood motionless in the doorway.

"Wear it."

"No."

"WEAR IT!"

"NO, DAMMIT, NO, I WON'T!"

The Rehmal bowed and withdrew, shutting the door after itself. From the outside it dogged it tight.

Feighan looked around, wondering what would happen next.

The Judges sang: "Then you must die." They bowed.

And water poured into the dome.

*　　*　　*

Milford Hommroummy stood with his face upturned. The screen showed the execution in three quadrants, and the black boy in the fourth. Hommroummy's cheeks were pale and sunken. "I've no idea," he said again. "He should have submitted. He has been indoctrinated!"

"Looks like it didn't take," said the boy.

"But he mustn't die!" He rubbed his throat.

"That's right, Gryll told you to bring him back alive, didn't it?"

He nodded. And put a finger on his carotid artery, as if to feel the beat one last time. "Stop it," he said.

"We can't. It's out of our hands, now." The boy chuckled.

He glared up at the screen. "What do you find so amusing?"

"The relationship between physiology and linguistics, for one thing."

"We've no time for that nonsense—save Feighan."

"We don't know about you, Hommroummy, but we have plenty of time. Putting a Flinger to death is strong stuff. It's going to scandalize the community, and cost the old female half her points. And her job, as well. Care to guess who's next in the line of succession?"

He made a sour face. "I assume you are, Gimpy. But that doesn't solve our problem—Feighan mustn't die!"

"No, Hommroummy, that's not our problem—it's your problem. You save him."

"Damn you, Gimpy. You'll pay for this. I guarantee it."

The boy laughed out loud.

Hommroummy whispered, "Get out of there, Feighan. Save yourself. For God's sakes, man, sa—" He gasped.

· Chapter XII ·

As the insurging seas crested his boot tops, Feighan flung himself to his own dome. Sherman, Maccari, and Sam were there, eating breakfast. Sherman looked neither surprised nor pleased at Feighan's abrupt entrance. He nodded, and swallowed the last of his food bar.

Maccari ran over and hugged the Flinger, pressing strength on him like a promise. "They set you free?"

For a moment he lost himself in her embrace. "Uh-uh—I teleported out."

"You shouldn't have done that," said Sherman.

He stared across the top of Maccari's head. "What, I should be a translator?"

"Or pay the fine." The newsman covered a burp with his fingers.

"Twenty-five thousand points?"

"No, I guess you couldn't have paid that. Then you should have taken your punishment."

Sam hissed his anger; Feighan shushed him and said, "I've got better things to do with my life than spend the next godknowshow many years wired to a fish."

Maccari released him to agree. "It would have killed him, Harry—a Flinger can't let his Talent stay dormant. The pressure drives him nuts."

"So now the Delu kill him," said the fat man gloomily. He wiped his hands on his green tunic, then spread them wide, palms up. "What's the difference, dead is dead, right?"

"They can't kill me." The tactile memory of Maccari's firm body whispered on his skin, invoking a surge of determin/elation.

"Hah!"

"They have to catch me first." He held back his temper as if he were talking to a child. "And how the hell are they going to catch a Flinger who doesn't want to be caught?"

"They have ways." Pessimism spread from him like a bleak mist. "These are the Delu, McGill, and they have ways."

Unhappiness washed across Maccari's tired face. "I don't know about ways, McGill, but they do have Anchors. And if they can pin you down—"

"They can't," he said, with more confidence than he felt.

"Look," said Sherman, "why don't you just skip the planet—go home, back to New York. They can't touch you there, and probably won't even try."

"Uh-uh." He folded his arms and planted his feet. "I came here for information. I won't leave without it—or without Taranya, either."

"You're being bull-headed."

"Maybe I am—but I don't feel like running. Didn't you once tell me that leaving's one thing, and having to leave's another?"

"Look, you can be back home in—" He snapped his fingers. "Otherwise they'll chase you around the planet trying to drown you. They won't feed you, they'll cut off your air if they get a chance—why risk it?"

He looked at the other for a long, unfriendly moment. "Tell me something, Harry—are you worried about me, or about you?"

"I, um..." His shrug threatened the seams of his forest-green tunic. "What can I say? I'm here on sufferance and—"

"A ten-year visa," Feighan said, "courtesy of yours truly."

"That's true, but...dammit, don't you see how this works? You think it's you against them, clean and simple, but it's not. It's also one faction against another, with you caught in the middle." He glanced up to look for eavesdroppers, then continued in a low, rapid tone: "Look. The fish who're running things set standards, and all the Delu have to stick to them. The other faction wants to change the rules: let more eedies in, downgrade the data-reliability classifications, increase the Network's economic dependency on the planet—"

"But why? It makes no sense—and what does it have to do with me?"

"Why? Because they're partners with your man Hommroummy. Combine Delu minds with Organization morals, and you get the original irresistible force. Let it last a while, and guess who's running the Galaxy?"

"That's what you were investigating?"

"Yes—the only way you can stop something like that is by publicizing it, but to do that without being sued into bankruptcy means facts. Evidence. Which I've been trying to gather for three years now; which I won't have enough of if I get thrown off the planet."

Feighan went to the wall and peered out. The sea was empty. "So how do I fit in?"

"They're making you a *cause célèbre*; they're trying to embarrass the ruling faction. To bungle a case like yours costs the administration points—in the monetary sense—and if they lose enough points, they lose their jobs. So Hommroummy's fish move into power, and . . ." He shrugged. "They also deport me, immediately, because dealing with an escaped criminal is a violation of the code. You've got to give yourself up."

The newsman's desperation hurt. Feighan turned to face the wall, and glanced straight into glaring eyes. A Delu had spotted him, and was presumably calling for reinforcements. "I understand what you're saying, Harry, but there's just no way—no way in hell—that I can yield like a meek little lamb. I've got my pride."

"Sir?" tweeted a Rehmal at the door.

He spun. "What?"

The orange-and-silver avian cringed, but did not withdraw. "Please go to the nearest translator for discussion with the authorities. Your safety is guaranteed until the end of the negotiations, if you promise to go."

He looked at the newsman, who spread his hands as if to say, *What have you got to lose?* So he said, "All right."

"This way, please." Talons clicking on the tiles, it led him down the wheel to the spoke. Every three steps it looked nervously over its shoulder, though it was neither the one he had kicked, nor the one Sam had bitten.

At Datadesk 1-12 sat Taranya, hair encircled with a tiara of wires.

He froze. The old female floated overhead. *Sure*, he thought. *They're squeezing her. She's got to lose either her job or her research project—just wish she hadn't brought Taranya.*

"Please inform her of your presence," said the Rehmal.

Through he approached down her field of vision, no life sparked in those azure eyes. "Hi." He reached across the counter to touch her with a gentle finger. "The bird said you wanted to see me?"

"Yes," she said, in a clipped, cold tone. Her hands moved as if to fend him off. "You did not submit to your sentence, nor did you accept death. The Delu nation finds itself in the curious position of having to declare war on you. This is not to our liking." A frown clouded her face. "We would prefer to arrive at a negotiated settlement before hostilities commence."

"They haven't already?" he said, trying to bring a smile to her lips.

The hands made pushing gestures. "That was a judicial matter—now it is a military one."

"Drop the charges and it won't be."

"Please!" She choked, then spasmed and went limp. Her face sagged forward.

He looked up. The old female was pulling away from the interface, allowing a smaller fish to replace her.

When it had donned its cap and tightened the wires, the translator sat up again. The stiff jerkiness in her manner manifested the new controller's inexperience. "I am accountant," she said, "and if we overgo the balance sheet together we able work out reasonable settlement."

"What do you mean, a settlement?"

The lips on the frozen face cracked to say, "You been found guilty of serious offense against civil code. Fine of 24,450 points been levied against you. Circumstances in your case indicate immediate collection impossible, and imposition of standard alternate sentences equally impracticable. Therefore, we work out payment schedule tailored to your abilities and special requirements." Clumsily, she took a pen and began to print laborious figures on a sheet of paper. "You continue to Fling, of course, and salary pay living expenses, as now. We located purchaser of your dreams, and you be paid 150 points night for them. The old female placed good bid for your daytime services—continuation of your present employment, as I understand—and continue to pay you 75 points a day. At such earning level, you pay entire debt to Delurc, including 10% simple interest, within 121 days." She drew a line across the bottom of the paper and placed an X at its left. "You sign here, commence immediately." She turned the paper around for Feighan's inspection.

"Crap."

She cocked her head like a bird hearing a catpaw. "Pardon?"

"No."

"I'm afraid don't understand." She reversed the paper again and studied it closely. "I left something out?"

"I'm not going to put up with that," he said firmly.

"Mr. Feighan—"

"It's involuntary servitude."

"It's repayment schedule, Mr. Feighan." She gave the impression of restraining anger on a frail leash. "And very fair, too. Not for your special circumstances, I point out, not even been offered to you."

"Yeah," he said, "but the thing is, my special circumstances make it impossible for you to force me to agree to that."

"Alternative is war, Mr. Feighan."

"So bring on the guns."

Almost at once pressure panels fell all around him, cutting him off from the the translator and the spoke. *Gonna flood me again*, he thought with a wry laugh. *Don't they know it won't work?*

As water began to jet into the dome, he made ready to Fling out—then stopped, for in the background pulled an Anchor. He couldn't teleport to safety, not yet. And the sea already slurped at his ankles.

Dammit. Carefully, he visualized a globe of water, and Flung that, instead. Imparting to it as much velocity as he could, he gave the velocity a small circular spin. *Oughta feel like a buzz-saw hit him*, he thought. Then, before the Anchor could recover, he took a deep breath and teleported himself back to his room.

"Hi, Gina," he said, shaking his head to clear away the cotton wool of fatigue. Water dripped from his pants legs.

"McGill!" She half-rose, then settled back. "Did you get it worked out?"

He laughed. "Not hardly." Going to the wall, his shoes squished. A puddle spread across the floor. He looked out at the gathering fish. "They just declared war on me."

She ran a hand through the black silk of her hair. "You don't feel too worried about it."

His breath fogged the glass. "They can't get me."

"I hope not."

"No, they— aah!" A fiery pain exploded in his skull. Slapping his hands over his temples, he dropped to his knees. It burned like a torch, but died out quickly. He squeezed his eyes shut, then opened them with caution. "Oh, wow . . . a bonfire between my ears . . . what the hell was it? Quiet, Sam."

The Rhanghan stopped hissing, and settled into a watchful pose.

Maccari was rubbing her own head. "A telepathic attack. And not too well-focused, either. They're trying to disorient you."

"They succeeded," he said ruefully.

Fingers to her lips, she listened to a sound he couldn't hear. "I'm only getting the outlines," she said after a moment, "but they'll keep hitting you with that while their Anchors hold you, and . . ." Her eyes widened. "They're trying to *kill* you!" Astonishment and outrage vied for dominance in her tone.

"Told you they'd declared war on me." Having a Minder for an ally emboldened him. "How do I fight back?"

"I don't know if you can . . ." Nibbling on a finger, she thought a moment. "Uh-uh. You'd have to be a telepath yourself. But the Delu aren't—"

His brain flashed white! The light blotted out his vision and, for an instant, divorced him from his body. Deaf and dumb, he floated in the heart of a cold sun. Then it, too, faded, leaving no after-haze on his retina. "Another attack?" he asked when he'd recovered.

"To put it mildly."

"You were saying?"

"Huh? Oh . . . the Delu aren't . . . they don't use their telepathy the same way we Minders do—I mean, they don't key it to a given brain, wherever that brain is; they key it to all the brains in a given area. I guess that's 'cause they know where each other is all the time— OH!"

This cut like a knife of ice. Clasping his hands across his belly, he doubled into a fog of anguish and whimpered. Maccari and the Rhanghan cried out with him. But like the other assaults, it passed quickly, and he was able to straighten up again.

"Gina, you'd better get out of here."

She rose to her feet, clutching at the desk for support.

"Take Sam, too, huh?"

"You going to stay here?" And she answered herself, "No, I can feel you're not . . . but what are you planning?"

He smiled, a trifle wanly. "I'm just going to stay around and free long enough to convince them that there's nothing they can do to hurt me—once they accept that, things'll settle back to normal."

"I think you're wrong."

"We'll see, won't we?"

She stepped up to him and planted a quick but real kiss on his cheek "Good luck, McGill—don't let anything happen to you."

"I'll do my best." He toyed with a lock of her fine black hair.

"Bye."

"Bye."

He waited till she was out of sight, then set another water-globe spinning beneath the nearest Delu. This time he did not graze the fish with it—rather, he dribbled it on the ocean floor so it would churn up mud and guck. Pwodees scrambled help-lessly in the vortex; a huge cloud enveloped the green-flashing Delu. "Try that in your gills." He laughed.

Then he sat on his pallet and tried to figure out what to do. He started to formulate a plan of guerrilla warfare—appear, attack, then disappear—but before he had worked out the first two stages— "AAH!"

Screams ricocheted through his head, agonized screams of dying men from all the galaxy, humans and Delu and Rhanghan and Timili and every creature he'd ever imagined, much less met . . . the shrieks echoed down the corners of his mind, falling and rising like banshee wails so there was no one volume he could adjust to, learn to accept, and . . .

. . . and water rose in the dome, gurgled on the floor as it swirled around the pallet, and already papers floated on the tide, while his pillow sank . . .

. . . and he could sense an assembly of Anchors outside, sense them through the clamor in his brain; he knew that he couldn't— no, yes he could, he *could*, he was McGill Feighan the Fearless Flinger and they were fussy fish, that was all, he could, just not kill them they were cops after all, just startle them, break their concentration . . .

PING and a chair slapped one on the tail.

PING the desk drove another through the water like a motor.

PING a dresser drawer scraped the belly of the third.

And the pressure of Anchors was gone, sliced like an ax-hewn hawser. If he could stay away long enough he could . . .

PING

His brain fell silent. He almost slept.

Over him bent a middle-aged woman with braided black hair and coppery skin. "Feighan! What the hell are you doing in my dome?"

After a long yawn he smiled weakly, and tried to look reassuring. "Very sorry to disturb you like this, Ms. Ambassador, but this was the first place that came to mind."

Reed's dark eyes hardened. "They told me they've arrested you, and that you're a fugitive from justice. You can't break their laws and expect to hide here—there is no extraterritoriality any more, nor even diplomatic immunity. Give yourself up."

"Not a chance," he said, stepping into the corridor. "I've got better things to do."

As he ran the long spoke, he wondered, for the first time, just how he would make it through the night. The daytime should present no problem—as he had demonstrated time and again, he could do 96 Flings every 22 hours, and do them well—but at night, when fatigue coaxed his eyes into shutting of their own accord and he could fend off sleep no longer . . . what then? Wake on a wire? Or worse, underwater?

His shoes slapped the floor like wet sponges; here and there a startled face peered out a doorway at him. What would he do, come night? Fling back to New York until dawn? But that would defeat the whole purpose of staying . . .

Ahead, a kidney-shaped translator caught sight of him, and changed color from red to green. "Feighan! Feighan, listen!"

He sprinted past its booth.

"We've arrested Maccari!"

He stopped dead. Slowly, he turned, back stiff, shoulders squared. "What?"

As he stalked towards it, the puppet plastered itself to the wall and spread out like pancake batter. Its color dropped into the violet. "We have arrested Gina Maccari and the little Rhan-ghan. Both are in a hidden place, one you do not know. With them is the translator of whom you are so fond. If you do not surrender yourself within one troom, the dome will be flooded—and all three will die."

As its color dropped out of the visible spectrum, it disappeared into transparency.

* * *

"Pretty good, hey Hommroummy?" said the boy.

"If it works," he said.

"It will, it will . . . you'd better get down there to pick him up. Don't waste time—we haven't been sworn in yet."

He switched the intercom on. To his pilot he said, "Tell the Ookinza to get ready—I am going down for our quarry."

· Chapter XIII ·

Feighan stood at that sterile intersection for what seemed like ages, and no one came near him. The eedies in the area detoured through other wheels, down other spokes. The translator stayed invisible beneath its cap. The fish swam elsewhere. He stood alone—with himself. And time sped by on unwatched feet.

Gina! For one brief moment he wondered if this, too, could be a ploy; if her arrest had been faked to make her seem his ally. But the moment passed and he knew the truth. She had been on his side all along; he had just refused to accept it. He had not wanted to trust her, or anybody: because he had not trusted himself. He had lost faith in his ability to distinguish friend from foe, and so he had kept her at arm's length when he should have held her close. *Gina, oh God I'm sorry I got you into this . . .*

And they had Taranya, too, she of the golden hair and liquid laugh and velvety gestures . . . of course, they had had her since he had met her, but this was different. Before, they had only had her to use her—now, her life was at stake. And it was his fault. All his fault. If he had not resisted . . . *if I hadn't loved . . .*

And Sam. *Helluva guardian I am, letting my ward get taken hostage . . .* He looked through the wall into the darkening ocean, where seaweed mocked him with its supple sway. *Shit.* He had promised Sahaang he would take good care of her child, and now, because he had been a bonehead, the kid faced death. *Why'd I have to kick that Rehmal? Why?*

He could not Fling home, that was for sure. He would hate himself forever. Cacti still prickled his dreams, and there he had not abandoned anybody—what would haunt him if he ran away now?

He had to surrender before they drowned his ward, his

friend, and his love...*but when I do run up the white flag, they'll wire me into a booth and that'll drown* me, *dammit, me!*

The fluorescents cycled toward green. *I can't let 'em die. It was okay to play tag with the Delu when nothing was at stake but my freedom, but now...I can't let 'em die.*

At last he sighed. His muscles had stiffened from tension. He stretched and, unaccountably, yawned. Then he said to the cap hanging in mid-air, "All right. Tell the fish I give up. Where do I turn myself in?"

The shape and color changer darkened into a fog. "You surrender?" it whispered hoarsely.

"That's what I just said, isn't it?"

"Yes, but I had to be sure I'd heard right. Very well." With a burst of boldness it blued itself. "Wait here. An Aronya will take you to where you're going."

Now that the decision had been made, he found himself impatient for its consequences. "Wait? Can't I go there myself?"

"You don't know where."

He cracked his knuckles and paced anxiously, while the dimmed image of his tunic curved along the wall. Odd. During his struggle with himself he had not noticed time's passage; now that he had to stand around and wait for...*the jailer*, he thought wryly...He wanted events to speed up because time itself had slowed down. He wanted to go before the judges, to hear the formal sentence read so the punishment could start and he could lose himself in the zombiedom of a translator...*Do they think?* he wondered. *Do they cringe inside their minds while the fish possess their bodies? What does it feel like, and can I stand something that feels that bad?*

Plodding feet brought him away from the wall. When he turned, the long squat Aronya grunted: "Put this on." Its hand proffered a collar, and a chain-link leash.

Feighan scowled. "No."

The plastic chameleon said, "You must, to prove the sincerity of your surrender."

"I'm not a dog, I'm a man!"

"No longer, Feighan. You're a convict."

"I won't."

"Then your surrender is rejected and the hostages die."

"Wait!" His hands trembled as he reached for the circle of

iron. "I'll...dammit. Give them to me."

They watched in smug silence as he fitted the collar around his neck, and clipped the heavy leash to it. Rough metal chafed his neck. Tears of rage sprang to his eyes; never had he felt so abased. "All right," he muttered, "It's on."

The translator said, "Hand the free end to the Aronya."

He obeyed.

At once the alien set off, clutching the leash and tugging Feighan behind. Its legs pumped a furious pace. The Flinger knew that if he once lost his balance it would drag him through the spokes and wheels like a sack of garbage. Panting, he ran; puffing, he gave thanks that the Delu hadn't cuffed his hands behind his back. *They did that, I'd have fallen by now.*

When the Aronya galloped past his old room, Sherman came to the door, a look of inexpressible sadness on his fat face and in his bloodshot eyes. "Luck, McGill!" He turned away immediately.

A half-kilometer farther on, the American Ambassador watched with blatant pleasure. "You deserved it!"

Angered, Feighan drew on the tattered remnants of his strength and Flung ten kilograms of water into the American's clothes. Her howl pursued him down the wheel.

Others emerged to watch his humiliation, but none were glad to see it. Kaleidoscopic flashes froze their horror and repugnance and fear. Each realized the Flinger's fate could be his own, if he offended the Delu.

At last, in a sector Feighan had never explored, the Aronya pulled up before a dome guarded by half a dozen armed Rehmal. It handed the leash to the blue-feathered one that seemed to command, and thundered off again, without so much as a glance at the being it had paraded through the city.

The avian yanked on the leash, yanked hard and down so that Feighan had to drop to his knees to ease the sandpaper pain on his neck. "Very good," it tweeted. "You're learning the proper attitude. Now follow me—but don't get up."

Gritting his teeth, he crawled into the dome. The bird locked the leash's free end to a post and stepped to the wall, where it donned a translator cap. Feighan looked around. The room was empty.

"Where are my friends?"

"In a safe and secret place," snapped the Rehmal.

"I gave myself up—I want to see that they're free."

It shook its crested head. "They will be freed once you have been wired. Not until then. Your capabilities are too laden with potential."

"Who are you?"

"You know who I am, McGill Feighan." A wingtip stroked his temple in a horrid parody of something dear and familiar.

"The old female," he said glumly.

"Exactly. Now—" The translator jerked suddenly. "What?" Feighan looked through the ceiling. An entire school of medium-sized Delu swam around the dome, swam circles around the solitary old female. If he didn't know better, he'd say they were threatening her.

"Well, well, well," said a voice he had not been expecting. "It has been a while, McGill."

"Hommroummy?" He twisted around to see.

"None other." The Organization man stepped forward and seized the end of Feighan's leash. With a pick he worked at the lock. "And you have just been delivered into my custody."

"The old female gave me to you?" He couldn't believe it.

"Her?" He rolled his eyes up. "Of course not. She'd not deal with me. My associates and I are anathema to her entire hidebound clique. Ah, well. One ignores the future at her own peril."

"I'm not going with you." He reached up and undid the collar, dropping it to clatter on the white tiles.

"Oh, but I think you will."

The Rehmal translator said, "You think wrong, Milford Hommroummy."

His suavity was something to behold. "I have a contract," he said, extracting a voice-record chip from his briefcase and holding it above his head. "This, of course, is a copy, but it states clearly that McGill Feighan is to pass into my possession the instant he becomes the property of the Delu."

Every feather on the Rehmal's body fluffed out, making it look three times as large. "The contract is null and void, because it cannot have been executed by anyone with the authority to negotiate it."

The Organization hunter looked calmly at the chip. "That's not my problem," he said, "it's yours. Those who signed it will be in positions of authority. The Organization will ensure that this contract is enforced."

Feighan tried the door. It was locked. Arms folded, he

leaned against the wall. He did his best to look untroubled.

But he projected a false image. Inside, where no one but a telepath could see, he sweated, and tensed, and shouted with all his might, *Gina! Gina Maccari! Where are you?*

Closing his eyes, he listened for some response—and heard only Hommroummy arguing with the translator: "... burn off your breeding grounds, if need be. We care nothing for the future of your race—in fact, we would be pleased to see you become extinct. So surrender him to us, or face ruin."

GINA! He visualized her smile, her friendly white teeth. *GINA!*

Still nothing but the Rehmal's reply: "... not be pressured, Milford Hommroummy. The Delu will not be intimidated. The Delu will not be forced to surrender their convict to anyone, at any time. Should hostilities commence, the mutual defense pact now extant between the Delu and the Flinger Network Control would come into effect; within hours our allies would have arrived to destroy you."

"Ah," said Hommroummy in a purr, "but within hours the entire next generation of Delu will have been broiled alive, and we, madam, will be long gone."

GINA WOULD YOU ANSWER ME DAMMIT?

Oww ... is that you, McGill? Though familiar, the voice sounded strange—like a friend's over the telephone the first time. Every medium, every mode of transmission alters reality by the act of conveying it, and telepathy behaves the same. The words welled into his consciousness like a vivid, vagrant memory, and partook so strongly of the texture of his mind that he could not tell if she had spoken or he had imagined. *How the hell did you get through to me?*

I thought real loud. The intonations felt genuine, and he felt good that they were still attuned to each other. *Where are you? I want to rescue you.*

I don't know. Her plaintiveness whistled like a lonely wind. *They took us down a maze, almost; I got lost ... can you locate me through my Minding? Like a ... a homing beacon?*

No ... for a moment a cliff of despair loomed over him, ready to topple. Then he stiffened. *I have an idea: use your telepathy to, ah—* He didn't know how to phrase it so it would make sense to a non-Flinger. *—to experience your environment. Better yet: if you can, hook me directly into your eyes and ears and other senses, and let me feel it for myself.*

Though kilometers separated them, she recoiled from him. *Let you into me?*

Swimming against the tides of her uneasiness, the waves of her near-fear, he thought, *Your physical senses. I don't need your memory, your mind, anything spiritual or emotional—just the physical, so I can experience your environment, your location, for myself.*

It's all or none— Her shudder induced one in him. *—I don't have that kind of discriminatory control.*

There's no other way I can reach you.

Oh, God . . .

Suddenly his pulse raced; a stranger's nausea fluttered his stomach. Hugging his belly, he slid down the wall. The knobs of his spine slithered along the glass. Squatting on his haunches, he opened his eyes. Hommroummy gestured through a shadowy Sam, and the Rehmal paced the length of the supine translator. *Stronger, clearer, sharper!*

A lemon-bite of asperity tinged her snap: *I'm doing the best I can!*

Of course you are, I know you are . . .

Sam's outlines misted as Hommroummy's voice knifed through Feighan's concentration: ". . . three cruisers armed with lasers; what they don't burn, they'll boil."

The Flinger wrestled his eyelids down. In the room of his mind the blonde's profile clarified, and he could discern the steady rise and fall of her chest. Her fanned-out hair gilded the tiles. The nausea strengthened; helium chilled her skull while making it lighter than air. In two seconds he would faint, which he had not done since that day at the Training Center . . . *what?*

I was never in a Training Center

no, but I was, and you're part of me, now

I'm sorry,
he said with all sincerity, because suddenly he felt like a pervert, skulking through a woman's head and squatting on female haunches and receiving from her nervous system very different telegraph messages, especially—

please, McGill,
no! And another awareness within that body seized the hand he had dispatched to explore, and he/she blushed, they blushed, he for his inconsiderate curiosity, she for her reflexive modesty.

I'm sorry, he said again, and once more meant it.

Just . . . this disorients me, I can't get used—

> *think how I must feel,*
Feighan, letting somebody else in and giving him free rein to—
> *wonder if Taranya*

feels this way when she's wired up?

> *God, I hope not, it'd be hell.*

Ignoring the physical distractions that teased him to investigate, Feighan focused the eyes he had borrowed. No help. The room recapitulated every dome of its size on the planet: eight meters at the peak, eighty square meters on the ground, white tiles rimmed in dark mildew . . . must soured the air, dank and clammy . . . in the ocean beyond, shifting pillars of bright precessed between Delu-shadows while seaweed shimmied and pwodees scuttled from stalk to stalk . . . but he concentrated, laser-tight and diamond-hard, working his Talent down the pipeline of hers; he had to bend it around the far elbow, working it from the point of insertion, bend it around the far elbow and twist it into the light . . . not easy, wriggle and push and contort and hold his breath until his Talent sensed or guessed something about this mass-produced dome, some intangible attribute of time and space that set it in some small way apart from every other dome in the planet. With that tiny uniqueness as a reference, the task became easier, but he still had no time for corporeal diversions, so when the haze of black hair fell burning into his eyes, Maccari took control of her hand and swept the stray lock back up over her forehead to its proper wave. He moved his finger to scratch a patch of mildew; he raised it to his nose where he sniffed it; she took her nail fastidiously and wiped it on a paper towel when he was done with it.

I think that's got it, he said.

> *Leaving so soon?* she mocked,
because, now that he'd laid her this bare, she didn't want him to go, yet couldn't permit herself to say so.

> *Be back in a minute, in person—*
I hope.

He withdrew from her, then. The perceptions they had been sharing dwindled into the invisible past; the warmth of her mind raced cooling away. He squatted on his haunches in the dome to which the Aronya had dragged him, and Milford Hommroummy still argued with the translator.

"Just surrender him," said the clench-jawed Organization

man for what must have been the twentieth time. "We shall quit your planet—ridding it, I should point out, of an element which you yourselves have already deemed highly objectionable—and nothing more shall be said of this."

Feighan had no time to listen to the Rehmal's rebuttal. He closed his eyes, summoned up the memory he and Maccari had manufactured—concentrated—visualized—felt—knew—

PING

Sam scrambled across the floor with happiness hissing in his throat. He hurled himself up Feighan's pants leg to his shoulder, where, curling within his tail, he nuzzled the human's ear.

Maccari got more slowly to her feet, and raised her face face. A flush still perfused her cheeks. Awkwardly, she shifted her weight from one foot to the other. A barrier parted them like a glass wall.

He lacked the words to apologize for his violation of her privacy; all he could do was seize her and hug her tightly.

And she did not try to pull away. Not once.

At last, he released her—reluctantly—and scowled at a Delu nosing up to the dome. "We've been spotted," he said. "We've got to get out of here."

"But how—" She laughed at herself. "Sorry, I keep forgetting."

"You and Sam—" He detached the saurian from his neck. "—sit on the floor next to her." He shooed them over with a flurry of hand sculls. "Ready?"

Maccari, the Rhanghan in her lap and her arms around him, bit her lip and nodded once.

PING

All four materialized in the private dome of the United States Ambassador to Delurc—who huffed angrily when she caught sight of them. "What are you doing?" She sprang from her desk and stalked over to them. Her braids swung back and forth, pendulums of petulance. "Get out of here."

"Sorry," said Feighan, "but it's you—"

PING

Maccari blinked. "Nasty woman . . . where'd you put her?"

"In your prison cell." Quickly he glanced through the ceiling; the largest fish in view measured only a meter. The Delu swam elsewhere. He ripped the blankets and sheets off the ambassadorial pallet and draped one over the unconscious translator. He stretched another over the backs of two chairs, pitching a small tent of it. "The two of you get in here; you'll be hidden for a while, and I hope that's all I'll need."

"I'll mind-shield us, too." Just before he dropped the fold to conceal her completely, she asked, "What are you planning to do?"

"It's sort of complicated. Besides—" He grinned. "—I don't know if it'll work, so just wait inside until I come back. Okay?"

"Okay, but don't be long. And— be careful, all right?"

"I promise." Cloth bunched in his hand, he swooped down to drop a kiss on her forehead. "Thanks."

The banket swished like an act's end curtain and locked her in darkness.

PING

". . . produce him immediately," Hommroummy was yelling, "we will—"

"Shut up, Hommroummy," snapped Feighan. "Hey, old female!"

The Rehmal swiveled its head and pinned him with its beady eyes. "Yes?"

"I'll make you a deal—I'll get rid of The Organization's ships for you if you'll pay enough to cover my fine, free the translator, and buy the answer to my question—but no juggling with the books this time." He ducked a vicious punch from the hard-faced older man, and kicked him in the stomach, twice. "Stop that," he said. "Well? Is it a deal?"

Sprawled on the floor, The Organization man barked orders into a transceiver mounted on a pinky ring, but before the acknowledgement crackled back, the Rehmal bobbed its beak. "Very well." It sighed. "We have a deal."

"Thanks." A distant Flinger pulled Hommroummy to safety. "I wonder what he's up to?" He gave a mock salute to the fish outside, then—

PING

—teleported himself into the observation dome.

"You!" The Rii-edsch translator squeaked. "You're wanted by the police."

"Not any more I'm not," he said, striding to the windowwall. He jabbed a finger towards the cloudless sky. "There are three eedie ships up there—"

"All ships orbiting this planet are extra-Delu—fish don't fly, remember?"

He shook his head in exasperation with the controller's childish literal-mindedness. "These belong to The Organization, and if I don't stop them, they're going to burn off every nursery they can find. Now. Do you think you can bring them into view?"

"I can but try," said the marsupial, nervously grooming its flank fur with its ninth and tenth legs. "Straight above your head I'll focus a patch—there. See it?"

A jewel-studded black circle blossomed in the middle of a blue sky. The Rii-edsch fine-tuned the focus. Delu optics transfigured the central gem into an aluminum-colored ball prickled with antenna.

"How high is it?"

"Five hundred kilometers."

That seemed low, but then, they were hovering in readiness for action, and a higher orbit would have delayed their arrival at the firing line. "What about the others?"

"To the left and right of your present field of vision—by the way, this is being charged to your personal account, isn't it?"

"Yeah..." He shifted his eyes. The Organization vessels ballooned in his sight, each as ominously innocuous as the first. Each had a small opening in its hull: the laser-cannon port. "Same height?"

"The same."

Now that he'd spotted them, a new question arose: could his Talent reach a place he had never been to? When he could see a location with his own eyes, he had no trouble Flinging to it—but through a telescopic wall? Experimentally, he scooped a globe of water from the sea outside, and—

PING

—light sparkled beside the middle ship as the waterball appeared and flashboiled.

He scratched his temple and contemplated the next step. He could Fling water at the ships, as he'd done to the landing craft that day which seemed so long ago, but he was not sure how the missiles would behave in frozen vacuum. If they turned to ice, no problem—but if they vaporized before they hit—

The Rii-edsch's gasp alerted him—or his body, because he had already dropped to the floor and rolled right before his mind began to puzzle at the sound's origin and significance.

He bounced on his shoulder as an anesthetic dart slapped the wall where he had been standing; it ricocheted and fell, needle flattened.

"Damn," said a hard bass voice.

While he scrambled for cover he risked a glance—four men crouched on the dome's far side, each swinging a leveled dart-gun that tried to track his frantic zig-zags.

"Freeze!" said the unshaven man in the front, the one with the bass. Raising his rifle, he squeezed off a shot that missed Feighan only because the Flinger skinned his nose on the tiles. "Hommroummy said—"

Christ they got here quick. He panted his lungs full, then threw himself into a hasty somersault. Another trigger clicked; another projectile twanged. *So what the hell am I— hah!* Even as he moved, he detached a portion of his mind from the task of survival and set it to concentrating, visualizing . . . feeling . . . knowing—

PING

"Bull's-eye!" said the Rii-esch.

To his companions' loud alarm, the bristle-faced man had disappeared. For one heartbeat the only invader with Feighan in his sights let his jaw go slack and his eyes twitch to his leader's last footprints. He began: "What the he—"

PING

The marsupial applauded with eight of his limbs. It sounded like a small crowd. "It's spinning and dropping and the crewmen are being sucked out the hole!"

TWANK popped a dart, and *TWANK* another, but they rattled into the corner as their target flopped away like a gaffed fish on a deck.

He felt like he had been breast-stroking through molasses for hours; his muscles screamed to sleep and to recover. A yawn forced its way up his throat, but before it curled the back of his tongue, he had—

PING

—Flung the third gunman five hundred kilometers high, with a velocity of two kps directed at the very heart of Delurc. And for the third time the translator hailed Feighan's triumph: "You put him right through the hull," it said, "and it looks like that ship's a goner, too. Congratulations—three bull's-eyes—that's fine shooting."

The fourth man snarled as he raised his gun. Feighan, so
fatigued that he could barely raise his chin off the cold floor,
chuckled, "Bye-bye."

PING

On a nursery reef two kilometers distant, the children
swarmed eagerly over this new kind of food.

"I guess that'll do it." The Flinger laid his cheek on the
clammy tiles and went to sleep.

*   *   *

Gryll was in the cabin, waiting. Its gases swirled faster than
Hommroummy had ever seen, but when it spoke, it seemed
calm. "Another failure?"

"Regrettably, yes." He stiffened his spine.

"Not your fault."

His jaw dropped. "Sir?"

"Whole planet reeks of Retzglaran. Lucky to escape with
life. Regroup. Rethink. Replan. Third time charm, yes?"

"Yes, sir," he said, holding his hands behind his back to
control their trembling. "Yes, sir. I shall not fail again."

"Your neck if you do, Hommroummy." The wall opaqued;
the speaker shut off.

And Milford Hommroummy shuddered.

• Chapter XIV •

Under the dome and the sky he awoke alone, save for the marsupial, which leaned across its counter to peer down on him. "About time," it said peevishly. "I should charge you rent for the floorspace. There are two messages for you, and both have already been debited to your account."

Woozily he sat up, and rubbed his eyes with his knuckles. They cracked as he flexed them; the same stiffness hobbled the rest of his body. "How long have I been here?"

"Fifty trooms." It settled back, wrapping its tail around its perch. "Do you want your messages, or don't you?"

"Go ahead." He stretched, and touched his toes. It made him grunt, but he felt better for it.

"I'll give them to you in order of importance. First, the old female says—" Its pose and pitch altered instantly. "—'Congratulations, and our gratitude. Your fine has been paid, the answer to your question is available at my desk anytime within the next five days, and you have been awarded a 5000-point bonus for having lured a traitorous faction into open action, thus allowing us to identify and eliminate it. Your translator is also free. I look forward to speaking with you soon.'"

"Where is she?"

The Rii-edsch waved its tail indifferently. "She's reachable through any datadesk; just request the chance to speak with her, and your message will be relayed."

After a moment's digestion, he said, "Not the old female, the translator who's just been freed."

"The second message might answer that question—from one Gina Maccari, who says, 'Sam, Harry, and I are in your dome with *her*, who woke up an hour ago. Please come as soon as possible.'"

He pushed himself to his feet and dusted off his pants. Scuff marks lightened the toes of his boots, and wrinkles shadowed his trousers, but his fingernails were fairly clean, and his tunic glittered like a Christmas ornament in the red light. He smoothed back his hair with anxious hands. "How do I look?"

"Terran. Wha—"

PING

A millisecond before materializing, he crashed through a shell of antipathy. Alarm jangled in his synapses and he tensed, ready for anything. The instant his feet felt cold tile, he got his bearings and looked around.

A static tableau uncoiled his muscles, though it prickled the hairs of his neck. On the pallet, herbivores cornered by a predator, sat Maccari, Sherman, and Sam. Their jaw muscles bulged.

The translator poised in the desk chair, dry palms on her thighs, a statue of patience. Her quiescence was a dormancy: a seismic fault, a well-honed blade.

The *otherness* of her shook him, yet he steeled himself. He nodded to his friends and stepped toward her. "Hi, I'm McGill Fei—"

"I know." She spoke levelly, spacing sounds and silence with an exactitude suggestive of enormous self-control. Still in the chair, she seemed four meters tall. "I am Jessica Bjornfjorken."

Then he knew. The Delu had lived too long in her; their outlook had become hers. Having no use for compassion, they had burned it out of her. All of it. Every bit. Like Pluto, she dwelled so far from caring's heat that ice crackled in her every part. Nonetheless, he held out his hand. "I'm pleased to meet you."

She gave the extended arm the attention paid to a stranger in an urban street: unless it did something, it was irrelevant. "I would like to leave." And in that, too, cracked the Delu will: she would have what she wanted, and had already counted its cost. The price to others mattered not.

"Ah . . ." He tucked in his chin, dismayedly aware that what he confronted was closer, now, to an elemental force than a fellow human. Still he clung to his hopes, like a mountaineer to his rock in a high wind. "Well, listen, we're probably going to be celebrating; would you like to stay for the party?"

"No." She raised her eyes. They were flat as cheap blue

paint. They looked into his without a flicker of acknowledgment. He meant less to her than would a wall. Or a pane of glass. "I am leaving now."

"Ah..." He swallowed a lump of something heavy and bitter. "Sure. If you want."

"I will not forget that you have freed me." She rose like the moon, aloof and unstoppable.

Sam hissed, and stalked towards her.

"Let her go, Sam," Feighan said.

The Rhanghan gave a disgusted wheeze. Settling onto his tail, he folded his arms as if disclaiming responsibility.

She walked steadily away, seeing nothing but her goal.

"Wait!" he said, as she stepped into the wheel.

She paused. Her head swiveled back like the turret of a tank. "Yes?"

"Why were you sentenced? What did you do to get them mad?"

She blinked. "I lied to them." Then her head pivoted forward and she moved away to pass through the world without its ever touching her again.

Feighan breathed, but it caught in his throat. His eyes stung. Half-buried in the rubble of his ruined dreams, he watched her proceed down the wheel with precise, acquisitive strides. He wanted to curl up in a closet and just hurt for a while.

"McGill," said Maccari softly.

Keeping his back turned, he held up his hand and waved her to silence. He was stunned by the reality of Jessica Bjornfjorken—and devastated that he had discovered it in the presence of his friends. His shoulders tightened as he waited for them to comment, to laugh. *I must look an absolute fool, falling head over heels for a— an alien like that.* He feared their laughter. Although he would have earned it, he was defenseless against it, and its harsh ringing would so deepen his pain that he could relieve it only by transmuting it into rage at those who took it lightly...*Don't laugh, any of you, 'cause if you do I'll hate you forever. Don't laugh—*

"We won't," said Maccari's caring voice.

"Won't what?" asked Sherman, instinctively curious even at delicate moments.

"Hush," said Maccari. "McGill?"

He cleared his throat, but still didn't turn. "I, ah...I'm going to go ask about the gastropod, be back in a while."

"Sure," she said gently. "I'll watch over Sam."

"Th-thanks." He squared his shoulders and marched out of the dome, arms swinging stiffly at his sides. Self-consciousness trailed him all the way down the wheel.

At Datadesk 1-19, a huge-headed Aronya shuffled about on a wooden platform. It raised its head from a water bucket as Feighan approached, and appeared not to notice when he stopped, and visibly hesitated, ten meters from the desk.

I better find another one, can't face the old female . . . naw, they'll just patch me through to her, set up a relay to carry the answer . . . but dammit, she made a fool out of me with her little translator games . . . He swallowed hard. *I'm gonna have to deal with her again, sooner or later, so I might as well get it over with right now . . .*

"This the old female?" he asked as he stepped forward again.

"Yes," lowed the Aronya, shifting its weight on its many feet. "What can I do for you, MmmuGill?"

He leaned across the counter, and tried not to wrinkle his nose at the bovine's earthy stench. "Tell me about the gastropod," he said simply.

"I could tell, or I could show. Which would you prefer?"

"I don't understand." His knuckles whitened as his hands curled into fists. Was this the start of another evasion?

"You have swapped mmmemmmories with mmme before," it said. "I offer you the opportunity to do so again, and experience the recollection of mmmy mmmeeting with the representative of the Far Being Retzglaran."

"Then he *did* work for the Far Being?" he said eagerly, forgetting his distrust.

"It refused to nammme its emmmployer, but—" The Aronya's tail dusted its speckled back. "—I had enough evidence to mmmake a respectably logical deduction."

"For example?"

"Let mmme show you." The monstrous head nodded towards a helmet in the corner. "I'mmm afraid, though, that because you purchased the formmmer translator's freedommm, suitable contact can be mmmade only through the cap."

He drew back unconsciously. "No."

"This is a dreammm cap, MmmuGill, not a translation interface. Please. If you don't, you will only hear a description of the reality you mmmight otherwise have experienced."

"But it—"

"I mmmake contract with you—which is to say that I prom-mmise on the honor of mmmy score—that when the mmmem-mmory has played itself out, you will be released frommm the cap, none the worse for wear."

He had to find out what the Delu knew about his gastropod—he *had* to. And if that meant risking his— his what? His whole-ness, his psychic integrity?—then, by damn, he'd risk it. "All right," he said at last. "But—" He shook away the last of his doubts. Slowly, anticipation replaced nervousness as the cause of his tension. "All right."

His fingers stayed steady as they lifted the cap, and he was glad for that. He didn't like to be embarrassed by tremors at crucial moments. The inner lip of the metal helmet fit his skullbone as snugly as if it had been tailored especially for it—which disturbed him, because it might have been. But he brushed away that final foreboding, and velcro'd the helmet strap under his chin. "Now what?"

"Just sit and wait," said the Aronya. "Close your eyes and . . ."

. . . and the fields that the helmet enlivened in his brain took effect. Gently they separated his being from his body, and nudged it down the path to the other body, the empty one, the big sleek eight-finned one that pumped its gills faster now that it couldn't swim circles for fear of breaking the fragile wires.

He got to the edge of usurpation and a force like a whirlwind enveloped him, turned and twisted and compressed him, pulled him like taffy until it dropped him right into—

"Taranya the Queerbeing Quotamaker," she projected at intervals defined by her scorecounts: "8,721 net," and inter-spersed with her datawants "Willbuy: annual Occleftian con-sumption of zinc-based sun lotions," and datahaves "Cansell: number of red-headed male infants born in North American Consortium daily."

She shrieked her pronouncements into the sea, yet still could listen to the other gabble her meter-wide aural membranes picked out of the waters. Like a hawker parked outside a mar-ket, she called, "Taranya the Queerbeing Quotamaker; 8,728 net; willbuy: profile of leading extrepreneur on Rehmal; cansell: pheroreceptor diagram of Terran nasal passages."

With another part of her mind she directed the singing of her latest name song, and pondered the speed of time in a space filled with anti-matter, and carried on a conversation with a large ocher tourist which could probably shape itself into something quite attractive, but which, at present, resembled nothing so much as an overgrown snail. The tourist filled two-thirds of the dome in which it humped, and trickled into the spoke in both directions.

"Ah, McGill Feighan," it said, in a cultured Oxford accent that the Flinger later recognized as having been supplied by his own concepts of the appropriate mannerisms for a divine emissary. "Now that you've traced me this far, don't you think it's time we had a little talk?"

"Why me?" It spilled out of him/her before she/he could think of anything more profound.

"And why not you? My master will work with any material that suits the Far Being's purpose—and you will."

"What is that purpose?"

It deformed itself to let a pedestrian pass through the intersection. "I say, have you heard of the uncertainty principle?"

"You mean that the observer changes the event by the act of observing?"

"An analogy can be drawn between that and yourself."

He waited for elaboration, but when none came, asked, "What's the analogy?"

"P'raps it would be best if you drew it yourself."

"Can't you tell me anything?"

"Certainly. You are not to continue the quest for the Far Being. Do you understand?"

"No . . ." She/he shook their head and scattered a school of bottom-browsers. "No, I don't understand at all. Why?"

"The Far Being does not intend to monopolize your life, McGill. My master has not ordered your ingestion to provoke your curiosity about the Far Being; my master has acolytes enough without going to such lengths to enlist more. You will not be called upon to comb the far reaches of the galaxy for the Far Being Retzglaran. Do you understand?"

"I know why I haven't been called," he said, "but what I still don't know is, why have I been called?"

"But that's just the thing, don't you see? You will not be called."

"But you—"

"I will ingest you, McGill—not ordain you, not enroll you, not call you. Can you make that rather fine distinction?"

"But why did you eat me?"

"Ah . . . that, my friend, I must confess is a mystery to me."

"You don't know why you did it?"

"I will do it because my master has ordered it," it said stiffly. "That is reason enough for me."

"But what did you do to me while I was in you?"

"As I have yet to do it, I really couldn't say."

"Not even a hint?"

"Just the one: you are not to waste your time investigating it. You are to lead a normal life in every way—get married, have children, pay your taxes—you are not to imagine yourself Galahad in search of the Grail. Can I make myself any clearer?"

He groped amidst his astonishment for words: "But then what's the point? Why did you bother to eat me at all?"

"If I knew that," it said with dignity, "I would be the Far Being Retzglaran. But I am not, so I do not know." It extruded a pair of pseudo-pods with which it lifted off the cap.

"Hey, wait!" said Feighan/Taranya.

But, as it could not—or would not—hear him, it set the cap on the countertop, flashed a jovial "Thank you," to the datadesk attendant, and followed sluggishly down the wheel.

That tornado of transformation ripped him out of his place in space, scruffed him into the air and shook him, prodding him back into his original shape and size. It set him on the passageway and shoved him towards his own body. As he tumbled into it, he rubbed shoulders with a fleeting, fleeing woman veiled in black.

And then he was easing the cap off his own head, and staring at the orange-eyed Aronya. "Whew! The transition's a little rougher with these things."

"Yes," mooed the bovine, "that's why earlier I used mmmy fingers, instead. But now that I have only hooves—" It raised one and let it clump back onto the platform.

"Thanks," he said, uncertainly.

"You're very welcommme . . . you'll be leaving soon, won't you?"

He nodded.

It turned its huge eyes on him. Soulful, expressive, their depths trapped wistfulness and humor and intelligence. "I'll mmmiss you," it lowed mournfully.

He could no longer avoid acknowledging the truth. "You

tried to manipulate me into falling in love with you." He gave a shaky laugh. "And almost succeeded. Why did you do it? Just to get a research subject?"

The great head swung from side to doleful side. "I'mmm sorry. We have a concept of love that mmmust differ greatly frommm yours, but frommm the mmmommment we mmmet I could see in you the qualities that enhance a mmmale. You are bold, confident, inquisitive . . . yet sensitive with women, shyly charmmming and charmmmingly shy . . . and your need for love is so palpable. Were you a Delu I would mmmate with you with joyfully, MmmuGill, for at least a full season. But I ammm sorry."

He looked at the tail-flicking Aronya, yet saw the veiled, scented shape of the true Taranya. "It's not your fault," he said, seeing himself as he was, too. "I, ah . . . I fell in love with the notion that love has to be sleek and regal and . . . and beautiful; then I extended it, and felt—felt that the person you loved had to be all that, and, ah . . ." He shook his head like he was throwing off his youth. "I guess I'd better be going."

She nodded. "Commme back anytime, this tour or in the future . . . you don't need the points any mmmore, but if you'd like to chat—or discuss mmmy new mmmodel of reality—I would welcommme you. Goodbye, MmmuGill."

"Goodbye," he said, and then, because he didn't like to linger over partings—

PING

—Flung himself back to his dome. Sherman had left, but Maccari sat cross-legged on the pallet, holding a small crustacean just out of Sam's reach. Neither noticed the Flinger's arrival. "Gina," she said patiently, "Gina."

Feighan kept silent, watching, wondering.

The Rhanghan snapped his jaws at the crustacean, but Maccari pulled it away. "Gina," she said, "Gi-na."

Sam's tongue flickered and he hissed, "Heeña."

"Magnificent!" She popped the baby pwodee into the open, toothy mouth. "Good boy, Sam. You did great." She waited till he'd swallowed it, then from a small box at her side took another and waved it over his nose. "Gi-na? Gi-na?"

Something swelled in Feighan's throat right then, and his eyes grew moist enough to require heavy blinking. "Gina," he said softly.

She jumped a good fifteen centimeters; the pwodee fell forgotten from her fingers. Sam nailed it in mid-air. "McGill!" She struggled to her feet. "What'd you find?"

He started to answer but decided that the big discovery could wait. Instead, he told her what he'd learned at the datadesk. "A dead end. The—the fish let me share her memory of the day she met the gastropod, and . . ." Moving across the room, he sank into the desk chair. "And it was weird. The gastropod talked to me—not her, me—as though . . . I mean, it came here twenty years ago or so, before I was born, but in this twenty-year-old memory, it acted like it was here right now." A sudden thought struck him: did Taranya know that the gastropod had been what she now sought—a being with random access to time? *Of course she does; it must be what started her on this* . . . "Anyway, it told me, I'm not supposed to be looking for the Far Being, or trying to figure out the reason for my ingestion or anything to do with the whole event. I'm supposed to pretend it never happened, and just lead a normal life." He gave a bitter laugh tinged with wistfulness. "As if I could . . . as if I would."

She put her hand on his shoulder, then slid it under his chin and lifted his face. "Are you going to give up the quest?" Her dark eyes bored into his. "No," she whispered slowly, "no, you're not, are you?"

"Uh-uh." He would have shaken his head, but he didn't want to dislodge her fingers. "I can't . . . you know that."

"So—?"

"I don't know . . . go back to being a Flinger, keep my eyes and ears open for leads, and in my spare time . . . I don't know, something like that. I haven't decided what, exactly."

"So I can expect that you won't be dragging Sam off to the Hub tomorrow? I mean, I've just got him started trying to talk."

That hurt. Not because she was doing a task he should have overseen himself, but because she inquired about his plans only out of a desire to spend time with Sam. "No," he said at last, masking his jealousy with a stiff amiability, "I expect you'll be seeing a lot of Sam for a while."

Her fingers circled on his chin. "Only Sam?"

"Well, I . . ." He caught the laughter in her eyes and scowled with mock severity. "You bum! Why do you tease me like that?"

"Because Sam's the one who seems to like me best."

"But you know how I feel! I mean, you're a Minder, you can read—"

"There are some things, McGill, a woman likes to hear said."

"All right." He stood, and took her in his arms. "Gina Maccari, there's something I want you to hear said. I—" The next word came out though he tried to stop it, but once it hung in the air between them he could hear for himself that it was, after all, proper and right. "—love you. I do. And, ah . . . I'm not about to Fling very far away from you, because suddenly I find myself wanting to spend just a whole lot of time standing somewhere exactly like this, all the world silent and your nose bumping mine."

Her eyes drifted shut and her mouth groped for his. Her warm, alive tongue came to his tentatively, hesitating before penetrating, but then touched and entwined with joyous abandon. *Oh, McGill,* she said in his mind, where only he could hear her, *I love you, too, and thank you for saying that, because while you felt it all along you kept trying to pretend it wasn't there, and so you wouldn't share it with me until you believed in it, too, but you wouldn't believe in it until you admitted it to yourself . . .*

Pulling away to scrutinize the richness of her irises, he took a deep breath. He'd never felt so happy in his life—or so scared. Now that he had his arms around her, he couldn't imagine ever releasing her, even for a moment. Yet he knew he would have to, eventually—she had a job, after all—and the thought depressed him. Once she left she might not come back. So he took another deep breath and asked, "Will you marry me?"

Her startled eyes popped wide. "Marry you?"

He tried for a light touch because gravity would choke him. "Yeah, marry. You know: church, rings, flowergirls . . . lots of champagne at the reception . . . marry."

She broke his hold on her and slipped lithely away. "No." Her words rang firm. Then sympathy softened her face, and she stretched out a hand. "There you go, taking it wrong again . . . I can feel you hurting like a dropped infant, but you've got no cause. I'm not rejecting *you*, McGill—just the notion of marriage right now."

He tried to speak but his throat was full of sticky splinters and he couldn't find a facile phrase anyway. He coughed into his hand; the action broke some of the tension. "I, ah . . . I'm sorry." The words rushed out of him as if to wash away what he'd just asked. "It was silly of me to ask you and I apologize for it, I guess I just got carried away and—"

She hushed him with a kiss. Holding his cheeks between tender hands, she said, "McGill, it wasn't silly of you to ask—it just would have been silly of me to accept. I'm not ready for it, not now. I love you dearly, but to love you right I'd have to give up my . . ." A frown creased her forehead as she mused along. "'Freedom' is the wrong word, because I can sense that when you love someone right you don't have to surrender that; love has room for it . . . it's just that to do a marriage right, you have to be able to explain everything you do, and to have a good reason for it, because marriage is this incredible tumble through time, like synchronized sky-fall ballet, only it lasts a helluva lot longer. Each partner's got to trust the other to make the right moves all the time, or at least to have a good reason for making a wrong move, but McGill . . ." She shook her head and her hair brushed his fingers. "I'm still growing up. I'm going to be doing a lot of things purely for the hell of it, and if something goes wrong because of what I do, it wouldn't be fair for you to get hurt by it. Do you understand what I'm saying? I love you, but I'm not ready to slant my decision-making along the lines that I should do what's best for *us*, or that I should avoid what will hurt *us*. Do you understand?" She searched his eyes.

He took yet another deep breath, and let it out slowly, resignedly. "I think I do," he said. "I think it's the same for me—I haven't been, ah . . . an individual, in the sense of doing what most fulfills *me*—long enough to appreciate becoming half of a pair. I'm not expressing it well . . . it doesn't matter. I know what you mean, and I think you're right—for both of us. For the moment."

She ran a finger down his nose, and smiled. "Thanks." She kissed him. "And if you ask again in four or five years, who knows? Maybe I'll have grown up by then."

Burying his face in the smooth follow of her neck, he felt peaceful. And yet, curiously . . . satisfied. "Four years, huh? I'll tell my computer to mark it on the calendar—in boldface bits."

"Maybe five," she murmured, as her hands stroked his back.

"If I'm ready in four, you'd better be, too."

"We'll see." And her smile vanished under his lips.

From the corner, Sam hissed, "Heeña! Heeña!" When they ignored him, he flicked his tail and trotted across the wheel to Sherman's dome. He was hungry, and if anybody around there would understand that, it would be the newsman. "Hawee," he tried, "Hawee..."

It ought to be worth a couple of pwodees, at least.